FRAZER LEE

GREYFRIARS REFORMATORY

This is a **FLAME TREE PRESS** book

Text copyright © 2020 Frazer Lee

All rights reserved. No part of this publication may be reproduced, stored in a retrieval system, or transmitted in any form or by any means, electronic, mechanical, photocopying, recording or otherwise, without the prior written permission of the publisher.

FLAME TREE PRESS
6 Melbray Mews, London, SW6 3NS, UK
flametreepress.com

US sales, distribution and warehouse:
Simon & Schuster
simonandschuster.biz

UK distribution and warehouse:
Marston Book Services Ltd
marston.co.uk

Publisher's Note: This is a work of fiction. Names, characters, places, and incidents are a product of the author's imagination. Locales and public names are sometimes used for atmospheric purposes. Any resemblance to actual people, living or dead, or to businesses, companies, events, institutions, or locales is completely coincidental.

Thanks to the Flame Tree Press team, including:
Taylor Bentley, Frances Bodiam, Federica Ciaravella, Don D'Auria,
Chris Herbert, Josie Karani, Molly Rosevear, Mike Spender,
Cat Taylor, Maria Tissot, Nick Wells, Gillian Whitaker.

The cover is created by Flame Tree Studio with
thanks to Nik Keevil and Shutterstock.com.
The font families used are Avenir and Bembo.

Flame Tree Press is an imprint of Flame Tree Publishing Ltd
flametreepublishing.com

A copy of the CIP data for this book is available from the British Library
and the Library of Congress.

HB ISBN: 978-1-78758-475-4
US PB ISBN: 978-1-78758-473-0
UK PB ISBN: 978-1-78758-474-7
ebook ISBN: 978-1-78758-477-8

Printed and bound in Great Britain by Clays Ltd, Elcograf S.p.A.

FRAZER LEE

GREYFRIARS REFORMATORY

FLAME TREE PRESS
London & New York

*For my sisters
Tamsin, Phaedra, Sarah
with love*

CHAPTER ONE

The Gray Girls

I'm on the prisoner transport bus again and the sky outside the window looks almost as gray as I feel.

I say 'again' because, well, I've been institutionalized a few times. All my adult life actually. I've had a few problems, shall we say. But before you ask, my meds are so strong I can't remember what any of my problems were, or are. I guess that kind of makes me an unreliable narrator? If that bothers you then look away. I know I would. Or at least, I think I would.

The five other girls on the bus have been real quiet since we crossed the county line into Dustbowl, Nowheresville. Not that any of them spoke to me at all in the first place, you understand. I'm not what you'd call the approachable type. A couple of them whispered to each other, some nonsense about 'making a break for it during the pee break'. Yeah, good luck with that in your handcuffs and leg irons, ladies. Probably just trying to style it out before they realized for sure that they were going to be banged up like the rest of us. No special cases here, just a bunch of head cases.

One girl, sitting two rows in front of me, is quieter than the rest. I clocked her when I got on, but couldn't see her face because she was lurking behind her floppy brown fringe. I wondered what she might be hiding. And then again I didn't wonder at all. I mean, what's the point in trying to figure that out anyway? We're all hiding something, that's partly why we're here.

I glance out the window and try to decipher where 'here' is, exactly. The window is almost as grimy as the sky, making me doubly separated from the landscape as it smears across my vision. I can see the skeletal forms of trees, clinging to the wind-battered hillsides. The country road begins to twist and turn, as if coiling in on itself to keep us moving into its spiral.

The driver makes a bad gear change as the road gets rougher. The torturous sound of the grinding gearshift gives way to a burst of static on the bus radio. The signal is weak, probably because of the mountainous terrain on either side of us, but I can hear a few faint bars of a song coming through the tinny speakers. The lyrics say something about ghosts, and regret, and about not saying sorry. Soon enough, the song becomes lost in another crackle of static and I turn my attention back to the window.

"Turn the fucking thing off if it's not working properly." The voice from the back of the bus is petulant, and clipped with indignation. I look around, on instinct, and my eyes meet the baby blues of the tall blonde who decided to take the entire back row for herself. She gives off that vibe, you know, where she's just daring you to sit near her so she can make a scene. Best ignored, those types. Which makes it all the more unfortunate that I made eye contact with her, I guess.

"Would you like a fucking selfie with that?" she says.

I break eye contact. Then I go over what I saw, but in my mind's eye. It's a thing I do. A thing I have to do, to try and make sense of whether or not what I'm seeing is real. Unreliable, like I said. One thing's for sure, that blonde girl wears her entitlement like a swipe card. She groans theatrically, and I think I'm in for an earful from her. But then I see the apparent source of her disappointment, looming dark beyond the small clear section of driver's window that isn't caked with dirt.

The building is solid looking, hunkered down into the landscape like it knows more bad weather is coming. A clock tower is the only vertical part of the structure, looming darkly at the center of the building. The bus swerves and the road narrows further as we approach the brick perimeter wall and wrought-iron gates. Lichen casts a rusty glow over the weathered bricks, and thick black paint is peeling from the iron railings. There's a sign next to the gate, the painted letters almost destroyed by the elements. It reads *Greyfriars Reformatory for Girls*. Whoop-de-doo. The way the paint has deteriorated makes the words 'Grey' and 'Girls' stand out. Yup, that's us in our drab uniforms I guess, the gray girls.

The driver slows the bus to a halt and a few seconds later, the gates swing open, activated by an unseen hand. The driver makes another horrendous gear shift and the bus proceeds through the gates and onto a graveled forecourt. The centerpiece of this gloomy space is a dead-looking tree. A few dry leaves flutter in the wake of the prisoner transport bus as we pass by. I glance back through the rear window, careless of the arrogant blonde, and see the gates swing shut behind us. They close with a loud clank, and the driver swings the vehicle around so we're adjacent to the front steps of the building. With a hydraulic hiss of the brakes, we lurch to a halt.

"Finally," the blonde says, with a wisdom beyond her years.

"Right, ladies, disembarkation time. Front rows first. Single file. No talking. Watch your step at the bottom."

The chains we're wearing tinkle like Christmas bells as we file off the bus. I'm ahead of the blonde, so I stand up but she gives me that superior look of hers and pushes past me. As the heat of her body rubs against me I notice that she smells overbearingly sweet, like a bag of boiled candies. I don't like the scent.

"Come on, come on," the driver urges, and I follow as quickly as my leg irons will allow me to.

The sky looks just as grimy as it did from inside the bus, but at least the air is fresher outside. I take a few calming breaths—

(*In, then out, count to three in your head, and breathe in again.*)

—like they taught me to, and then line up with the others alongside the bus. The reformatory looks huge now, up close, its dark windows giving nothing away. The front steps look cracked and worn. Several hopes and dreams must have been deposited there on the way into that—

(*And I'm just being honest here.*)

—frightening shithole of a building.

But even more terrifying is the woman waiting for us on the steps.

She's in her fifties, and wears a functional black trouser suit. Her auburn hair is bunched and her lips pursed, making her look pretty tightly wound. She carries a clipboard, tucked under her arm. In her free hand I see a bunch of keys on a dull, silver ring. They too make the sound of little silver bells as she walks across the gravel to face us. She doesn't look at us yet, instead giving the driver a sharp nod. The driver clambers back onto the bus and I hear the engine grumble back into life behind me. The air around me fills with exhaust fumes. After a hiss of the brake release, the bus moves off, kicking up dust as it goes.

The woman quickly pockets the keys, pulls out her clipboard and makes a show of leafing through the pages of the document that is clamped to it. She shakes her head, slowly.

"More lost souls," she says. Then, after taking a breath, she begins to walk the line of girls.

"I am Principal Quick. Welcome to Greyfriars Reformatory. Your new home."

I can see the blonde's smug, smirking face poking out from beneath her plumage-like fringe at the head of the line. The principal stops still and stands in front of her. Glancing at her clipboard, she says, "Name?"

The blonde flinches for a second. Blink and you'd miss it, but I didn't.

"Saffy," she says.

"Full name," Quick replies.

Then Saffy speaks her full name, real fast so it almost comes out as a single word.

"Saffron Chassay."

I'm not the only one who sniggers. I mean, who wouldn't? *Saffron Chassay*. What a ridiculous-ass name. It suits her. She rolls her eyes at the barely contained laughter from me and a couple of the other girls. But she does look rattled. Interesting.

Quick takes a pen from the little holder on the clipboard and makes a ticking motion on her document before moving on to the next girl. She's the waif of the group, real skinny and pale. I notice her tousling her hair as Quick approaches, which makes the older woman purse her lips even tighter.

"Hands by your side, girl. Name?"

"Jessica Hope."

Another tick, then Quick moves off. Jessica starts fiddling with her hair again as soon as Quick's back is turned.

"Name."

I hear a loud hawking and then spitting sound as the next girl deposits a ball of freshly drawn phlegm onto the gravel. I lean forward a little so I can get a better look and see that the girl has spat right in front of Quick's feet. Oh, boy. I remember seeing her on the bus because the dark circles under her eyes stood out. I recall thinking that she looks as though she has grown up way too fast. She has the punk rock look about her, and could pass for thirty thanks to those dark rings.

I see Quick reach out and for a moment I think she's going to whack her. But instead, Quick places a finger under the girl's chin and lifts her face until their eyes meet.

"Nasty habit," she says. "Name?"

The girl jerks away from Quick's touch, then stares at the floor. "I'm…Lena Turner," she says, and I'm surprised at the defeat in her tone.

"Yes, I suppose you are." Quick makes her mark on the clipboard again.

I become aware of a slight movement beside me. Glancing that way, I can see that the girl who was hiding behind her fringe on the bus is shaking. Even her knees are trembling. I wonder if she's going to faint. Quick is standing in front of the girl next to the one who has the shakes.

"Name."

"Annie. Annie Chastain."

Quite perky sounding, this one. And I can see a distinct look of displeasure on Quick's face before she makes another ticking motion with her pen. Then she walks a couple of steps along the line until she's face-to-fringe with the trembling girl.

"Name."

The shaking gives way to uncontrolled sobbing and, at the far end of the line, Saffy laughs. It's an unpleasant, birdlike sound, and loud enough perhaps to overcompensate for the giggling her full name received.

"Your name, girl."

I look at the girl. At her hands. She's balled them into fists and her knuckles have turned white. Her shoulders have almost folded in on themselves, and she's trying to hold her sobs so deep inside she looks as though she might burst open. A tear trickles down her cheek, which has turned a vivid shade of pink.

Quick sighs, then checks her list.

"Victoria Kim?"

The girl nods and her shoulders drop slightly from the relief. I see Principal Quick looking at Victoria in the same way a cat might regard a mouse, before ticking her name off the list. Then Quick moves to the end of the line. It's my turn.

"Emily Drake. Surprised to see you back here so soon."

I can almost sense Saffy's ears pricking up at this. A couple of the others seem pretty interested, too. I can see them out of my peripheral vision, but I try not to look away from Quick in case she interprets it as a sign of weakness. I vaguely remember Principal Quick, and this place. But I'm not sure if I really do remember, or if it's just my meds messing with my head again. I try my breathing exercises again.

"You will learn," Quick says, her eyes on me, "someday." Then she takes a step back and addresses all of us. "You will *all* learn, as I live and breathe."

Quick tucks the clipboard under her arm with military precision.

"Inside. Single file."

One by one, the girls ahead of me file across the gravel forecourt, up the steps and into the main entrance of the reformatory. I'm last in line and as I follow the others, a shadow catches me. The sudden chill turns my skin to gooseflesh and I have the compulsion to look upward. The clock tower looms over me, obelisk-like against turbulent skies. The increasing wind is bringing with it dark clouds that look heavy with rain. I notice that the clock's hands are not moving – stuck close to seven. Above the clockface is an arched window, open to the elements. For a moment, something gray flutters within the archway. It looks like a girl, standing there in an inmate's uniform and watching me through her long, dark hair. The wind is making my eyes water and I blink to clear my vision.

No one there after all.

I keep walking, eager to be indoors and away from the biting wind.

CHAPTER TWO

Routine Clarifies Mind and Body

I pass over the threshold and into the building and it's as though Greyfriars Reformatory is a shroud wrapping its darkness all around me. The air is stale and thin and the corridor is possibly the gloomiest I've ever seen – and believe me when I say that I have trudged down some pretty depressing corridors in my time on God's green Earth.

Principal Quick stands beside the door and, once we're all gathered inside the entrance hall, she turns and then reaches up to tap a gray plastic switch mounted on the wall next to the door. The principal has to stand on tiptoes to do it and I find myself thinking maybe she's not as big and imposing as she'd have us believe. I hear a faint clank from outside and realize the switch must operate the iron gates. She then shuts the door and locks it using three different keys from her bunch. Principal Quick keeps her back to us the whole time, shielding the keys with her body so we can't see which ones she's using. I think she's been doing this job for a long time because she's less concerned about being jumped from behind than she is letting us know which keys unlock the front door. Maybe it's a weird display of power, keeping her back to us. None of us bothers to try anything, of course. We're in the middle of nowhere, after all. Nowhere to run to all the way out here.

Principal Quick turns to face us. As if she's heard my thoughts, she says, "You will have noticed by now that there are no guards at Greyfriars. And before you get any ideas, be aware that this is precisely because there is no need for them. If you try to leave this place, you won't last longer than a day on the outside. There are no vehicles. No houses. Only empty, endless roads and harsh, unforgiving wilderness. This is an experimental facility, and one that is built upon the one thing you have each been denied during your incarceration thus far—namely, trust. I am your caregiver. Your ticket to rehabilitation and survival in the big, bad world. The first cohort didn't work out. Abject failures, all. But Emily, you have apparently been given a second chance here. I hope you will lead by example."

I can feel their eyes on me again. I do not like it.

"I trust that each and every one of you will allow me to do my job," Quick says.

It is more a statement than a question, so we each remain quiet and just watch her affix her keys to her belt. Another subtle display of power.

"Come along, girls," she says.

Then Quick marches past us, her heels clicking on the hard reflective surface of the floor. We follow dumbly behind and I notice that Annie keeps her head down the whole time she's walking. She has the beginnings of a stoop that already makes her look like one of those old street ladies you see pushing around grocery carts filled with crap. I put on my best shuffle to keep up, but also to maintain a safe distance from any of them. Personal space really becomes a priority when you don't have it. It's currency for the institutionalized.

And if there's one thing Greyfriars Reformatory has, it is space. Quick leads us down one corridor after another and they all look the same with their polished floors mirroring dark ceilings. The drab walls are painted in a fetching—

(*Or is that retching?*)

—off-white shade that may have been intentional, or may just be years of accumulated dust. The principal takes a right turn and I'm completely lost. But then I'm amazed to see what lies beyond the long, narrow window set into the interior wall of this corridor.

"Our swimming pool affords us the luxury of indoor exercise, whatever the weather – and it does get quite rough out here on occasion," Principal Quick says.

I move closer to the glass to take a better look, and become aware that the other girls are doing exactly the same thing. The still waters of the pool, artificially blue from its tiled interior, reflect squares of light from the skylights high above. Deep shadows meet the deep end, making the pool room look even larger than it perhaps is.

"Each of you will maintain a strict regimen of vigorous exercise. Every morning."

I hear a couple of sighs and groans from the others. I don't feel anything either way. I mean, what's the use in complaining about an exercise regimen? We've all been there before. And here we all are now. No point fighting it, or trying to get a pass because it's your period. Disciplinarians such as Principal Quick don't give a rat's ass whether you have stomach cramps or not. And I bet the pool isn't even heated. Quick doesn't even seem to notice the groans of protest anyway – or maybe she's just ignoring them.

She leads off again and I glance back at the pool. My reflection in the glass looks hollowed out. A silhouette person with no face. I turn my back on it and catch up to the others.

Our guide slows down as we enter an adjacent corridor, and then stops beside a door. Principal Quick appears to be well and truly in her element – school matron and prison warden made one, as she selects another key from her bunch and opens the door.

She leads us inside and I see that the room is a classroom, set up with two rows of desks and chairs. The furniture is worn and old, and I wonder how many girls like us have sat at them over the years. A blackboard dominates the wall behind Principal Quick, its surface cloudy from accumulated chalk residue.

"After your morning workout, you will have personal development classes. Followed by chores."

Chores. The word that sends terror into the hearts of us all. I hear the others muttering and moaning again. Principal Quick doesn't rise to the bait; she just ushers us out of the room and we wait while she locks the door. I notice that she doesn't bother shielding the keys from us this time. I mean, who would want to break and enter into a classroom? Especially one that has bars on its windows. I can hardly wait for our first 'personal development class'.

Muted daylight washes over the next corridor, which has similar observation windows to the swimming pool running along one side. A glass-paneled door leads outside onto an exercise yard. Principal Quick opens the door for us and gestures for us to head outside. We file out, and the principal has us line up against the far wall.

A glimmer behind the spot where Principal Quick is standing catches my eye and I see what looks like a mirror set into the connecting wall nearest the door. Then I realize it's a window, paned with reflective glass. For surveillance, I guess, so we lucky inmates can take our exercise under strict observation at all times. The walls are high, and cast long shadows across the already rather grim space. A single, bare tree stands crooked at the center. Its trunk and branches look diseased. Any bark left on it is hanging loose like post-liposuction skin. Maybe it's been killed off by lack of natural light.

(*I wonder if that's the fate that awaits us all.*)

"Supervised recreation helps you to absorb the day's learning," Quick intones. "Two thirty-minute periods per day."

(*Ah, no such luck then. I think we're doomed to be kept alive to endure her 'vigorous regimen'.*)

Principal Quick has us exit the recreation yard and then follow her along yet more nondescript corridors. I begin to zone out for a bit, the gray walls and viewless windows merging inside my head until there's just a sickly pale mist drifting across my eyes. I guess I should probably explain that I have these out-of-body things fairly regularly, so I've learned to just ride them out. It's less alarming that way, if I just try to accept them as and when they happen. Everyday sounds usually bring me out of them and, true to form, I become aware of the swish of a sliding door opening on its runners.

The sound brings my surroundings back into sharp focus, but it's only when the bright lights hit me that I even realize we've entered the refectory. A row of plastic bowls stand waiting for us on a Formica table. Each bowl is covered with cling wrap, and has a disposable spoon next to it. Single-use plastics seem to still be a thing at Greyfriars Reformatory. Gray bucket seats are attached to metal frames, which are bolted to the floor. It's like a motorway service food court, only a million times more depressing than that.

Principal Quick instructs us to sit down, and then to remove the cling wrap – and eat. The only thing on today's menu is some pretty ghastly, lukewarm porridge, I discover. The principal waffles on, with no apparent sense of irony, about the importance of nutrition. She says the dining staff aren't around to cook for us right now, but that we can soon look forward to 'a nourishing breakfast'. Those words strike fear into my heart, based on what lurks in my bowl right now. I manage to swallow some of the sludge and can almost feel it expanding in my stomach like a medical balloon. Whoever prepared this gruel – Quick herself? – has never heard of seasoning. I glance around the drab space, hoping some salt or sugar might magically appear. But there's no magic here, only the miserable faces of the other girls. I return to my meager meal and attempt to turn my gag reflex into another swallow.

"Evening meal before washing, then lights out," Quick recites. "Routine clarifies mind and body. Heals the soul."

(*Yay, she sounds like a life coach for the recently deceased.*)

I lift my spoon and see a congealed lump of porridge at its center. I give up the ghost and place my spoon back into my bowl. The refectory has fallen silent, save for the clicking of plastic spoons. Jessica, I notice, hasn't actually eaten any of hers. Although she is admittedly very good at manipulating her spoon to make it look as though she's eating, I can see she's just moving the spoon in an elaborate series of circles-within-circles. It's as though she's performing some kind of spell, with the plastic spoon her magic wand, hypnotizing the onlooker into thinking she's joining in with the tepid porridge feast. Maybe there is some magic here, after all.

I look away, and see that Saffy is watching Jessica too, very intently and with that silver-spoon smirk all over her chops. Saffy sees me looking and takes a huge scoop of porridge onto her spoon and then, with theatrical relish, into her mouth. She chews and swallows like she's enjoying a fine steak.

(*You go, girl.*)

A true survivor that one.

Disgusting meal quickly and thankfully over with, Principal Quick has each of us place our bowls in a stainless-steel wash-down area. We each then rinse them out, creating a thin sludge of porridge around the plughole. The principal watches over us in the manner of a cooking-show host who is about to critique our work.

(*Beautiful sludge, girls. But I think it needed more flavor.*)

After we're all done, Principal Quick crosses to the door, then slides it open and beckons us out. I'm last, as per usual. Quick glances around the refectory as I approach her, and her expression strikes me. It looks like she's mislaid something. I hear the door click shut behind me, and then hear the jangling of the principal's keys as she locks it.

★ ★ ★

If the refectory was depressing, the dormitory beats it, hands down. Neatly made camp beds stand in rows beneath barred windows. Thin, pale gray drapes flutter in the breeze from the partially opened windows, high above. At least there's some fresh air I guess, but when the sun comes up there'll be no hiding from it. Principal Quick directs each of us to a bed, and tells us to stand beside it. Mine is nearest the door. Drab, uniformly gray nightclothes lay folded atop each of the beds. Each bed has been crisply made up with white sheets and gray blankets. There is a small locker beside each bed.

"You will find all the essentials required for personal hygiene in your lockers," Principal Quick says. "You are responsible for the care of each of your own items. No replacements will be issued."

The principal then gestures to a door at the far end of the dormitory.

"Scrub up and get changed," she says, and then pauses at the end of Saffy's bed. As usual, Saffy has that smirk on her face. Principal Quick stiffens, and it's as though her entire body is demonstrating her dominance over Saffy. What an exciting pissing contest *this* is.

"Lights out in thirty minutes," Principal Quick concludes, before leaving the dormitory.

All the other girls, except Saffy, set about investigating their lockers. Saffy just stretches and yawns, looking like a cat. I decide to open my locker. Inside, I find a small bar of soap, a bath towel and a clear plastic toothbrush with a tube of toothpaste. I bundle the soap, toothpaste, and brush inside the towel and then place the bundle on top of my nightclothes. A couple of beds away from mine, Victoria throws herself facedown onto her bed and begins sobbing into her pillow. She's really going for it – I mean, full-on snot and tears.

"What's her fucking problem?" Saffy asks.

She glances around, looking to each of us for some kind

of reaction. Receiving none, Saffy opens her own locker. After retrieving her things, she tosses her towel onto her shoulder and trots toward the bathroom, humming an annoying tune as she goes. I wait for the others to follow before tucking the towel bundle under my arm. The sound of Victoria's sobbing echoes around the dorm as I walk to the bathroom door.

The bathroom is just as gloomy and authoritarian as the other 'highlights' of the reformatory we saw on Principal Quick's whirlwind tour. It has an unpleasantly moldy odor to it. Cracked tiles and musty mirrors hang above a row of sinks, opposite a line of gray-doored toilet stalls. At least the bathroom is big enough to allow each of us some space to do our thing. I cross to the nearest unoccupied sink and place my towel beside it. After unwrapping the contents, I pick out the toothbrush and rinse it under the tap. I squirt a line of toothpaste onto it and begin to brush my teeth. Uppers first, front then back, followed by my lower teeth. I have never had a filling in my life and would like to keep it that way. While I brush, I glance at the reflections in the other mirrors.

Saffy is attempting to style her hair, it seems, and I wonder why on earth she would be doing that. No one is going to be looking at her except her fellow inmates, and I doubt if any of us will give much of a shit what her hair looks like. Jessica appears to be doing the opposite of Saffy. She's actively un-styling her hair, back-combing it with her fingers and pulling the tousled strands forward until they are obscuring her face. Lena just stands there, hands on the sink and staring straight ahead with unblinking eyes. I notice how muscled her arms are compared to the rest of us. She looks like a prize fighter waiting for her next knockout bout. Annie ducks into a bathroom stall and closes the door.

I finish brushing my teeth and change into my reformatory-issue smock. It feels rough against my skin and I wonder how I'll ever sleep in it. On the bright side, at least skin exfoliation will be a feature.

Saffy voices her displeasure at the reformatory-issue clothing, and a couple of the other girls join in, making a chorus of disapproval. The sounds of their whining and sarcastic laughter echo around the bathroom. This, coupled with the ever-pervasive moldy odor, begins to make me feel a little queasy. I splash my face with cool water and then dry off with the towel. As I blink away the last of the moisture, I hear the door creak open.

Reflected in the mirror, I see Victoria step into the bathroom. Her shoulders are rounded and her head hangs low as she clutches her toiletries to her chest. She sniffles, and the other girls fall instantly silent. The only vacant sinks are right at the far end of the bathroom, and Victoria has to walk the gauntlet past each and every one of us to reach them. All the other girls are standing stock-still now, watching her. I lean forward slightly so I can see her better, and watch her place her stuff on the side of the sink before turning on the tap and filling the sink with water. She soaks her flannel and sets about washing her face, which is pink from crying.

I hear the sound of a toilet flushing and seconds later Annie emerges from the stall. She walks over to the only remaining unoccupied sink and washes her hands.

Saffy stops messing with her hair and makes a big show of sidling up to Victoria.

"Feel better now?" Saffy asks. But her tone is the opposite of caring.

Victoria glances at her nervously and, right under her nose, Saffy reaches out and snatches her toothbrush away. Holding it aloft like a trophy, Saffy dances across the tiled floor, grinning in triumph. She taunts Victoria with the brush, then backs up to the bathroom stall that Annie just vacated and bumps it open with her ass. Chuckling, Saffy dances into the stall and holds the toothbrush above the toilet bowl. She raises her arm, teasingly, then drops the brush into the bowl. It makes a loud 'plop' as it hits the water in the bowl. Saffy turns and approaches Victoria, who recoils from her.

"Don't forget to brush your teeth," Saffy says. "Retard."

Saffy marches over to the door, accompanied by howls of amazed laughter from the other girls.

"Come on, girls," Saffy says, "let's give Moaning Myrtle some privacy, shall we?"

I listen to their laughs as they follow Saffy out of the bathroom. I can see Victoria's forlorn reflection in her mirror and it strikes me how laughter can sometimes be such an unhappy sound.

When I return to the dormitory I find Saffy waiting for me. She's sitting on the end of my bed, her legs crossed casually. She supports her body weight on one arm. For some reason the flat of her hand pressing down onto my bed bothers me the most. It's like she's invading my personal space in the most subtle, yet completely arrogant, way possible. Which is, of course, exactly what she's doing. I stop still a few feet away from her, and from the end of my bed.

"We haven't been formally introduced," she says, her voice silky smooth.

I glance over to the door and see Lena standing beside it, staring through a narrow gap in the doorway. Oh, I get it. She's the lookout, in case Principal Quick comes to check on us.

Saffy moves, and I see she has extended her right hand for me to shake. It hangs there in the exaggerated space between us, and that ringing in my ears starts again. The air around me grows thick somehow, and my eyesight blurs slightly. Then there's only the ringing sound and Saffy's hand, haloed in my swimming vision like some alien artifact on display in a museum. I see the vague outline of Saffy's face. Her already indistinct features begin to melt, dripping like melting crayon across the gray of her nightclothes. The dark oval of her mouth starts to swallow the rest of her face, and—

"Whatever," I hear Saffy say through her distorted mouth, and someone behind me sniggers. The two sounds snap me back into the room, and into reality.

"I'm not one to stand on ceremony anyway," Saffy asserts.

She withdraws her hand and I realize she's trying to style it out – the fact that I didn't shake it. My out-of-body moment has left me feeling a bit numb, and I just want to climb into bed. But I can't, because she's still sitting on it. Saffy tosses her hair back and puffs her chest out. It's quite a sight, let's just leave it at that.

"This is how it's gonna work," she says. "You've been in here before. That's potentially useful to me. Think of me as the real principal, yes?"

Her voice trails off and I see her looking over my shoulder. I follow her glance and see Victoria enter, shoulders hunched as though she's trying not to be noticed. I turn back to Saffy, who watches Victoria with a sly grin on her face. I hear Victoria's bedsprings creak as she climbs onto it, and Saffy returns her unwanted attention to me.

"If you do good by me, you won't have anything to worry about," she goes on, apropos of nothing, "but if you don't...."

She's really grinning now, showing all her perfect white teeth as she stares across the room again.

I turn to see Victoria pull back her bedcovers. Her face falls into a look of utter dismay. She pulls an object from inside her bedcovers. It's a roll of toilet paper. Saffy shrieks with laughter and the other girls join in. Victoria drops the toilet roll to the floor, climbs into bed and hides under her covers.

I turn back to face Saffy, who is wiping tears of laughter from the corners of her eyes. She blinks and looks at me – and I mean really *looks* – frowning for a second as though she can't figure me out. I guess it's because I'm not laughing along with the rest of them. Nor am I crying like Victoria was.

"So, who *is* she?" Saffy asks.

I'm not sure what Saffy means. I glance around the room. "Who?"

"The other inmate."

"We're all...here, aren't we?"

"You tell me."

"I don't understand," I say. And really, I don't.

"You're the old timer," Saffy goes on. "Come on, you must've seen her, up in the clock tower, watching us when we arrived?"

I think back to when we arrived. I remember the hiss of the hydraulic brakes, the dust cloud when the bus drove away. The hands of the clock in the tower stuck on seven o'clock. Was there someone watching me from the clock tower? I can't be sure. My mind conjures the fluttering of cloth, but maybe it was just a curtain.

"Do not fuck with me," Saffy says.

I lock eyes with her through my confusion and I see something twist, and turn, in her expression. Her lips draw thin with anger. She reaches out and grabs my wrist.

"Actually I *do* stand on ceremony, particularly when it comes to social skills," Saffy says, her voice dripping with bile, "and when I offer you my hand, you take it, bitch."

Saffy twists my hand around sharply. It feels like my bones are going to snap.

"You feel me, Emily darling?" Saffy snarls, and her grip tightens.

I open my mouth to breathe, but the pain stops the air in my throat. I try to pull away, but it makes the pain even worse. She's strong, and she's hurting me. This is who she really is, under all the blonde hair and sideways smirks.

"She's coming!" Lena says from her position by the door. Lena closes the door quickly, but quietly, and the other girls each snap to it, climbing into their beds.

Saffy makes a show of slowly releasing my wrist from her painful grip, then prowls over to, and into, her bed. Jesus, she's like a trapdoor spider returning to its lair.

I get into my own bed and then I hear the door open. From my vantage point in my bed, I see a long, dark shadow fall across the floor. I look over to the doorway to see Principal Quick standing there.

"Lights out, girls. Morning inspection at zero-seven-hundred, followed by exercise, and then – and only then – breakfast."

With that, Principal Quick turns out the lights and closes the door.

I listen to the principal's footfalls as they echo into the distance down the corridor. My wrist still aches from where Saffy twisted my hand over. I tuck it under my pillow and close my eyes. I doubt I can sleep until the throbbing pain subsides.

After a few moments, Saffy's whispering voice pierces the semi-darkness.

"Hey, crybaby...."

I open my eyes and see something gleaming white fly across the room. I blink, and then I realize that Saffy has hurled the toilet roll at Victoria. How depressingly childish of her. It rebounds, off Victoria's head. Victoria just pulls her blanket up and over her face.

"Sweet dreams," Saffy purrs, and a couple of the other girls respond with more cruel taunts.

I pull my covers over my head too, hoping to block them, and their games, out.

CHAPTER THREE

The Seven Virtues

I'm drifting in blackness when I hear a faint musical sound.

It sounds like a child's music box, the kind with the little handle you turn to make the chimes ring out. I open my eyes and find the dormitory is still shrouded in darkness. In all honesty I don't yet know if I'm dreaming or not, so I sit up in bed. I feel groggy and dehydrated. At least the ache in my wrist has gone away.

I swallow dryly and then yawn. The musical sound persists, and it sounds like it is coming from the corridor outside the dormitory. There is another sound too, and this one is fainter than the music. It sounds like a girl is sobbing. I assume it's Victoria, until I look over to see her still lying asleep in her bed. All the other beds are still occupied, so who is it making that noise? I'm awake now, and too intrigued to go back to sleep, so I clamber out of bed to investigate.

The eerie musical chimes continue as I steal out of the dormitory. And, as I emerge into the corridor, the plaintive sobbing grows louder too. The night sky beyond the high windows is pitch black. The only light comes from some eerily green emergency lighting at the far end of the corridor, where the sounds of the chimes and the sobbing are coming from. Then I see the shadow of a girl flit across the wall.

I pursue her, following the corridor around to the left. The music and the moans lead me on until I'm walking through a longer corridor. I fight the instinct to call out to the mystery girl, for fear that I might alert Principal Quick to the fact that I'm out of bed and roaming the hallways.

(*Is that dream logic? I wonder. Am I still asleep after all?*)

I round another corner and see a dark shape set into the wall up ahead. As I get nearer, I see that it is the dark entrance to a stairwell. I hear echoing footfalls climbing the stairs, and a sharp sniffing sound before the mournful sobbing continues on. I look down at where the scant green glow of the emergency lighting gives way to the black shadow of the stairwell. I step across the shadow's threshold and I'm engulfed in the darkness. Cool air washes over me from somewhere above.

I climb the steps, each of which feels rough and cold beneath my feet. The darkness is almost impenetrable as I climb the stairs, and I have to feel my way around as the staircase spirals up to the next level. A cold breeze blows through my hair, giving me goosebumps, and all the while the chimes grow ever louder and more distorted. The sound makes me think of a child's toy with the batteries running down, making the pained sobbing I can hear all the more disconcerting. A few more steps and I can see a little better thanks to a faint, silvery light at the summit of the staircase. I push on and reach the top. Holding on to the side of the open brick doorway, I pause to catch my breath.

And then I realize the sounds have stopped.

I enter the room and take in my surroundings. The reverse side of a large clockface is to my right and the moon is shining right through it – the source of the silvery light that guided me to the summit. The stairs have led me right the way up to the freaking clock tower. A chill breeze blows through open arches on each side of the clockface, making me shiver. The clock mechanism ticks rhythmically, a counterpoint to the ebb and flow of the wind. The clock's hands are a minute before seven o'clock. That strikes me as strange. How can it still be so damn dark if it's almost seven?

I feel both exposed and enclosed up here, somehow. The tower room smells musty. Dust, debris and an old, gray blanket litter the floor. The breeze lifts the blanket and for a moment I feel a chill as it looks like someone might be lying there, underneath it. I blink away the illusion – but then I hear something.

The sobbing sounds break the quiet. I look to the source of the sound and feel a shock of surprise to see a girl standing on the precipice in one of the open archways. How she got there, I can't explain. The clock tower was definitely empty when I entered. No way I wouldn't have noticed if she'd come up the stairs behind me. I feel more gooseflesh pricking my arms as the girl turns my way. She's clad in a dirty, gray reformatory uniform. Her dark, tousled hair hides her facial features. She looks strangely lifeless standing there in the archway – a shadow-person. But her shoulders convulse as she sobs uncontrollably, betraying her humanity. She turns her back on me and teeters on the edge.

I reach out my hand to her on instinct, though I'm still a few meters away. *No*, I try to yell, but I can't speak. Then the girl just *drops* suddenly. One moment she was there, standing in the archway, and the next she's gone. I rush to the side of the precipice and, placing my hands on the cold brickwork of the archway, I peer over the edge and down at the ground. But there's no sign of the girl who fell. I lean, carefully, a little further over the edge, scanning the recreation yard below for the shape of her body. Nothing. Just the skeletal shape of a dead tree.

Then I feel a freezing chill at the nape of my neck.

A hand grips my shoulder tight.

I whirl around to see the girl, her face hidden in hair and shadow. But her eyes are just visible through the veil of hair. And they are brimming with hatred. Her fingernails dig into my shoulder painfully and I try to cry out, but again no sound will come.

I try to lift my hands, to fight back, but they dangle numbly at my sides. My ears begin to ring, as though the music box chimes have become a single, discordant note burrowing through my ears and into my brain. Her hateful eyes narrow to spiteful slits, and she shoves me hard. I fall back from the archway, my arms and legs feeling as distant from me as the tower becomes with my descent.

My heart beats faster.

The wind blasts my back as I plummet toward the ground.

I try to scream, but all I can hear is that terrible ringing, on and on in my ears.

* * *

I wake with a jolt. My bedcovers are tangled around my wrists and legs. I sit up and wriggle free. Saffy's face is the first that I see, unfortunately. She's already dressed in her uniform, and is wearing that trademarked, shit-eating smirk of hers. A couple of the other girls are getting dressed, and I hear running water coming from the bathroom.

I blink away the last remnants of my nightmare and prepare to hit the shower.

I hope the water's hot because I feel so damn cold.

* * *

Principal Quick is waiting for us when we arrive at the refectory door. She stands with her back to the door. As she eyeballs each of us, I notice her caressing the bunch of keys she holds in her right hand. She has a leather-bound book tucked under her left arm.

"At Greyfriars, we *earn* our meals. You will follow me."

With that, she's off, and we each have to walk fast to keep up with her. I'm just guessing, you understand, but I suspect

Principal Quick may have already *earned* her breakfast. I bet she eats like a queen, somewhere, while we're all still in bed. Stomachs gurgling audibly, we each line up in the exercise yard under Quick's instruction, our backs to the far wall. The sky looms gray overhead, and there's a damp smell in the air. I look down at the ground and see that the concrete at my feet has green patches on it where moss and mold have taken hold.

(*Hey, that rhymes!*)

"Jogging detail. Single file. Saffron Chassay, you will lead."

I can barely contain myself, hearing her call Saffy by her full name again. It'll never get old – unlike me, stuck in this rotten, depressing place.

"Emily Drake! Step in line."

Principal Quick's command goes straight to my feet and I follow the rabble around the courtyard. I hear the jangling of keys behind me and, as I round the courtyard, I see that the principal has pocketed them. She has a cigarette between her lips, which she lights. She exhales a plume of smoke into the morning air like the dragon she really is. We all have to jog through her secondhand smoke. If I was at all cynical, I'd think she had planned it that way. Reminding us that we have no privileges. Surely not though. The principal glances at us as we pass, then takes the book from beneath her left arm, opens it and begins to recite.

On and on she drones, turning the pages as we each huff and puff our incarcerated asses around the exercise yard. We begin to bunch together, and I can feel the heat of other bodies around me. It's not an unpleasant sensation in the cool damp of the morning air. Then Saffy's voice cuts through in a harsh whisper, and I feel like running faster to put some distance between us.

"Be good to know where she keeps her stash of smokes, eh girls?"

Quick continues reading, oblivious.

"Well?" Saffy says, and I realize she's right beside me.

"What?" You have to agree, it's a fair question.

"Where does she keep 'em?" Saffy whispers.

"I don't know."

"Oh, sure you don't. Like you don't know a thing about the mysterious other inmate. Allow me to *jog* your memory."

Before I can react, I feel Saffy's hand on my elbow. She shoves me hard, and I lose my footing. I crash into Victoria, who tumbles to the ground as I half run, half jump over her falling body. I have a split second to avoid smashing into the wall. I put my hands out in front of me and come to a standstill.

Saffy and the other girls have stopped jogging too and are standing around Victoria, shrieking with laughter.

Quick looks angrily at Victoria, then snaps her book closed. "Am I interrupting you? Get to your feet, clumsy girl."

Victoria gets to her feet, rubbing at her badly grazed hands. She glares at me like it's somehow my fault. Saffy, I can't help but notice, looks delighted. For one, brief moment, I feel something burning in my chest. It's the truth about what happened, trying to get out. It's tempting, I have to admit, the idea of landing Saffy in hot water by telling Principal Quick how she shoved me into Victoria and made her fall. But I swallow the truth down inside of me and let it dissipate.

"Back to it, girls." Principal Quick finds her page again, unfortunately, and continues reading aloud.

No sooner have we passed by the principal, than Saffy draws alongside me again.

"Good to know you're a team player," she whispers, and I realize it was maybe another of her weirdly ritualistic tests like when she offered her hand for me to shake. "I'm going to be running a tight ship here, don't forget it. You're either with me, or…." Saffy clams up as we jog past Principal Quick.

The principal finishes her cigarette and stubs it out beneath the heel of her shoe. She raises her head and has a faraway look in her eyes. I glance upward too and see that her eyes are fixed on the clock tower above the courtyard.

I cast my gaze back down at the courtyard and feel a chill pass right through me as I jog under the tower's shadow.

* * *

After exercise detail, we had breakfast. Well, I say breakfast, but in reality I don't know what it actually was that Principal Quick served up. I think it was supposed to be porridge, but the absence of any discernable flavor would make it anyone's guess. Rest assured, it satisfied no major food group requirements. I can still feel it, heavy in my stomach, as I sit at my desk in the classroom.

Principal Quick stands at the head of the class and her back is to all of us as she's writing something on the chalkboard. She finishes what she's scrawling with a flourish and steps back from the chalkboard before turning to face us.

The heading reads: PERSONAL DEVELOPMENT – THE SEVEN VIRTUES.

The look on her sharp face is one of immense pride. She clearly feels a sense of accomplishment when writing things, especially when using chalk.

(*You go girl, too.*)

"You will learn the seven virtues," she announces. "You will embrace and embody them. Only through this learning can you hope to salvage something from your lives."

Principal Quick turns her back on us and begins writing on the board again. Beneath the heading, in immaculate handwriting, she is writing a list:

Humility. Chastity. Temperance.

Oh good, I do love a list. Everyone does, don't they? Wow, her handwriting is really neat though, I'll give her that. And while she's writing, I glance carefully at the other girls. Victoria looks even more fucked up than she did yesterday, like she hasn't slept. I see her idly rubbing at her wrist, which looks red raw from her fall in the exercise yard. Saffy sits bolt upright, her posture perfect, wearing her power-smirk. Annie appears to be looking for a window that isn't there to stare out of. Lena slouches over her desk, absentmindedly picking her nose.

(*Atta girl.*)

Principal Quick turns back to face the class and I snap back to attention again. She takes a couple of steps forward to address us, revealing the rest of her beautifully rendered list:

Mercy. Kindness. Charity.

"The first step in your rehabilitation will require?"

It's a rhetorical question, *obvs*. I stare at the blank page of my notebook. None of the others makes a sound. Well, all except for Lena, who yawns. I look up at the sound and my eyes meet Principal Quick's. She scowls, then finishes adding a final word to her list:

Diligence.

The principal turns from the blackboard and stares at me. I don't really know how to react. Does she expect me to say something? It's like her gaze is burrowing into my brain and poking around in there for anything of use.

Good luck with that, I think.

And the burrowing becomes a burning sensation, like I'm burning on the inside, and then the ringing in my ears starts up and I feel numb at my extremities, like I'm falling but not falling and just hanging there, an empty vessel being carved out hollow from the inside until there's nothing left of me but a shell and even that is tenuous, I mean I'm hardly even there at all and—

★ ★ ★

The ringing echoes out and my seat feels softer beneath me than it did in the classroom. And the room's darker, too. I blink and then, lowering my hands flat either side of me, I find the springs of a mattress pushing back. The echoes fade away and I'm in the dormitory. Around me, the other girls are getting ready for bed. I see Lena keeping watch again by the door.

I wonder how much time has passed since I began to completely zone out this time. A taste, like mashed potatoes, on my tongue. That heavy feeling in my stomach again, only different from the breakfast gruel. It must be after dinner, because they're all getting ready for bed. Saffy is sprawled on her bed, fiddling with her blonde hair. She's already in her nightclothes.

"Let's play a game, ladies," she says.

(*Oh, please, let's not.*)

"What kind of game?" Annie asks. She's sitting cross-legged on her bed.

"Why are you in here?"

Lena snorts. "Wouldn't you like to know?" she says from her vantage point by the door.

"Yes, I would, matter of fact," Saffy snaps back. "And that's why you're going first. Well volunteered."

"Screw you," Lena says.

"Screw me? Ugh. I knew it would be dyke-related." Saffy wrinkles her nose theatrically.

Lena flips her the bird, which only encourages Saffy to play to the room all the more.

Victoria pads over to her bed, then places her toiletries into her bedside locker.

Saffy watches her with the attitude of a bored predator. "How about you, retard?" Saffy asks.

But Victoria pretends not to have heard.

"Earth calling retard," Saffy says, louder this time. "I said how about you?"

Victoria pulls back her covers. Her face falls as she pulls out another toilet roll from beneath her bedcovers. She tosses the toilet roll out onto the floor and then climbs into bed. She grits her teeth in apparent anger and frustration before pulling her covers over her head.

Saffy laughs and the others do too. I don't find it that funny, to be honest with you. They've made that lame joke before. Maybe they need a new one. Then Saffy looks at me with a cruel smirk on her face and I wonder if *I'm* going to be their new joke.

"Hey, bitches," Lena says, "Principal Quick's coming."

Saved by the principal. Hallelujah.

Saffy gives Victoria a parting shot. "I'll get it out of you, I always do," she says, before getting into bed.

"Lights out, girls." I hear Principal Quick flicking the light switch. She pulls the door shut, and then I hear the heels of the principal's shoes beat a tattoo as she walks away down the corridor. I lie awake in the near-darkness and, after Principal Quick's footfalls die away, I listen to the mournful sobs coming from Victoria's bed.

CHAPTER FOUR

Victoria

Victoria slept fitfully, as she always did. It was a source of consternation to her mother that she always had dark circles under her eyes.

"Your bedroom is as pink as the womb," her mom had told her. "I don't know why you can't sleep through."

Victoria knew why. And she wondered if her mother knew too, but chose to ignore it. *Ignorance is bliss.* Wasn't that how the saying went? Even now, Victoria was drifting out of sleep and back into wakefulness. Her nose wrinkled at the persistent smell of something. And the something awakened her.

She sat up in bed, all pink pastel and plush throw cushions. All her gender-stereotyped belongings, neatly laid out on cerise shelves. The little alarm clock, also pink, told her it was still nighttime. Just before one a.m.

Confused by the strange smell, and half-asleep, she pulled on a robe and drifted out of the room. Holding on to the handrail because she was feeling so woozy, Victoria yawned her way downstairs and headed for the kitchen. She passed the line of framed photo portraits on the wall. A half-dozen versions of herself, pictured through the years from fat-faced kid to young adult. Smiling. But not really smiling.

Victoria entered the kitchen. The lights had been left on, their reflections gleaming off the polished tile floor. Squeaky clean, just how Mom liked it. But instead of the quiet of the hour, Victoria could hear an intense hissing sound. As she moved into the domestic space, she saw her mother sitting on a breakfast stool. Her upper body lay slumped across the kitchen island, with a near-empty liquor bottle next to her. She appeared to be unconscious.

Victoria yawned, and a bad taste clung to the back of her throat. She needed that glass of water, still, but thought maybe she'd sit next to her mom for a while. Her limbs were so very heavy, and she felt so tired all of a sudden. She approached the kitchen island, reached out a leaden hand to her mother. And all the while the hissing grew louder and louder until—

Victoria jolted awake from her dream. She sat up and looked around the dormitory. No shades of pink pastel here, only gray. At least that horrid hissing noise had stopped. She swallowed, dispelling the acrid taste at the back of her mouth from her dream. The other girls were asleep.

All except for one.

Victoria saw that one of the girls was out of bed. She was standing a couple of meters away from Victoria's bed, her face hidden by her dark hair. How strange that Victoria hadn't noticed her before. Moonlight from the high, barred window accentuated the paleness of the exposed skin of the girl's forearms. Victoria felt a sense of dread seeing her standing there. Not because she was afraid, but rather because she was tired of being tormented like this. She wanted it to stop, and to stop now.

"Go pick on someone else, okay?"

The strange girl instead took a couple of steps toward Victoria's bed, making Victoria wish that she could have summoned more confidence into her wavering voice. The girl's movements were unnatural, somehow. Each step was accompanied by a series of clicks, as though a puzzle of bones was attempting to solve itself. Her limping, lurching gait seemed disconcertingly like her body was twisted and broken. Seeing her reach the end of her bed, Victoria felt terror clinging at her psyche.

"Leave me alone!"

But the girl did not take heed. Instead she clambered onto Victoria's mattress, her limbs scuttling across the bedcovers like the legs of a monstrous spider.

Victoria screamed as the girl crawled right up to where she lay.

CHAPTER FIVE

Fuck Her Up

I open my eyes to a cacophony of screams. I sit up, then swing my legs over the side of my bed. I see Victoria, thrashing around beneath her bedsheet. For a moment, it looks like someone dressed in gray is curled up at her feet. How weird. But then I realize it's just her blanket, bunched up into a ball at the end of her bed. She's still screaming, deep in the throes of a nightmare. I would have thought she'd be awake by now. The noise has woken up the other girls, and I hear a couple of them cursing Victoria drowsily. I see from the dusky light through the high windows that it's not quite daybreak.

I climb off my bed and cross to Victoria's. Her screaming could wake the dead. Honestly. I have no idea how she can still be under while she's making such a racket. I reach down and grab her by the wrist before shaking it, hard. Victoria wakes with a start and stops screaming. She opens her eyes and then recoils at the sight of me. She looks terrified.

"You were having a bad dream."

"Leave me alone," Victoria says, her voice sounding raw from all the screaming. "Just leave me the fuck alone."

Bit harsh, I think, given the circumstances.

"Ewww! Gross."

I look over my shoulder to see Saffy gloating. "Looks like you're not the only carpet-munching *freak* around here, Lena. Get a room, bitches." Saffy settles down onto her bed again. "Another room, far the fuck away from me." She rolls over, turning her back to us.

I look down at Victoria. She's sitting on her bed, arms folded tight around her legs. The fear is etched into her eyes, like she's somehow pulled her nightmare into the day with her. She looks almost catatonic. I wonder what she could have been dreaming about to be in such a state. But I decide against attempting to ask her about it, and beat a retreat back to my own bed.

* * *

After showering and getting dressed, we each line up in the refectory for breakfast under Principal Quick's watchful gaze. A sharp nod from the principal is our prompt to proceed to the self-serving station. It's a stainless-steel breakfast buffet of—

(*You guessed it again, you* are *getting good at this, aren't you?*)

—lumpy porridge. I hear the refectory door slide open on its runners and look to see Victoria enter, looking sullen. She waits for the stragglers to go ahead of her in the queue. I let them pass, too. I'm second-to-last, with Victoria behind me. I reach the pile of plastic trays and take one, still damp to the touch from having been washed. I take another and offer it to Victoria. She just stands there, arms fixed at her sides.

"You okay?" I have to ask, if only because I genuinely don't know what to do with the spare tray now. Awkward.

"Don't.... Don't start," she replies, agitated. "Just let me get my breakfast in peace."

She sidesteps me and passes in front, grabbing a tray for herself. I watch as she fills a cup with orange juice before placing it on her tray and slouching off on the long, lonely walk to a vacant table at the back of the room. Saffy and the others make fun of her as she passes.

I ladle horrid, gloopy porridge into a bowl. I rock on my heels a little until I can watch the others out of the corner of my eye. I notice that Jess is again taking even-sized spoons of porridge and transporting them around her bowl, without eating.

Saffy has noticed, too. "Careful, Jessica dear," she preens, "you might get sick, eating so much."

Jess blushes and scowls at Saffy. "Fuck off, *Saffron*," she says.

(*Atta girl.*)

The others laugh and jeer and Saffy waves her hand at them dismissively, as though they are flies buzzing around her.

I place the bowl of porridge on my tray and walk toward Saffy's table.

"Make some room, bitches," Saffy says.

I see the other girls shuffle up a bit at Saffy's behest, making room for me to sit with them.

But I just keep walking and, to Saffy's visible disgust, decide to sit down opposite Victoria at her table. She looks at me, shocked and embarrassed.

"You can't sit here," Victoria says.

"I already am."

Victoria looks me fully in the eyes for the first time since this morning.

"Well, I said you can't," she counters.

"There's more room over here." I shrug and then take a sip of my juice.

A slow burning rage creeps across Victoria's face.

"Get the hell away from me," she cries.

Her lips narrow and her gaze becomes one of pure spite. Then she stands up and hurls her entire glass of orange juice all over me. The juice trickles over my face, cold and sticky. It stings my eyes before I can wipe it away.

I hear Saffy and her cronies react with gleeful astonishment. My ears start ringing. I stand up, and, allowing my legs to lead the way, I cross the room to Saffy's table. Jess's juice is still untouched, just like her porridge. I take it from her tray. Saffy and the others look at me, incredulous.

"Hey...." I place the fresh drink in front of Victoria. "You spilled your juice. Here's another."

"What the actual fuck?" Victoria looks incensed, and her rage peaks again. She knocks the drink flying off the table, then slaps me, hard, across my face.

Now my ears really are ringing. I hear the other girls gasp. Or, maybe, it's my own sharp intake of breath that I can hear. My face stings from the blow. I touch the tender area on my cheek. It reminds me of something. A tactile response I've experienced before. But I can't be sure. My mind is drifting as the ringing undulates, like the looping pealing of a bell. I face Victoria, who takes an instant dislike to my facial expression. But you have to understand, I don't even know what my facial expression is. It's like I have no control over it. In much the same way that I allowed my legs to take me to Saffy's table to grab Jess's drink, my facial muscles have a life of their own, too. When the out-of-body thing happens, I have to just let go. Unfortunately this seems to make Victoria angrier than ever. She launches herself at me, across the table. Kicking and shrieking, she grabs my hair and pulls me to the floor. I feel the dull sensation of her fingernails scratching across my cheek. I feel her yanking at my hair as we tumble together across the hard floor, and my scalp begins to throb. And all the while, the ringing in my ears echoes on.

Then I feel a new sensation – something approaching actual pain – and I realize I am facedown now, with Victoria's knee in my lower back. She's pulling at my right arm as though she wants to twist it out of its socket. Seems a bit extreme. The ringing diminishes, and then other sounds begin to penetrate my hearing. A cacophony of voices, Saffy and the others, shouting at us to "Fight!" and to "Fuck her up!" I gasp for air and can taste only spilled orange juice, which would be funny if it were not for the fact that I can't actually breathe.

The pressure lifts from my back. I feel my arm twist again, before it's released. I allow it to drop to the hard floor, the sensation helping me to orientate myself back into the physical world. I place the flat of my hand against the floor and push and roll over onto my back. The ceiling seems so far away, a distant and gray sky punctured by sickly yellow lights.

"Both of you. My office, now."

I push myself up into a seated position and see Victoria being dragged away by Principal Quick. Victoria is putting up quite the fight, but the principal is much stronger. Much fiercer. I notice that the principal is clutching on to Victoria by her hair. That's got to hurt. And that's also what I'd call poetic justice.

Around me, Saffy and the other girls cheer and applaud the unexpected breakfast floor show. Ignoring their taunts, I get back to my feet and dust myself down.

Without looking at any of their jubilant faces, I follow Quick out of the refectory.

* * *

It is absolutely peeing it down with rain as we both kneel in the exercise yard with our hands on our heads. My knees have gone past the burning-with-pain stage and are now into an unpleasant cramping sensation. I kneel there, willing my ears to start ringing, but of course they don't. It's Murphy's Law that an out-of-body excursion won't happen when I most need it to.

"Don't think I can really take much more of this," Victoria mutters through chattering teeth. "My hands are freezing."

I give her the side-eye through the rain, and see her frowning at me.

"Are you actually a real, live human person?" she asks. "I mean, you're not even shivering."

Oh, but my knees are burning. "Think warm thoughts," I say.

Victoria's lips curl into a bitter smile as rain water pours down her face.

"Warm thoughts," she replies. "That's a good one."

"You lack focus." Now I *am* just fucking with her. You'll forgive me. There's not much else to do out here.

"And you sound like Principal Quick," she says, and then sighs. "But I suppose I do lack focus. I lack a lot of things. Guess that's why I'm here."

Ah, here it comes. I wait.

"I have a bit of a temper…" she says, then trails off.

"I noticed," I say.

She chuckles wetly before asking, "So why are you in here?"

Still, the ringing in my ears won't come, however much I wish it would. "I don't play that game."

"Oh?" Victoria says, but she can't disguise the inquisitiveness in her voice. "Have it your way." She leans forward and searches my face for something. Her eyes darken, and I wonder why. Over her shoulder, I see Quick through the courtyard window, ever watchful, and I realize that I'm beginning to see the light.

"What is it?" Victoria asks.

* * *

We trudge down the hallway after Quick. Both soaked through, we leave wet footprints on the floor behind us as we walk. My legs are still a little wobbly from kneeling so long in the exercise yard. I guess Victoria's are too, as we're both having difficulty keeping up. We follow Principal Quick around a corner, and into a wider corridor where scrubbing brushes and buckets filled with soapy water await us.

"Now that you have cooled off," the principal announces, "you are both on cleaning detail. I will be back in one hour for inspection. Make it spotlessly clean, or you will only have to do it again."

She pauses for a moment, then glares at us sternly before she walks away.

Victoria sighs heavily. She kneels down on the floor beside the bucket and grabs a brush. I watch, still standing, as she soaks it in suds from the bucket, then begins to scrub the floor. There's an awful lot of floor, folks. It'll take hours to clean it all. My head begins to ache at the thought.

"Some help?" Victoria asks, and I neglect to answer.

I'm looking beyond Victoria and watching Quick's shadow as

it moves across the far wall, accompanied by the click-clack of her shoes across the hard floor of the corridor. The shadow disappears along with the noise of her footfalls.

It's time to make my move.

"Hey! Where you going?" Victoria asks as I walk past her.

Ignoring her apparent frustration, I continue on, past the dark staircase set into the side of the hallway. I duck inside the stairwell to watch and wait for a moment. From my darkened vantage point I can see along the length of the adjacent corridor without being seen. It's all clear. I feel a chill on the back of my neck, like a cold breath. I turn and see nothing except the stone steps leading up into the gloom. I return my attention to the corridor. Satisfied that no one is there, I take a deep breath and break cover. I move stealthily. My movements are controlled. I'm focused, watchful, and alert. I spy a crack of light in the main doorway. It's ajar. I pad over to the door.

Just as I hoped, Principal Quick is standing outside puffing on a cigarette. I wait for a second, calculating my next move. But the principal is stubbing out her cigarette. She turns and heads back to the door. There isn't much time. I must act now – or never.

As Principal Quick reaches the door, I kick it open. The door hits her, square in the face, and knocks her off balance. I see her put her hand to her nose, which is gushing blood. She makes a strange kind of garbled, gasping noise as I dash past her.

It's a satisfying sound. Like music to my ears.

I sprint away into the rain. I'm not bragging, you understand, but I'm fast – really fast. A quick glance over my shoulder and I glimpse Principal Quick, clutching her bloodied nose, watching me go in shocked surprise. The damp air chills my throat. It feels pretty good, like the afterburn of an ice-pop. I run between the gateposts and out into the wilderness.

CHAPTER SIX

The Path to True Rehabilitation

I keep running until I'm deeper into the stark wilderness.

Wild grasses and tall, slender trees surround me in the otherwise rocky landscape. I begin to feel a tightening in my chest, and then the pain of a stitch starts burning in my left side. I slow down to a jog and then to a walking pace. I turn, still walking, and look back at where I came from. No sign of Quick, of course; there's no way she could keep up with me if she tried.

(*Okay, maybe I am bragging now. Sorry, not sorry.*)

And there's no way on earth she'd trust one of the other girls to come find me, either. Not even golden girl Saffy. Or especially not her, if you know what I mean. I stop walking and turn to face the landscape ahead. Gray clouds are churning overhead and they dampen the daylight from the sky. The wind whistles through the tops of the trees, a siren song beckoning me to higher ground. I walk on, toward a steep, grassy bank. My calves are throbbing from the climb when I reach the top. I look down, and see a stony path winding its way along a ravine. The path is too narrow to have been formed by human traffic, and it is strangely comforting to speculate about which kinds of animals have trodden this path before me. I'm one of them now, let loose in the wild and free to follow the undulating land. My stomach growls and I do my best to ignore the accompanying hollow sensation in the pit of my stomach.

I follow the path, enjoying the scent of the damp grasses

growing in random clumps on the slopes either side of me. But, all of a sudden, the pleasant smell gives way to something foul. I hear the buzzing of insects and, pretty soon, my eyes find the source of the stench. The ruptured, broken carcass of a hare lies at the side of the path up ahead. Its gray-brown fur is loose, like a woolen sweater that's been stretched, and is absolutely swarming with flies. I pull my clothing over my nose and mouth and hurry on by. I can't help but see the hare's body laid out as though it's been dropped from a great height. I remember my dream about the clock tower and the girl. The hands, stuck at seven. And I remember how it felt to plummet toward the recreation yard, and a shudder passes through me, chilling me to my marrow.

(*I tell myself that it's just the wind making me feel cold.*)

And so I hurry on, eager to be away from the dead hare. High above me, the sky boils with thunder clouds. I can almost feel the pressure of a gathering storm crushing down on me. Instinctively, I fold my arms around my body and, my head tucked down against the elements, I push on along the path. A few minutes later, and to my utter relief, the path leads me under tree cover.

With the canopy of trees above me, I feel hidden from the world. The trees are densely packed together, growing wild from wherever they've taken root. All the scents of the forest are alive in my nostrils and I breathe them in eagerly. Fresh pine blends with damp earth and the freshness of the wind, which becomes a gentle breeze the farther I walk into the forest. Twigs snap beneath my feet and leaf litter rustles. Pretty soon I'm walking on a soft, springy carpet of pine needles and I realize that the path has disappeared completely.

I'm lost in this forest, strolling all alone. Stark nature is all around me. It's actually really glorious.

Then, I hear the pitter-patter of a few raindrops as they begin to fall on the leaves. Oh, crap. Nature might be glorious, but it is also unpredictable, and unforgiving. The sound of the rainfall builds as the heavens open.

I dive for cover under the largest nearby tree I can find. For a little while I just sit there, arms around my knees, listening to the rain. There is a loud *splosh* as a particularly large raindrop penetrates my shelter and lands on a leaf beside me. The leaf bounces up as the raindrop falls to earth and I notice something clinging to its underside. I pull the leaf gently toward me so I can take a better look and see that the object is a chrysalis. Its light brown fabric makes the little cylinder look rather like a cigar.

I stroke the surface of the chrysalis. It's incredibly fragile, and yet it looks so strong, as though it could survive anything nature can throw at it. Thunder rumbles and I swear I can feel it vibrate the earth beneath me. The wind picks up, and there's a sharp scent of electricity in the air. A flash goes off with all the intensity of a lightbulb, and momentarily the chrysalis looks as though it is glowing orange with a spark of life burning from deep inside of it. There's a thunderclap, incredibly loud and much too close for comfort this time. The wind blows more ferociously, bringing horizontal rain with it. My already-quite-wet clothes begin to stick to my arms and legs. I take the chrysalis in my hand and then pull the leaf away from its branch. Folding the chrysalis up inside the leaf, I tuck the little bundle inside my clothing next to my breast. The rain is blowing in all directions now, so I walk away from the tree, intent on outrunning the thunder and lightning.

No such luck.

With some effort I make it to the tree line, but the storm continues gathering in strength all around me. As I pass through the trees, the land drops away into a steep and muddy slope. I slip and slide in the stuff as my feet try to gain purchase on the sodden terrain. I decide to try to circle the perimeter of trees, to see if the ground levels out further along. The howling wind and rain lash unforgivingly at my limbs as I try my utmost to push onward. My face stings from the icy rain and my clothes are plastered to my legs. I swear I could just lean forward and find myself supported by the wind, it's that strong. I'm being battered by the elements. Maybe leaving the dubious shelter of the tree was a mistake after all. And then, as if to prove my thesis, a gust of wind knocks me off balance. My feet slip from under me in the wet mud and I take a tumble down the slope. At the bottom, I fall headlong into a cold, muddy puddle of rainwater.

Kneeling on all fours with the murky water directly below me I see my reflection, dark and indistinct. The wind moves the surface of the puddle's dark mirror, distorting my facial features. Ripples form with each raindrop, furthering the effect. I dislike the way my strands of hair take on the aspect of water weeds. I can't see who I am anymore. The lashing rain beats against my back, willing me to just give up the ghost and fall headfirst into the water. I look up and see an impassible quagmire stretching out before me. Placing a hand at my breast I feel the little chrysalis there, still swaddled in its leaf. My skin is so numb from the pummeling rain that I can't tell if I should feel cold or not. I smash the water with my right hand, shattering my muddied reflection.

A ringing in my ears begins. It starts to drown out even the sound of the rain.

I glance over my shoulder, back the way I came.

* * *

Night is falling by the time I get back to Greyfriars Reformatory. The relentless rain falls in cold sheets. My drenched clothing sticks to my skin. Quick was right, there is nowhere to run to beyond the reformatory gates, only harsh wilderness. I kind of wish that Quick had a guard detail that could have hunted me down and then carried me back. I would have gone willingly. I'm tired and my body aches. Energy all but gone, I trudge over wet mud and stones to the main gate. It's shut, so I try a shoulder against it, to see if it will open just enough for me to slip through. But it won't budge. I peer between the bars of the gate and see lights from windows casting a sickly yellow glow on the surfaces of puddles in the forecourt. The gate is really high, with sharp points here and there in the ironwork. I decide to look for a place where I can climb the wall.

Rainwater squelches in my shoes with every step I take. My right sock has sprung a leak and I can feel a blister forming between two of my toes from the constant rubbing.

I find a section of wall that has crumbled away at the top and use the fallen bricks as a platform from which to mount my bid for renewed incarceration. The hammering rain does little to aid my ascent, but on my second attempt I manage to get up and over. Half-falling and half-rolling to earth on the other side, I disentangle myself from the hedgerow that has broken my fall and take stock of my surroundings. I've entered the grounds to the right of the building, which stands indomitably alone in the landscape. Rain gushes from overflowing gutters beneath the clock tower, soaking me further, and it feels as though I'm being punished for trying to escape from this place. This is the second cold shower I've been subjected to for my indolence today.

But what did I really expect, I wonder? That I'd find the road, hitch a ride with some understanding, forward-thinking individual who was not averse to giving rides to convicts before living my best life on a beautiful island with my faithful animal sidekick? I reach for the chrysalis at my breast, reassured somehow by its presence. It has a vague warmth to it. Or maybe my fingers are just numb from the rain and the cold. It doesn't matter which. All that matters are those few moments in the forest, when I felt like I was free. I try to hold on to that feeling but it is, even now, leaving me.

The rain from the gutters skitters in my ears and trickles down my back. I walk up the steps and try the main door. It, too, is locked. I lean against it for a few seconds, feeling tired to my bones all of a sudden. Exhausted now, I bang my head against the door.

Once. Twice. Three times....

My head is still against the cold, unyielding surface of the main door when I hear, and feel through the door, a key turning in the lock mechanism. The door opens and I almost tumble inside, reaching for the doorframe to halt my fall. My clothes and hair drip rainwater onto the doorstep. I peer through the soggy strands of my fringe at Principal Quick. Her face is an impenetrable mask. She does not exude any sympathy, let me tell you. If anything, she looks like she has been begrudgingly expecting me. A parent or guardian staying up late to berate a drunken teenaged daughter back from her revels.

Principal Quick stands back from the door and I trudge inside, wet through. I hear the jangling of keys and turn to watch as the principal locks, and then bolts, the door.

"Come with me," she says.

* * *

Principal Quick's office smells of a peculiar and unpleasant blend of cigarette smoke and bleach. There's an empty seat opposite her desk, but she doesn't invite me to sit in it. So, I stand adrift on the periphery of her personal-slash-professional space.

The walls are drab and largely featureless, the paintwork old and discolored save for an unstained oblong area where a picture frame used to hang – but doesn't anymore. Principal Quick's desk is uncluttered, playing host to only a landline telephone, a pot of pens and pencils, and a stack of paperwork. In the corner, behind the desk, is a tall cabinet.

Principal Quick crosses to the cabinet and unlocks it using

a small key from her bunch. The cabinet door creaks open and the principal takes a towel and some fresh nightclothes from the shelves. She walks over to her desk and leans across it to hand them to me. I approach her cautiously, wondering if she will snatch the items away when I try to take them before giving full vent to her fury at my behavior. But there are no such power games at play with Principal Quick. She is in charge, and we both know it. She allows me to take the towel and the clothes.

"Not the first time you've attempted a breakout, Emily," she says, casual as anything.

My eyes are drawn to the empty space on the wall. I wonder what kind of picture used to hang there. Then I catch the expression on Quick's face and realize she is expecting some kind of response from me.

"Is that a question?" I ask.

"You don't remember?"

"No."

I don't.

I get the sense that the learned principal doesn't believe me. I look down at the pile of paperwork on the desk. There's a thick manuscript on the top of the pile. The title is upside down from where I'm looking at it. I peer at it, deciphering what it says. 'GIRL A: A CASE STUDY' by Dr. Mina Quick'.

Then I realize she's been talking to me. And I haven't been listening to a word she's been saying.

"The same old memory problems," she says. Then, she raises an eyebrow. "Or selective memory problems?"

"I don't remember," I reply. Well, at least I'm consistent, and it does seem apt.

"You know why you're here, though. Surely you remember that?"

Something about Principal Quick's tone suggests an urgency, like she just expects me to rifle through my brain and pull out what she wants to hear. But my brain is a bowl of swirling fog right now. Her intent expression is freaking me out a bit to be honest, so I try.

"I remember something about a disorder. I remember doctors. Meds. Tests...."

I realize I'm holding the towel and the fresh clothing tight to my chest. I ease off, concerned about the fate of the little chrysalis concealed at my breast.

"It is called acute dissociative disorder, Emily. It causes a disconnection in your emotional responses, lapses in concentration, self-imposed memory gaps which become plugged by flights of fancy. The root cause of your diminished responsibility."

She frowns at me. I gaze once more at the manuscript on her desk. Principal Quick moves closer to the desk and removes the manuscript. She then carries it over to the tall cupboard in the corner.

"In short, you keep making the same mistakes. Over and over, it seems. That is why you are here," she says, "again." Then, unlocking the cupboard, she files the manuscript away. She closes and locks the door once more. "The path to true rehabilitation is to learn diligence."

Returning to her desk, the principal slides open a drawer, and takes out a box of matches and a pack of cigarettes. She selects a cigarette, and puts it in her mouth before sparking it up. I like the sound that the tip of the match makes when it scrapes across the matchbox and erupts into flame. It sounds vibrant and alive, when everything else in this room feels stale, and dead.

"You will keep an eye on the other girls, Emily," the principal says. "You will keep me informed about what they are up to."

She holds the pack of cigarettes and the box of matches out for me to take.

(*What the hell?*)

She smiles slyly. "Tell them you stole these when I had my back turned."

I hesitate for just a moment, and then step forward to take the smokes and the matches. I do it quickly, in case she changes her mind. Or in case this is some kind of mind game after all. The principal watches with an approving smirk as I tuck the contraband items inside the neatly folded towel.

"Earn their trust," Quick says, exhaling smoke. She brightens, becoming the efficient matron once more. "Now, go and get cleaned up, then off to bed with you."

I'm at the door when I pause for thought. There's a shadow in my mind's eye that I just can't seem to shake. I turn to face Principal Quick. I have to ask her. I can't leave the room without doing so.

"Is there another inmate here?" I ask. "Another girl?"

The principal's expression is one of impenetrable stoicism again. "Whatever gave you that idea?"

"The others said they saw someone."

"Where? When?"

"In the clock tower. Shortly after we arrived here."

"I assure you it is just you and me," Principal Quick replies, before fixing me with a level gaze. "I remind you that the clock tower is out of bounds. It is dangerous. You and the other girls would do well to remember that. Close the door after you."

I turn my back but I can almost feel Principal Quick's eyes burrowing into me, before I slip through the door. I pull it shut behind me and take deep breaths, relieved to be out of Principal Quick's claustrophobic office and its bad atmosphere. I stand there in the lonely corridor and check that the cigarettes and matches are still tucked safely inside the towel. Reassured that they are, I start walking back to the dormitory. *Earn their trust*, the principal had said to me, and I begin to wonder if that's even possible.

* * *

The dry clothes feel good against my skin. I have moved the reassuring little lump of the chrysalis that I found in the woods into the waistband of my underwear.

I'm warmer now, even in the slight damp of the dingy bathroom with its cracked tiles and dripping taps. I cross to the sinks, toweling my hair dry. As I pass by the toilet stalls I'm surprised to hear a sharp retching sound coming from inside one of them. Only a couple of the doors are closed. The noise of more retching, followed by the unmistakable sound of vomit hitting the water in a toilet bowl, reveals that it's the center stall that's occupied.

"Hello?"

I hear a faint sob from behind the toilet door. Maybe I should just leave whoever is in there alone. But they really don't sound too well. I approach the door, and reach out my hand cautiously to test if it's locked. As my fingers brush the surface of the door, it swings open on its hinges and bangs against the interior of the stall.

Jess emerges from the stall, her face wet with tears. She wipes her mouth with her hand. As she does so, I notice that Jess's knuckles are red raw. I've seen abrasions like those before. They happen when a girl repeatedly makes herself sick. All that stomach acid leaves its mark. Jess has clearly been making herself vomit pretty regularly. Just as I'm considering all of this, Jess fixes me with a challenging glare of defiance.

"What you looking at?" she asks, and it sounds much more like an accusation.

I just stare at her blankly, and then at her knuckles. Just then, I hear the main door to the bathroom open and turn to see Victoria.

Jess scowls at her, then glares back at me.

"Freak. Robot fucking freak," Jess says before storming out

of the bathroom. She pushes past Victoria roughly, and then slams the door in her wake.

"What's eating her?" Victoria says, without realizing what a truly fantastic gift for comic timing she has.

I shrug, deciding not to go there, and then grab my spare towel — with the cigarettes and matches still safely stowed inside — and head back into the dormitory.

Jess is the first person I see, and she shoots me a loaded look. Her eyes are brimming with so much guilt that I think the only thing she can possibly do with it is to turn it into anger against me. Against anybody. I break eye contact.

"Oh look, girls, the drowned rat returns," Saffy sneers.

She's sitting cross-legged on her bed. Queen Bitch on her blanketed throne.

As I walk closer to the foot of her bed she says, "Enjoy your jailbreak? Tell me, how *is* that bid for freedom working out for you?"

I decide not to answer. Not in the way she might want me to, anyway. Some people thrive on chaos and confrontation. Saffy is one of them. And I'm all too aware of the delicate chrysalis I have hidden in my underwear. I don't want it to come to any harm. It's all I have of the outside world. So, I just stroll over to my bed, then sit down. Saffy watches me intently as I reach into my spare towel and take out the pack of cigarettes, followed by the matches. I light one up and kick back. Her face is an absolute picture.

"Get. The fuck. Out," Saffy says, incredulous.

I purse my lips and blow a smoke ring. It floats above my bed, toward my feet. I think it looks like a little cloud. A pretty one, unlike the rain clouds that drenched me earlier.

"The sun will be shining when I leave this place," I say, as I watch the cloud dissipate.

The other girls all whisper and giggle, sounding astonished. Even Jess.

Saffy laughs too. "Freak," she says. Then her tone takes on that air of entitled authority that she does so well. "Gimme."

I take another drag, then I toss first the cigarettes, then the matches, to Saffy.

"Help yourselves," I say.

She lights up and breathes the smoke so deep into her lungs it's like she hasn't enjoyed one for years. I watch Lena sidle over, on the make. Saffy keeps hold of the contraband, enjoying the power, but then allows Lena to take a smoke. Saffy strikes another match and Lena takes a drag before exhaling smoke around her grinning face.

"You're still on watch, remember?" Saffy tells Lena.

Something silent passes between these two titans before Lena, cigarette poised between her lips, returns to keep watch beside the door. I think she could take Saffy, and I think Saffy knows that. But Lena is happy to play along for whatever her reasons are. She's pretty impenetrable, that one.

While they're distracted, I slip the chrysalis from my underwear and hold it, unseen, in the palm of my hand. I tuck it beneath my pillow. Then, I see Victoria carrying her towel and toothbrush and I wonder if she saw me hiding it. If she did, she's being discreet and for that I'm grateful. Victoria pads over to her bed and silence falls over the room as Saffy and her accomplices watch – and wait. Victoria pulls back her covers. I can see that her bed is completely soaked through. Water drips from the mattress onto the floor. They must have emptied an entire sink full in there, somehow, the cruel bitches.

"Oh dear, dear," Saffy says mockingly. "Soaked the bed again, crybaby?"

She and the others burst into laughter as Victoria stands next to her bed, looking like she's trying, and failing, not to cry.

"Shit!" Lena exclaims. "She's coming!"

We each take urgent last drags of our cigarettes, then stub

them out and hide the butts under our beds. And just in time as — only seconds after the last cigarette butt has been safely stowed away — Principal Quick arrives to turn out the lights.

"Quiet down, girls. Lights out," she says in that officious way of hers.

Victoria still stands next to her bed, with her back to Quick. Our eyes meet. She looks pleadingly at me. I feel kind of sorry for her.

"Victoria?" Principal Quick prompts.

But Victoria doesn't budge.

I hear Saffy chuckle evilly, under her breath. As Victoria's expression grows all the more pained I break eye contact and then pull my covers around me.

"Into bed this instant," the principal commands.

From behind the protective barrier of my blanket I see angry tears well up in Victoria's eyes. She has no other option but to climb into her sodden bed, to the quiet delight of her tormentors.

"Settle down now, girls."

Principal Quick stands watching from the doorway as each of us — except Victoria, of course — gets comfy in bed.

I lie down on my side and slip my hand under my pillow. I can feel the reassuring shape of the little chrysalis against my hand. I have my face turned toward the doorway. The principal glances at me and I see her sniff at the smoky air, a smile curling her lips. She says nothing further. Then, she turns out the lights and closes the door.

In the half light, Saffy whispers. "You did good today, Emily."

I prop myself up on my elbow and I'm about to ask Saffy to toss the cigarettes and matches back to me when I see Victoria, her body shuddering with heavy sobs. I don't expect Saffy to hand over the smokes, you understand, it's just that I sense I can make her feel even more trusting of me if I ask for them back – and then accept her inevitable refusal. Mind games. They're Saffy's stock-in-trade after all, aren't they? But when I see Victoria, sobbing into her pillow like that, my bravado falters and I fall silent. Somehow, any business with Saffy seems trivial compared to how much Victoria is suffering. I know I can't do anything to help, though. She hardly…welcomed my advances in the refectory, after all. And any demonstrative attempt to show kindness to Victoria would undermine my progress with Saffy. These interpersonal interactions are becoming so complex to me that I'm beginning to wish I was locked away from the lot of them in solitary confinement, when I sense someone looking at me.

From across the room I can see Jess – her eyes twinkling with fury in the gloom. She glares at me, then pulls her bedclothes tightly around herself before she turns over, and curls up into a fetal position.

CHAPTER SEVEN

Jess

Jess awoke with a jolt. She sat up and blinked at her surroundings. The room was as clinically clean and white as the hospital bed she lay in. Jess felt a familiar burn and scratched at her sore, dry knuckles. They began to bleed again.

She reached under her pillow and pulled out a fresh tissue to swab the blood with. As she did so, her fingers found a candy bar tucked beneath the pillow. Forgetting her bleeding knuckles and the tissue, Jess took out the candy bar. She stared at the confectionary, its bright wrapper tempting her to indulge in the pleasures beneath. Jess bit her lip, trying to resist. No use. She glanced at the door as if to remind herself that it was shut. Then she ripped open the candy bar wrapper in one, swift movement.

The first bite was heavenly – a thick layer of milk chocolate giving way to gooey caramel that oozed sweetly across her tongue. She shoveled more candy into her mouth. Within a couple more bites, it would be gone. The pleasure spike would be over all too soon. But Jess knew there was yet more hidden food beneath her pillow. She pulled back the pillow as though it were the lid to a treasure chest, and dived in.

Jess tore open the wrappers, gorging herself on candy bar after candy bar, tearing into and adding packets of chips and fistfuls of popcorn to the feast, before sloshing it all down with a can of soda that she had carefully concealed behind the leg of her bed. She let out a triumphant, celebratory belch. Then, just as suddenly as it had started, her gluttonous reverie stopped as she heard another sound from across the room.

The door creaked open. A sudden breeze blew through the room, lifting empty foil wrappers and plastic packets off Jess's bed and onto the floor. How could she have eaten so many? There were hundreds of them – a dizzying rainbow blur of colors.

Jess launched herself from her bed and scrambled to the floor. The breeze had gathered in strength, becoming a howling vortex of wind. She reached this way and that in a vain attempt to catch the fluttering candy wrappers. Dropping just as many as she picked up, Jess was desperate to hide the evidence of her weakness, before anyone came into the room. Before they saw the remnants of her shameful binge. Her fingertips brushed the edge of a particularly large candy bar wrapper, but she only managed to send it flying underneath the bed.

Reaching beneath the bed to retrieve the wrapper, Jess saw a shadow. And the shadow *moved*. Something else was beneath the bed. Something much larger than a candy bar wrapper. Jess's heart began to beat harder, a warning signal to recoil from whatever was lurking under her mattress. She felt her breathing becoming ragged as the shadow began to take on a more discernible shape as it darted toward her – and into the light.

A hideous apparition was clawing at her. A gray-skinned girl, with dark hair covering her face. Jess screamed as the foul apparition grabbed at her and clamped its cold, clammy hands around her face. Each fingertip was as shockingly freezing as an icicle and her nerve endings became conduits to a flow of icy despair that seemed to flow – unstoppably – into her entire body through her face.

Jess gasped as a flood of flashing images invaded her mind, carried by the rush of cold.

She felt herself convulse, and then saw herself reflected in a mirror of sheet ice. Only it wasn't a reflection of how she looked now. She was as thin as a rake, her skin pale and mottled. Her lips were yellowed and dry. Heart rate monitors flatlined with a steady, piercing whine. In the reflection, she saw a medic pumping frantically at Jess's bony chest, trying to revive her heart. The medic leaned over her on the gurney and administered the kiss of life. But to no avail – the heart rate monitors continued flatlining. The reflected image shimmered to reveal another figure standing, watching her. With a jolt of raw emotion, Jess recognized her mother. She recognized the stricken look on her mother's face as she cried in anguish, unable to do anything to save her teenaged daughter, her baby.

The searing cold and the painful images were all too much for her now, and Jess clamped her eyelids shut for a second. She opened them again and the reflection shattered – the ice of memory dissipating into a desiccated whiteout of snow.

Jess's vision cleared, and she was looking once again at the terrifying gray girl from under the bed.

Jess recoiled against the clammy fingers clutching her face, trying to wrestle free from their unwelcome touch. She scrambled back on her hands and heels, then lashed out with her left foot. She felt those ice-cold fingertips disengage. Propelling herself backward and then up against the wall, Jess turned toward the door. She grabbed the handle and, after wrenching the door almost from its hinges, launched herself out of the room.

She was already standing in the bathroom before she fully recognized where she was. The tiles were cracked and grimy. The grouting was a moldy green color. A broken lamp flickered overhead. The leaky faucet dripped, echoing off the hard surface of the sink in time with her pulse. Then she heard the eerie sound of sobbing coming from a stall closer to the far wall, where mirrors hung.

Jess walked over to the stall and pushed the door open a crack so she could see inside. The stall was empty. She was about to close the door and retrace her steps out of this creepy old bathroom when she heard the toilet flush. She hadn't touched the handle. She wasn't anywhere near it, still standing in the doorway to the stall. But sure enough, the water was spiraling around the toilet bowl. She took an instinctive step forward, and saw that the water in the bowl looked odd somehow. It was still spiraling around, but in the opposite direction to how it normally did.

Intrigued, she entered the stall fully, and heard the door slam behind her. She turned on her heels and tried to unlock the door, but the mechanism was jammed shut. The spiraling water behind her seemed to howl, hurricane-like, and she turned around to see that it had escaped from the toilet bowl. The tornado of water had brought something with it, too – a chaos of candy bar and other snack wrappers. Then, the spiraling column of water dropped back into the bowl, scattering the wrappers across the stall. Strewn all around her on the filthy floor were enough confectionary wrappers to fill a dumpster. Jess felt her stomach heave and raced to the toilet, falling to her knees before throwing up.

She felt her stomach muscles convulse one last time and heard her throat expel the last remnants of her binge. The sound of her own sobs echoed around the cramped bathroom stall. She flushed the toilet. Exhausted, she brushed her sweaty hair away from her face and sat back against the stall partition. Her breathing slowed. Disgusted with herself, her sobs became a full-on torrent of tears.

Then, inexplicably, the door to the stall creaked open.

As though nothing had happened.

Jess exited the stall and trudged to the sink. She opened the faucet and took handfuls of water to rinse the acid aftertaste of stomach bile from her mouth. Spitting into the sink, Jess splashed more fresh water on her face. She watched the water swirl away down the plughole. Closing the faucet, Jess looked at herself in the broken mirror.

The faucet dripped. She looked dreadful – as though ravaged by a wasting disease.

Drip.

She stroked the skin on her lips with her fingertips, then her cheeks, before running her fingers across her throat.

Drip.

She felt a dryness at her throat. Something more than the aftereffects of her old binge-and-purge routine. The dryness quickly became a scratching sensation. Her breath began to rattle as she gasped for air.

Suddenly she choked, as if all the air had left her body.

Drip.

She gagged, clutching at her painful throat. Surely there was nothing left to throw up?

Drip-drip-drip.

Watching herself in the mirror, Jess's eyes filled with terror as – impossibly – a dead, gray hand pushed its way out of her mouth. The momentum of the hand pulled her face with it toward the mirror and she made a strangled screaming noise as her forehead smashed into it. Broken glass fell into the sink. Jagged shards of it hung in front of her disbelieving eyes. From between her lips, the gnarled fingers reached desperately for the mirror. They grabbed at a piece of the broken glass.

Jess tried to scream – but only a dry gagging sound would come. She bit down, as hard as she could, tasting cold flesh between her teeth. But the hand protruding from her mouth did not flinch, instead making a fist around the section of broken glass. Jess watched the reflection in the fractured mirror, in mortal dread of what was to come next.

The gray-skinned hand yanked the shard of glass violently down into Jess's throat. Jess began choking on blood. Her eyes widened. She saw the gray girl looking back at her from inside the mirror – the broken glass multiplying her malevolent eye into a legion of hatred.

Jess's throat gushed blood, and pain, and total fear.

And, with a final bloody gasp, she lost consciousness.

CHAPTER EIGHT

The Other Inmate

I wake up and feel sleep trying to pull me back down again, but for some reason I fight it off and sit up. The vague light of daybreak casts a dirty halo around the high window opposite my bed. Around me, the other girls are asleep. Lena is snoring softly, and I wonder how she can do that without waking herself. I quickly check under my pillow for the chrysalis. It's still there. Feeling its surface against my skin connects me to the outside world somehow, to the soil and the trees beyond the window. Perhaps I'll walk among them again one day. Sleep has well and truly lost its hold on me now. I yawn, then clamber out of bed. I grab my towel from the little bedside cupboard, along with my toothbrush and toiletries. As I cross to the door, I realize that I'm not the only one awake after all. Jess's bed is empty.

The bathroom door squeaks open as I enter. One of the lights is flickering, and I hear the steady dripping of a leaky faucet. The flickering light reveals something else – something major. One of the mirrors is smashed to bits. Shards of it lie on the washbasin and floor. I walk toward it, treading softly. Don't want to cut my bare feet on the broken glass. Then I see red. Pooling from beneath the bathroom stall nearest to the mirror.

I walk on tiptoe to avoid the glass, then push against the door to the stall. It creaks open slowly, and the sound seems to stretch out across time. Jess is on the floor of the stall, lying in a bloodied heap with her throat cut. The gash across her neck is a deep, wide, scarlet rictus. A broken piece of bloodstained mirror lies on the floor next to her. I stare at Jess's body, and the creaking of the door—

(*Horrid sound, why won't it just damn well stop?*)

—becomes a ringing in my ears. My vision turns watery. The palms of my hands become cold and wet. I think I'm still standing on tiptoes, but I can't be sure and now I feel distant from the floor tiles like I'm levitating above them. The ringing is all around me, and it's as though I'm in a bell jar. Maybe I formed my own chrysalis in bed last night and now that I've awoken I've taken flight, only to become trapped under glass.

Another sound cuts through the ringing, sharp and intrusive. The shrill, unwelcome sound wants to drag me back into the present, and I don't want to go. But it's too late. I can hear her now. I can hear Saffy scream.

"Emily? Jesus fucking Christ."

Saffy is right beside me at the door to the stall. I turn to look at her. She's looking at Jess's body. Then she looks at me. Her eyes are wet. She looks really scared, and I wonder why.

* * *

Quick watches over us as we scrub the last of the blood away from the wall and floor. I return my cloth to the bucket of soapy water. There are hardly any bubbles left, and the water has turned red. I squeeze the cloth over the bucket and see Quick's face reflected in the surface of the water. The drips from my cloth make the water ripple, distorting her face. I wipe around the base of the toilet bowl, where a couple of blood smears remain untouched. Quick's shadow falls over me.

"Better," she says, surveying my work. I get to my feet and she passes a broom to me.

"Sweep up the last of the broken glass, Emily. There are a few pieces under the sink. We can't have anyone cutting their feet."

Or their necks, I think, trying to dispel the image of the red gash from my memory.

I sweep up the remaining broken glass from the mirror. Victoria crouches beside me, collecting up the tiny fragments of mirror with a dustpan and brush. She moves the brush in slow, deliberate strokes, like she's an automaton.

"Well done, girls. As good as new."

(*Like nothing happened!?*)

"Report to the recreation area for your morning's exercise."

"We've had our exercise already," Saffy pipes up, "helping you carry Jess's dead body outside. Then mopping up all this blood."

Much as I hate to back Saffy up, she does have a point.

"Do not cross me."

I look at Principal Quick and see her face wrinkle with barely suppressed anger. A chink in the armor.

"Courtyard in five minutes," the principal says, "or you will all be confined to your dormitory."

"We're just going to carry on as though nothing happened?"

Saffy and Lena look just as surprised as I am to hear Victoria's voice.

Principal Quick looks really livid now. She purses her lips, and then releases a controlled breath. "We shall continue with your rehabilitation. Discipline is what matters. All that matters. Now more than ever."

The principal moves over to the stall where I found Jess. She shuts the door with an air of finality. Discussion over, I guess.

Victoria throws me a troubled glance. I can't read her look, so I just look back at her.

Principal Quick says, "Give the floor a thorough mopping, girls. And then pack away the cleaning equipment."

Then she fixes her cold gaze on me. I wish she wouldn't.

"Emily, you will come with me," she says.

* * *

That stale tobacco smell still lingers in Principal Quick's office, but the bleach notes seem even stronger this time. After a little while, I realize the smell is coming from my skin. Scrubbing the bathroom has made me stink of it. But I can't shake the metallic scent of blood that lurks somewhere beneath all the competing sensory layers. I blink and recall how wet Saffy's eyes looked. Like she was going to cry, which is ridiculous because, well, because *Saffy*. I cross and uncross my legs, and then rearrange my hands in my lap. I don't know why I can't sit still. I guess it's because Principal Quick is making me feel nervous. She hasn't said a single word to me since telling me to sit down. I sneak a glance at her and see that she's hunched over a drawer. She's rooting around in it, searching for something. After a while, she stands, and I see what she was looking for. In her hands is a tall metronome. It has a little lightbulb on top. She carries it over to the desk and positions it in front of me. She unclips the slender metal arm on the front of the device and sets it off in a rocking motion. Then she reaches around the back of the device and I hear the click of a switch. The little lamp on top lights up, pulsing in time with the metronome arm.

Principal Quick crosses to the window that looks out onto the recreation yard. She operates a thin, metal pulley and closes the window blind. The room becomes gloomy, save for the rhythmic, pulsing light from the metronome.

"Settle back, Emily," she says, and her voice sounds softer than usual.

She takes her seat behind her desk and I watch as she picks up a notepad and a pen.

"Don't look at me, girl. Look at the light," she says, her voice now almost a purr.

The rhythmic swoosh of the metronome arm grows louder as I look at the light, which has a warmth to it that is inviting.

I find that I don't want to look away, even if instinct is telling me this is a pretty freaky setup that Quick has going on in her office.

"Feel your heart, beating in time with each pulse of the light," the principal says.

I sit and watch, and feel my heart rate skitter, before settling into a pulsing rhythm with the flashing of the lamp. And as I watch, it seems to slow down – the metronome, and my heartbeat – and I wonder if that's really true, or if it is just a result of the strangely hypnotic effect of the flashing light and the swinging arm.

"Be at one with the light. Feel it pulse within you. From inside of your eyes. You don't need to blink, because you are making the light come from out of you."

I exhale, and feel warmth rush through and out of me. The swishing of the metronome takes on an eerie, whining quality, and it builds into a high-pitched ringing in my ears. My sense of touch begins to deteriorate, the chair beneath me no more than a dull ache. And even that recedes eventually, leaving me floating.

"You are perfectly comfortable," Principal Quick purrs. "You feel perfectly supported. Weightless. Unfettered by thought or deed."

Oh, and I do. As the ringing in my ears grows, so too does my feeling of weightlessness. I feel a smile spread across my face. I must look like an idiot, floating around Quick's office, grinning like a loon, but I don't care. It feels so nice and trippy.

"It is your deeds I want you to float above now, Emily," she says, her voice sounding so quiet I can imagine her crouching beside the filing cabinet at the back of her office space. But I see only the light. In my mind's eye and all around me, like I'm both its source and shadow. That's actually really weird, but I'll go with it.

"Look down on your world as you float above it. Picture yourself...in the bathroom, earlier. Before you found Jessica. What did you see?

I saw the flickering light, I think. I can't seem to speak out loud. There's only the ringing. And my voice inside my head.

"Good. And?"

How Principal Quick can even hear me is beyond me. But I feel so lightheaded now I just switch to a kind of mental cruise control. It's as though something has a hold over my mental faculties. My brain is on autopilot.

I see the broken mirror. I can see myself, from above, walking toward it. I see myself hesitate, avoiding the fragments of broken glass that litter the tiled floor. And all the while, the light flickers on. I drift across the scene, and over the cubicle where Jess lies with blood pooling around her. The flickering light makes a shadowy strip across the floor. I watch as the shadow begins to warp into a more distinct shape. It undulates like a length of ribbon, and then swings like a jump rope before settling into a familiar silhouette. The shadow is a girl, I think.

"A girl? What does she look like, Emily? Describe her to me."

She doesn't have a face, I say – or rather, think.

"Go on."

She's just...gray, like the walls.

"And what is she doing?"

She's just standing there, watching. I don't really like her.

"Is she not your friend?"

I don't know. I don't like her. Can I float away now? Somewhere else. Somewhere that she isn't.

"I want you to float down, Emily. Float down into your memory. Into your deeds. Look at yourself in the mirror. Look at what you did."

I don't want to. But the flashing, flickering light draws me down. I am a moth, in thrall of the flame. I drift down and hover above the tiled floor. My body turns slowly, in mid-air, until I am facing the shattered mirror.

"Look."

I don't want to look. But I am compelled to by the soft voice that crouches somewhere in the dark. The flickering light quickens and I feel my heart beating more rapidly with it. I hear an echo of breaking glass. The sound is coming from within the broken mirror itself.

"See."

I look. And I see. For just a moment, I see. I see myself, but not myself. A dark vision of a girl. I realize with fright, but also with relief, that it is not me at all, but the strange and shadowy gray girl. She has a shard of mirror glass in her hand. She is holding on to it so tightly that it should be cutting into her flesh. But there's no blood on her. *Maybe there isn't any in her,* I think. *Maybe she's made of shadows and dust.*

She seems to sense my thoughts and I see the dark glint of her eyes, from some dark place behind her hair. She beckons me closer to the mirror and I float toward her, unable to stop myself. I begin to feel heavy, and feel the tips of my toes scrape across the cold, hard surface of the tiles as I float forward.

She thrusts the shard of mirror out at me, and slices through the air. I wonder if she has cut my throat, but I can't raise my hand there to check. There's this strange vibration in the room, like she has eviscerated reality, then a sucking sensation that starts pulling me in. It's as though I'm in the depressurized cabin of an airplane, in freefall.

Then, I'm somehow on the other side of the broken glass, looking out. And I can see her, standing over Jess's body. The gray shadow girl. She slashes at her with the glass and blood trails through the air. Jess is cut to ribbons before me. I scream, but the sound is contained because I'm trapped inside the mirror. I watch as the gray girl, no more distinct than a shadow, drags Jess by the hair into the bathroom stall. I watch the blood pool beneath the door and across the tiles. It makes me feel queasy inside. But it keeps on coming.

So much blood.

"That will be all for today," Principal Quick says.

I am awake, and in the chair in her office. The window blind is open again. Quick is over by her cabinet. I look at the desk and the metronome is gone.

"I don't...I can't...."

(*How long have I been in here?*)

"You may feel a little disoriented after the hypnotherapy," Principal Quick says, her voice sounding characteristically hard again. "It is perfectly normal, and will pass."

I get to my feet, and she points me to the door.

"Now return to your dormitory and get changed. It is almost time for your exercise in the recreation yard, and you must not miss out on that, must you? Clarity of mind and body."

I sense that hers is a rhetorical question, and so I don't answer.

As I leave her office, I wonder why I'm feeling so nauseous. Sick to my stomach and green around the gills. I hope that the sensation will pass before I hit the recreation yard.

* * *

My breathing becomes ragged as I struggle to keep up the pace. Quick has had us out here for what feels like an age, running around and around the courtyard. Lab rats in a maze. Or rather, I feel like one of those horses you see being trained in a paddock. And now I think of it, I'm pretty sure Quick would be cracking a whip if she had one to hand.

My ankles ache from the continued pounding of my feet against the concrete surface of the recreation yard. The air seems to be charged with electricity, like a storm is coming.

My pulse throbs in my ears so hard that I feel my eardrums might actually burst. I haven't been feeling so well since the principal put me under with her weird metronome gizmo. I can sense the onset of another out-of-body event, but instead of my ears ringing I hear something else as I run. It sounds like a discordant nursery rhyme.

On instinct, I look up and see the clock tower silhouetted against the sky. I slow down because my legs feel heavy, as though I've waded into thick mud. My hands drop to my sides and I feel something alarming. A slender little hand holds on to mine gently. It is cold. I look down at my hand.

Nothing there.

I slow to a strolling pace, and then look up at the clock tower. There's a girl up there – and she's staring right at me. The pallor of her skin has a disturbing quality. It looks totally gray, like she's dead but alive. I wonder then if she's looking at me, or behind me. I turn to look in that direction and my eyes meet Principal Quick's.

"Keep up the pace, Emily," the principal intones, before scowling at me.

I prepare to start running again, but first I feel compelled to return my gaze to the clock tower.

The gray girl is gone.

* * *

I sit on my bed and watch the shadow of a treetop swaying in the light from the moon. It casts spidery shapes on the wall. They're mesmerizing, but not so much that they can distract me fully from Saffy's droning voice.

She's sitting on her bed and smoking a cigarette demonstratively, while holding court with the other girls who are lounging around on their beds. Even Lena has abandoned her post, trading keeping watch at the door for the comfort of her bed.

"Christ," Saffy says, "I can't get the image out of my mind. All that blood. I swear I still have some of it under my fingernails. *Eww*, so fucking gross. Why did she have to choose such a messy way to top herself?"

"That's a bit insensitive, even for you," Victoria says.

"Did someone just hear something?" Saffy asks, her voice dripping with sarcasm. "It sounded like a mouth fart."

Victoria rolls her eyes. No one else dares speak.

"One thing's for sure, I'm going to need more smokes," Saffy continues, "for my nerves. Don't worry, Emily's got it covered, girls. Haven't you?"

I know she's talking directly at me now, but I just keep my attention fixed on the shadow of the tree on the wall. I think back to earlier, when I saw the girl high up in the clock tower. Or *thought* I saw her. I wonder if it's possible to imagine such things. And if I am, then does that mean I'm insane?

"Is it just me or is everyone going stir crazy already?" Saffy says. "Hell-o?"

"Did any of you see her today? The other inmate?" I finish the sentence before I've even realized I started it.

"You saw her too? When? Why didn't you say anything?" Saffy asks.

"During exercise," I say. "She was up in the clock tower, like you said she was before."

Saffy looks emboldened. "See, I *told* you gals there was someone else here. Did you get a look at her face?"

"Nope. Her hair was in the way. She looked kind of sick."

"Fuck me, that's all we need," Lena mutters. "Some weird sicko. Probably gonna give us all leprosy or something."

"That's not contagious," Annie says.

"Yeah it is," Lena says.

"*Whatevs*," Saffy retorts. "Like today wasn't fucked up enough already. Thanks a bunch for facilitating my restful sleep, bitches."

"Anyone else see her?" I ask. If Saffy did, and I did, then maybe others have – but have been too nervous to say anything yet. I cast my eyes over each of their faces, until my eyes meet Victoria's.

"I did," Victoria says quietly.

"Really? When?" Saffy asks.

"Our first night," Victoria says. "I woke up, and she was watching me sleep."

"That's just really fucking creepy," Annie says, and she shivers. A master of understatement, that one.

"Then what happened?" Saffy has forgotten all about her cigarette. The fragile cylinder of ash looks like it might fall onto her bedclothes at any moment.

"Emily woke me up. For real." Victoria pauses for dramatic effect, and then cracks a sly smile. "It was a dream!"

Got to hand it to her, revenge is sweet.

"You bitch, you had me going there—" Saffy looks really annoyed, but before she can say another word, the lights suddenly click off, plunging us into darkness.

"Settle down, girls."

Holy crap.

Principal Quick has been standing there for who knows how long. I wonder if she heard our discussion. I climb into bed and listen to her walking away. The other girls are restless. I can hear them moving under their sheets. The moon slips behind a cloud and the shadow of the tree is gone, leaving just a blank, gray wall. I close my eyes.

CHAPTER NINE

Smoke Run

The swimming pool changing room is ridiculously cold. I hug my body with my arms to keep what little body temperature I have left from escaping.

Principal Quick has us each line up by the benches, looking over us with her characteristic sternness. Her pursed lips and uncaring eyes make it clear that she is not at all concerned about how cold we are.

"Today you will swim lengths," she says. "Nothing balances the mind quite like regimented exercise."

I hear groans from a couple of the girls. Principal Quick does not like that. She holds her hand up in the manner of an orchestra conductor calling for silence. It works, too. She has a way with people, the principal. A way of shutting them up, that is. We all know the futility of rebellion, even if the occasional groan of complaint does escape our lips.

"Ten minutes to get ready, girls, then line up by the pool. You will remain silent. You will carry out my instructions. You will learn."

Principal Quick walks out of the changing room, leaving a heavy atmosphere behind her. I catch Saffy making furtive glances at the other girls as we each begin to get changed in uncomfortable silence. There's something deeply unpleasant about being forced together in a room like this, freezing cold and starkly lit, and being expected to strip. It's dehumanizing. And that, I think, is precisely why Principal Quick is making us do it. She wants to reduce us to what we are, ultimately. A group of frightened little girls.

I change out of my gray uniform and into my equally gray swimming costume as quickly as I can.

(*At least we're consistently* on-trend *at Greyfriars.*)

My exposed skin is a nest of goosebumps. I keep my distance from the others as I use a hairband to tie up my hair. Principal Quick obviously thinks swimming caps are not required. I think my hair might freeze when we come back in here to change after our exercise detail. At least we have towels, although they're cheap, old and rather worn out. I drape mine around my shoulders. Anything to protect myself from the chill.

I glance across the changing room and notice that Victoria looks the most frightened of us all. She's actually trembling as she undresses, and I don't think only the cold is to blame. She looks so awkward in her own skin that it's almost as if she might take that off, too. After she has peeled her uniform away, she keeps it clutched to her body. I'm wondering why she has tears in her eyes.

Saffy sidles over beside Victoria. She has that look on her face. That thoroughly mean look that indicates she is about to do something unpleasant. Admittedly, it's a look she wears on her privileged face most of the time, but the way she's stalking Victoria is nothing short of predatory. Victoria turns away, but as she does so the towel slips from her shoulder, revealing a section of bare arm. I see row upon row of razor-line scars there. And Saffy sees them too. Before Victoria can react, Saffy grabs the towel and yanks it away from her shoulders.

"Ooh, nice scars! Look girls! We have a self-harmer over here – how last season...."

Victoria trembles, folding her arms as she tries to cover her scars with her hand.

"Give me my towel back," she says, and the bravery in her voice makes my stomach twist in the most peculiar way.

Saffy is having none of it, though. She just mocks Victoria some more, dangling the towel in front of her.

"What, this one?" she taunts.

Saffy swings the towel to-and-fro. I hear laughter from the other girls and wonder if they really are as cruel as Saffy, or just as bored as she is.

"Just give it back, okay?" Victoria says, sounding fed up.

Saffy takes center stage, climbing up onto one of the benches before giving the towel a long, demonstrative sniff.

(*Missed out on stage school, this one.*)

She looks so happy to have an audience once more.

"Smells funny, this towel," she says theatrically, and then offers it around to the other girls. Annie takes a sniff and then recoils in fake disgust. It's audience participation, Saffy's show.

"Wonder what it is, that smell?" Saffy asks. She reclaims the towel and wafts it in Victoria's direction.

"Don't...." Victoria is about to speak further, and then appears to think better of it. She just breathes out, long and slow, anger bubbling under the surface.

Saffy sniffs the towel again. She's on a roll. "Oh, I *know* what it is…" she says.

Victoria closes her eyes, and clenches her lips tightly shut, apparently in anticipation of the insult to come.

"It's soaking wet with your piss, bed-wetter! It stinks. *You* fucking stink."

She throws the towel at Victoria. It hits Victoria's face and then falls to the floor.

Victoria is on Saffy like a flash. She rushes her, shoves her across the tiles and up against the nearest locker door with a metallic clang. Saffy laughs and tries to fight back, but Victoria is too agile. She dodges Saffy's clawing fingers and punches her hard in the stomach.

(*Not going to lie, I have to laugh at that.*)

Saffy doubles up, the wind knocked out of her. She drops to her knees and the look of shock on her face is an absolute picture.

"Grab the bitch," Saffy says, her voice quivering with anger and pain from having been punched so hard.

Victoria takes a couple of steps back away from Saffy, her threat now neutralized. She turns to face the rest of us, her eyes daring us to get in her way. No one does at first, but when Victoria walks between us and toward the door, Annie steps into her path.

Annie raises her hand to grab Victoria. But Victoria is faster, and grabs Annie's wrist. Victoria twists her hand over and exposes a scar on Annie's wrist. Annie looks from Victoria's face to her self-inflicted razor scars, and then back to the source of her own shame. Annie looks aghast. We've all seen it, and she knows.

Pushing Annie aside in disgust, Victoria leaves the changing room.

Saffy crouches on the floor against the lockers, spluttering and holding her belly. If I didn't know her better by now, I'd say she might even be crying. Just then, Annie walks over to the lockers, where Saffy crouches. She offers a hand to Saffy to help her to her feet, but Saffy swats her hand away angrily.

"Fat lot of use you are," Saffy says.

Annie backs off—

(*Smart girl.*)

—before rolling her eyes and following the others out of the changing room.

I follow along, too.

At the pool, I join the line of girls and wait my turn beside the water. Principal Quick prowls along with the air of a predator stalking a watering hole in the savanna, signaling to each swimmer when it's time to dive in.

Saffy appears, uncharacteristically quiet since her standoff with Victoria in the changing room. Saffy stands in line beside me, clutching her arms around her body protectively. Maybe Victoria's punch to the gut was harder than I thought it was? Saffy is normally such a show-off. Then I notice that she's actually shivering. Her knees are trembling. She's like a frightened rabbit. Saffy sees me looking, and can't hide her obvious fear. A question forms in my mind and I am compelled to ask it, even if it risks provoking Saffy's wrath.

"What's wrong?" I ask.

Saffy frowns, still holding on to herself. "I don't like the water," she says, her voice strained.

It's my turn next to dive into the pool, so I ready myself. But then I see someone at the opposite end of the pool, where the shadows meet the water. Her hair obscures her face, but the pallid gray of her skin is instantly familiar to me from the last time I saw her, looking down from the clock tower.

She just stands there, watching me from the perimeter of the pool. Then she starts walking toward me, toward the edge of the pool. Incredibly, she steps down from the poolside onto the surface of the water—

(*Hell no, that's just not possible.*)

—but I can see her with my own unblinking eyes, walking toward me across the pool like it's made of solid glass. She's only a few meters away now, and my instincts finally kick in. I back away from the weird girl. But in doing so, I knock into Saffy. Our limbs entangle for a moment and Saffy, taken by surprise, shoves me away. She realizes her mistake with a yelp, and falls backward into the water.

I look down into the pool, expecting to see that Saffy has fallen onto the gray girl. But the girl has gone. Disappeared.

Principal Quick has heard Saffy's splash and is marching her way over to where I'm standing. She has a tin whistle around her neck on a chain and she puts it to her lips and blows a shrill note of displeasure. Then she turns her viper-like eyes to me.

"What are you doing? Swim, girl. I said lengths. Get in there and put your back into it!" Principal Quick commands.

I bend my knees and dive into the water. For a fragment of time, I'm free, isolated from sound and sensation under the water, which is refreshingly cool, but not cold. Then my head breaks the surface of the water and the noises invade my ears. Principal Quick's echoing voice, and the splashing of the other girls as they swim ahead of me, are deafening after the pleasant solitude under water.

I reach out with the flat of my right hand, then my left, and begin to swim my first length. Still stalking the poolside, Principal Quick supervises, holding a stopwatch and shouting at us to dig in, to swim faster.

Reaching the other side of the pool, I kick off onto my back and begin my return trip, swimming backstroke. I pass Saffy, whose ungainly splashes have her coughing up water. I turn my head to see Saffy reach the side of the pool, where she grabs on to the edge, catching her breath. A shadow falls over her and I see the creepy gray-skinned girl, leaning over the side of the pool and looking down at Saffy.

I complete my length and stop at the end of the pool. Out of the shadows and beneath the pool room's skylight, the gray girl's pallid skin looks as though it's stretched over her oddly distended body. Her hair is tangled like she's just crawled from out of the grave. Saffy sees me looking. Her puzzled expression gives way to a yelp of shock as she glances above her to see the weird girl gazing down at her. Saffy gasps and kicks her legs hard in a panic, making great splashes in the water.

"No time for breaks, Emily! Another length!" Principal Quick commands from across the pool.

I kick off into a front crawl. Saffy swims past me in a flurry of splashes and foam when I'm a third of the way across. Her terror has made her more of a swimmer, at least. She'll be at the side of the pool in no time at the pace she's going. I finish my length and pause to take a look. Sure enough, Saffy has reached the other end and is treading water, all the while looking around fearfully. The gray girl is nowhere to be seen.

But Principal Quick is omnipresent. "Shall I get you a sun lounger?" she asks Saffy, who just grasps on to the overflow ledge behind her like it's a life preserver.

She looks bloody terrified.

"Please. I want to get out," she pleads with Quick, and you can hear the raw fear in her voice.

"You've hardly even started," the principal says dismissively. "Get to it, girl, swim! Reach and kick, breathe and repeat!"

"Please! I need to get out!" Saffy's anguished cry almost has me feeling sorry for her. She sounds genuinely distressed. I notice that she isn't looking at Principal Quick, but is instead gazing down into the water directly below her.

There's a muffled cry as suddenly, and inexplicably, Saffy is pulled under the water, as if by a shark. She rises momentarily, screeching for a second before going under again. Seconds pass, and some bubbles arise and break on the surface of the water.

Saffy is still down there.

The principal peers down into the pool with a look of mild resentment on her face. It's as though Saffy's apparent drowning-in-progress is just another inconvenience to her. What a bitch.

I glance around at the others and see Lena is nearest to where Saffy went under. Lena takes a breath and then dives underwater. The pool room is quiet now, save for the lapping of the water around the sill behind me.

With a sudden splash, Saffy resurfaces, followed quickly after by Lena, who spits out a mouthful of water like an Olympian.

Within seconds, more arms are grabbing her and Saffy is hauled up onto the side of the pool. She's a coughing and spluttering mess. I think she's actually crying. Principal Quick and the other girls stand around Saffy, trying to calm her as she kicks and convulses.

"Get away from her," the principal commands, before stooping down and sliding a supportive arm under Saffy's shoulders. Quick drags Saffy to her feet and leads her away. The other girls follow, crowding around their leader. Victoria stops and looks at me, hesitant for a second, then she joins the others.

I'm all alone in the pool now. I look in the direction where I saw the gray girl. No one is there. But my flesh still tingles as I tread water. I swim to the side of the pool and clamber out.

After wrapping myself in a towel, I follow the sounds of Saffy's sobs and moans and find her in the corridor that leads from the changing room. Principal Quick looks to be having real difficulty holding on to Saffy as she walks her down the corridor. Saffy is still really freaking out, and her garbled murmurs are barely understandable. I do catch the words 'coming to get me', though. Saffy glances feverishly around, seemingly oblivious to Quick, or Lena and Annie, who follow close behind. Victoria, I notice, is keeping her distance.

"Pull yourself together, girl," Principal Quick says, before slapping Saffy hard across the face.

Wow. We're all a little shocked by that.

But not quite as shocked as Saffy, who slumps into a swoon.

"Hold her," the principal commands. Annie and Lena snap to it, propping Saffy up.

Quick takes her bunch of keys from her belt, then unlocks the door. I catch up to them and the principal gives me a cursory look.

"You," she says, "in here with me."

I step past catatonic Saffy, still being held upright by Annie and Lena, who looks entranced by what she sees through the open door. I'm in a storeroom, lined with shelves and cabinets, filled floor to ceiling with various medicine cartons. I glance back at Lena, whose eyes have lit up at the sight of so many meds.

Principal Quick unlocks a tall cabinet, opens it, and then selects a couple of cartons from inside. She then closes and locks the cabinet before unpacking the cartons. After a few moments, she returns with a freshly prepared syringe in her right hand, and a bottle and some cotton wool in her left.

"Hold this," she instructs, and I take the loaded syringe from her.

I can almost feel Annie and Lena's eyes on me. I guess they're willing me to stick the needle into Principal Quick so we can escape or something. But they've forgotten that I escaped already, and there's really nothing much to say for it save for mud, rain, and disappointment. So I just watch as Principal Quick swabs Saffy's inner elbow with antiseptic. She discards the cotton wool ball and places the bottle in my free hand before taking the syringe from my other. Holding Saffy's arm tight, the principal squeezes to make the vein pop out a little. Then she injects her. Saffy murmurs something unintelligible and visibly relaxes into a slump.

Lena watches with a weird kind of hunger on her face, as Principal Quick tosses the used syringe into a sharps bin. The principal shuts and locks the storeroom door.

"Help me carry her to the dormitory," she says.

* * *

Night has fallen over Greyfriars Reformatory by the time we get Saffy settled.

I brush my teeth and get changed into my nightclothes. When I return to the dormitory, the room feels so desolate and cold.

Saffy lies on her bed, looking worse for wear after her ordeal at the swimming pool. At least the sedative seems to be doing its work – she's stopped mumbling and thrashing about. Her eyes seem fixed on a point somewhere in the middle of the room. She's staring into space, in other words. Still, the other girls stand silently by. Saffy's loyal troops. Only Victoria keeps her distance, hanging back, looking awkward and out of place. I walk toward my bed and something unexpected happens. The other girls, except Victoria, form a line in front of my bed – an impenetrable wall of bitches.

I steel myself and try to push through them to get to my bed. Lena and Annie lock arms—

(*Yes, they actually lock arms!*)

—and shove me back.

I'm new to this game, but not defeated yet, so I beat a quick retreat and then attempt to skirt around the line of girls in order to approach my bed from the other side. But my different-angle idea fails. Too quickly, they extend the line and once again, they shove me back.

Then, I hear Saffy's voice cut through the tense silence.

"And you."

Victoria, head lowered, joins their ranks. When it was just her versus Saffy earlier, Victoria's anger gave her the upper hand. But without the element of surprise, and with Saffy's crew putting on a united front – let's just say I don't blame her for playing ball this time.

Saffy looks bolstered by her little triumph. She nods at the others.

"Grab her," she orders.

They grab my hair and the pain is so bad it feels like my roots are on fire. The pain forces my head down and I feel rough hands twisting my right arm behind my back. That hurts too, and I'm dreading hearing a tearing sound because it feels for sure like they are going to twist my arm from its socket.

Slowly and deliberately, Saffy gets up from her bed. She stands over me, a surrogate Principal Quick, and I begin to wonder if the two aren't related.

"Quick's aren't the only rules here, Emily," Saffy purrs, as though reading my thoughts.

The grip on my hair tightens, and all I can do is swallow the pain.

Saffy crouches until her cruel face is in my eye line. "What did you see? At the pool?"

Considering my position, I decide that honesty really is the best policy, however odd it might sound.

"I saw *her*. That strange girl." I try to breathe through the searing pain at my scalp and elbows. "Then she...well, she disappeared."

"Any of you lot see her?"

Saffy glances around at her cohorts. No one speaks.

"I don't know what you're playing at," Saffy continues, "but I do know you're up to something." Saffy glares at me, and then glances over her shoulder.

"Both of you," she says, and I know she's referring to Victoria, who's still cowering a short distance away. "You get lucky, throw a punch to wind me, and then…. One pushes me into the water, causing a distraction while the other—"

I look at Saffy, who seems to have drifted off into some other, darker place. To be honest with you, she looks a bit stoned. Must have been one hell of an injection. I'm almost jealous.

"The other does what?" I ask.

Saffy blinks as though she's banishing unwelcome memories. Her expression hardens again.

"There's only one way to redeem yourselves, get back in my good books."

Saffy looks around at the engrossed faces of her foot soldiers with a sly grin. She mimes smoking a cigarette, putting the imaginary cigarette to her lips. The girls giggle approvingly.

"Smoke run," Lena says.

"Smoke run?" I ask. Fair question, I'm sure anyone would agree. I mean, what the heck is a smoke run?

"Cigarettes, dear," Saffy says. "Currency. The only thing worth a damn round here. You made light work of it before, lifting a pack from old Quick. This time see if she's got any booze as well. Bet she has, sour-faced old hag."

"But she'll miss it," I counter, "and anyway her office will be locked for sure."

Saffy just smirks at me.

"You need to learn to use the eyes God gave you. The door to the courtyard is unlocked. From there you can access Principal Quick's office through the window. Don't forget to close the window on your way out."

"Smoke run," I repeat.

Saffy nods. "Perfect for someone *shifty* like you."

Well, now. I've never really thought of myself as being *shifty*. I'm not sure I like the connotation. And I think maybe Saffy can guess that I don't from the way her eyes are twinkling at me.

Then she turns her attention to Victoria.

"And you. Come back with the goods and maybe I'll be willing to overlook your little dog and pony show at the pool."

I don't feel like asking her what she'll do if we come back empty handed.

* * *

We steal down the hallway, treading as softly as we can, trying not to make a sound. It's going pretty well until we both see a huge black shadow moving across the wall. Victoria freaks out and I think she's going to scream, so I clamp my hand over her mouth. I can feel her trembling, and the rise and fall of her breathing getting quicker. Still holding my hand over her mouth, I poke my head out around the corner to take a furtive look. I release my hand and gesture to Victoria that the coast is clear. We round the corner together and, looking fearfully to the window, Victoria sees what I just saw. The source of the shadow is just a tree outside, its branches swaying in the wind. Victoria sighs heavily with relief. We move on together in the direction of the exercise yard.

I open the door and quickly move into the courtyard. I hang back in the shadows and check the coast is clear before waving Victoria through. Then, I close the door behind us quietly.

Ominous shadows dance across the stone surfaces of the eerily quiet space. I watch their darkly fluid forms – phantoms cast by the moonlight and clouds. Victoria looks alert, and completely on edge. She creeps over to the window, shoulders hunched. I'm still watching the shadows until she hisses at me under her breath to get a move on.

I join her over by the window. We check it over and find it's unlatched. I keep watch while Victoria slides the window up and open. With our point of entry secured, Victoria cradles her hands together and mimes giving me a leg up. I nod before placing one hand on the windowsill, and the other on Victoria's shoulder to steady myself. I lift my right foot and Victoria bends her knees, lowering her body so she can cup my foot in her hand. I push down with my foot and my hands, and up I go. I wriggle through the window and then drop to the floor. I give the office a cursory look, making sure it really is unoccupied and half expecting Principal Quick to be asleep at her desk. Satisfied that she's not around, I turn back to the window and raise it higher, widening the gap. Then I reach through with my hands and upper body. Victoria grasps my hands in hers, and I pull her inside.

Something white on the desk catches my eye. I walk over to take a closer look and see the thick manuscript that Principal Quick filed away before. Right next to it is Quick's clipboard. I begin to leaf through the papers that are mounted on the clipboard. Each one has a mugshot of one of the girls, and a bunch of handwritten case notes. Curiosity makes me want to read them, to know what path brought each of them here. I'm just wondering if my own case file is included among them, when Victoria waves at me to get my attention.

"We have to be quick."

I look back down at the case files. Quick would come down on us like a ton of bricks if they went missing. Oh, but it is tempting though.

"You know what I mean," Victoria says, and this time I catch the urgency in her voice. She looks really anxious. Then I see her nod at Quick's desk drawer. "In there?" she asks.

The smoke run. I almost forgot that's why we're even in here.

As Victoria keeps her ever-anxious eyes on the door, I slide open the desk drawer. Can't see any cigarettes in there. A picture frame lies facedown in the drawer. I lift it out and turn it over. The image shows a younger Principal Quick with a man who looks a few years older than her. Principal Quick is dressed in doctoral graduation robes, complete with ridiculous floppy hat. Wow, and her hair. It's so big. The older man's robes look ostentatious, and I wonder if that must mean he is, or was, a professor. The frame is roughly the same size as the empty-space stain on the wall. I cross to the wall and hold the picture up against the stain. Perfect fit.

"What's that? What are you doing?" Victoria sounds like she might burst open from anxiety. "You're supposed to be looking for cigarettes, not old photos."

I shrug, then return to the desk. I'm about to pop the picture frame back inside the drawer when I notice something else. By lifting out the picture, I have inadvertently uncovered a key in the bottom of the drawer.

"No ciggies in here, I'm afraid," I say, "only this." I hold the key up so Victoria can take a look at it. Then, I glance across the room and see the closet door. "I wonder," I say, before placing the picture frame back inside the drawer.

"Wonder what?" Victoria asks.

I cross the room to the closet door, making eye contact with Victoria for a second as I pass by. Victoria's eyes snap back to the main office door as though she fears being discovered at any moment.

I push the key into the lock and turn it.

It clicks open.

CHAPTER TEN

Saffy

Even in that limbo state somewhere between sleep and waking, Saffy knew she was dreaming. But as the warmth of a soft, shimmering day washed over her, she allowed herself to become subsumed by it.

She rolled over in her bed onto her side and, as she did so, left any connection to the physical world behind her. She entered her dream unconditionally, because she knew in her subconscious that he would be waiting for her. He was always waiting for her, whenever she closed her eyes and gave herself over to the oblivion of sleep. She could hardly wait. The control that she yearned for, even demanded, in waking life did not apply in her dreams. Here she could let it all go, let herself go, into his arms again.

And there he was. Jeff. His bare skin beaded with droplets of water from the outdoor pool. He blinked the water away from his eyelashes and his eyes shone in the sunlight. He smiled, revealing his lovely white teeth. A perfect smile, just for her and her alone, a beacon in her otherwise shitty and meaningless existence.

He beckoned to her and she took the bait, letting loose a laugh before kicking off into the water and swimming to him. The noonday sun caressed her bare back with its glow. She cut through the water until she was upon him. She placed her hands on his shoulders and reared up above the surface of the water. Saffy enjoyed the way he looked at her bathing-suited body. He looked like he wanted her all over again. And maybe he could have her, but not yet. She threw back her head and whooped in victory before pushing him back into the water. His mouth made a circle of surprise as he plummeted under the surface of the pool with an enormous splash. Giggling, she kicked back away from him and rolled over in the water, beginning to swim toward the other side of the pool where the rails of the shiny steel ladder cast their rippled reflection.

She heard him call out to her, his deep voice softened by the fact that he'd taken on some water during his impromptu dunking. Saffy swam faster, then felt his powerful grip holding her back. He pulled himself along the length of her body, hand over hand along her leg as though it were a rope. His hands found her waist, then moved across her torso, before his fingers entwined into her wet hair. He pulled her to him in the warm water, and she felt his heat against her. Laughing, he nipped at her chin with his teeth. She wrapped her legs around his waist. He carried her through the water. She felt weightless in his arms. Then, she felt the steel steps of the ladder at her back.

He kissed her, deep, and their tongues intertwined until they were exchanging the same hot breath. Her fingernails dug into the firm flesh of his shoulder blades as she felt his fingers find her beneath the water. Her other hand was already on him, freeing him from his swim shorts. She felt him move her bathing suit aside, exposing her to him. He put his arm around her waist and lifted her into place. Their bodies locked together, wet upon wet, and it felt so good. It felt right. Saffy gasped as they began to make love, rocking deeper into the throes, until—

Not this part. I don't like this part. I want to wake up.

—the sun disappeared as a shadow fell over them. Saffy's skin prickled. That felt good, too. A blast of cold amidst the heat of their lovemaking. But something was wrong. Jeff pulled away from her. She felt a sharp ache as their bodies separated.

She looked into his eyes and saw a figure reflected in his black irises. A woman looming over them.

Saffy leaned back her head onto the top step of the ladder. Even upside down, from her point of view, she recognized the woman in an instant. A woman the same age in years as Jeff, but so much older in Saffy's eyes. Those sharp features. The streak of gray in her fringe. Jeff's wife wasn't supposed to be back for a couple of days. Yet here she was. Standing large as life beside the pool where Saffy had been boning her husband. Great.

And in a way, wasn't it great? Saffy reasoned that this had to happen at some stage or another. Jeff had already told her he loved her, twice. The first time they had both been high as kites, and she'd just given him the mother of all blowjobs in the backseat of his car, so that hadn't counted – and she had told him as much. The second time did count. She had just been busted for cutting class again and had no one to turn to except him. He had asked her to wait for him at their usual meeting place, the bus stop near the mall, and had come to pick her up as soon as he'd finished at the office. He had held her as she sobbed into the collar of his shirt and told her that it would be all right, and that he loved her. That had been one of the worst, and one of the best, days of her crummy life. He loved her, and he clearly didn't love his wife anymore, so yes – it was a good thing that she had come back unexpectedly. Now he would make a clean break and they could be together, as they were meant to be. She felt lightheaded at the prospect of them seeing each other whenever they wanted to, rather than whenever they could get away with it. Jeff would be hers, and she would be his equal. They would have a lot of fun, and to hell with his old life. Her mind was reeling with the excitement of it all when she felt him detach from her completely. It took a few moments to figure out what was happening, but he appeared to be pleading with his wife, and trying to reassure her that he was sorry and that it wouldn't happen again. Saffy felt sick as she—

Please let me wake up now.

—reached down below the waterline and pulled her clothing back over her exposed, most intimate, self. The water lapped at her chest as Jeff launched himself up and out of the pool. She watched him clamber up onto the poolside where they had drunk cocktails together only an hour ago. Saffy spoke his name and she saw him stop for a moment. He looked at her and she saw no love in his eyes, nothing. Like the shadow of his wife blotting out the sun, it was as though someone had gouged his eyes out, they were so empty. He told her he thought she'd better go and she really did feel like she was going to be sick now. She protested, telling him she had nowhere else to go. He lowered his head, and his voice, and said that he'd get her a cab. Saffy told him to please go and fuck himself. Then he was gone.

Day turned to night—

Dream logic I guess. Jesus Christ, just let me wake up!

—as Saffy wandered blank landscapes that seemed to go on forever. The desolation of arid land echoed how lost and betrayed she felt. Her stomach squirmed at the feeling of Jeff pulling away from her. She was cut off, adrift from the only person who understood her in the whole world. Separated from the one man who never judged her. It was all wrong, this state of being. And with that thought, she began to fight against it. The endless circling became a faint path in the dust at her feet, and one which she followed. The cold light of the moon shone down on her, casting her long shadow before her. She heard faint voices and watched as her shadow stretched out and met the familiar wooden gate of Jeff's garden. It creaked open and the dust solidified into the paved path that led down to the pool house. The voices grew louder, and clearer. Saffy padded—

Barefoot. I'm still barefoot.

—down to the pool house and stopped by the nearest of the windows. Little fairy lights twinkled from inside the snug little space. Jeff was kneeling on the floor. His wife sat on the wicker furniture, looking guarded. Then Jeff was crying – actually crying, and Saffy had never seen him do that in front of her and it hurt to see him doing it now – and she saw his wife's guard drop. Then they were hugging, and then kissing, and both apologizing to each other through their tears and it was sickening. Saffy felt the weight of a liquor bottle in her right hand—

Have I been drinking? I feel a little like I have.

—and took a slug from it, before wiping cold tears from the corners of her eyes with her other hand—

Actually, I'm smashed. Fucking loaded. Feels good. Feels like control.

When she saw Jeff and his wife lie down on the floor of the pool house together, Saffy knew just what to do. She retreated to the edge of the pool and looked down at the water. She saw her reflection there, dark and indiscernible. She wasn't his anymore, and he was no longer hers. But she was damned if he'd be anyone else's either. Saffy refused to be the catalyst for dear old Jeff and his wife getting back together—

Jesus Christ no, how completely fucking gross.

—she smashed the bottle on the side of the pool. Didn't even hear it break. Clutching the jagged remainder like a dagger, she marched toward the pool house.

Jeff was telling her *No, don't, Saffy, please stop*. The woman was screaming, over and over. But she was deaf to their cries. She could smell the metallic tang of blood, and the musk of fear. It smelled gloriously new. And there was so much blood. So much power. And control. It was overwhelming. Saffy could feel it coursing through her veins. Her vision swam red.

"*Saa-ffyyy….*"

She blinked, and found herself in semi-darkness.

The sheets of her bed were a wet tangle beneath her. Stark white where, seconds before, there had only been dark red.

"*Saffy….*"

The whisper grew louder, like a rattling breath. Afraid of the voice, Saffy looked around the darkened dormitory fearfully. She looked at Victoria's empty bed, then at Emily's, and all of the others. She was alone in the dormitory. Where were the other girls?

Smoke run. I remember. Thank heaven I'm awake. But—

There was someone else, or something else, in the room with her. Standing in the shadows. The *someone* giggled, and Saffy's skin prickled with fear.

"*Saffy...*" the voice whispered again, and it sounded to Saffy like it was inside her head.

She bolted from her bed and ran. At her heels, the darkness of that voice had become a predatory shadow. Saffy ran down the hallway in her nightclothes, desperate to escape from the shadow bearing down on her. The strangely playful whisper pursued her, and whether it came from within her own psyche or not, Saffy pushed on in the hope she might outrun it.

"*Saffy.... Saaa-ffy....*"

Turning a corner, Saffy sprinted for the first door she saw. The swimming pool. Saffy wrestled the door open and slammed it shut behind her. Leaning against the door for a moment to catch her breath, she hoped the noise she had made would wake Principal Quick. Even a punishment for being out of bed at night would be preferable to her current, waking nightmare.

Hearing a swishing noise, Saffy turned and glimpsed a dark shadow flit across the wall between the changing room benches. Laughter filled her ears, piercingly loud. Saffy clamped her hands over her ears in an attempt to block out the sound. But inside her head, the noise only grew louder. Convulsing at the noise in her brain, Saffy struggled across the changing room and reached the door to the pool. It took all of her concentration to grasp the door handle, she was shaking so badly. With a cry of agony at the rising cacophony in her head, Saffy pushed through the door and into the pool room.

Silence. Saffy exhaled a nervous sigh at the relief she felt not to have the screeching laughter echoing around her head. She padded over to the edge of the pool, mesmerized by the red glow of emergency lighting on the water's surface. Saffy saw her own dark reflection there, on the red water. Unwelcome memories of that night at Jeff's pool house began to encroach upon her short-lived calm at the water's edge. Saffy could almost feel the weight of the broken bottle in her hand. The weight of what she had done hung heavy on her heart. She felt her skin turn cold—

Just as it had after she'd cut Jeff's wife.

—and uncontrollable sobs came out of her in waves. Her cheeks were drenched with stinging tears and her nose was running. She was just a snot-faced girl, a stupid girl—

Evil bitch. Hope you rot in hell.

—she had to breathe, to stop wallowing in the misery of what she had done, or she'd lose herself to it forever. She had to regain control—

"*Saaa-ffyyyy....*"

That voice again, whispering from the shadows.

Wiping her nose on the back of her hand, Saffy glanced around the pool room fearfully. She heard something, like broken glass scraping against tiles, and sensed movement. A shadow on the wall opposite her seemed to expand and contract, like all the darkness in the world was taking a breath. A sharp whisper from behind her made her whirl around. Saffy backed away, terrified, her eyes searching the dark corners of the room for answers she could not find.

Saffy failed to realize how close she was to the side of the pool until it was too late.

She heard a splash as something emerged at speed from the water. Felt the ice-cold grip of bony fingers around her ankle. She screamed as the hand pulled, hard, and her foot slid back over the side of the pool. Caught off balance, she toppled forward. Her arms flailed out in front of her uselessly. Everything went red as her face smashed against the hard, tiled surface at the side of the pool. Saffy tasted blood, and then chlorine as she was pulled under the water. She struggled and cried out in pain and terror as the bony hand gripped tighter around her ankle, pulling her down ever further.

Water invaded Saffy's lungs. She realized her screams made no sound at all down there in the depths as she drowned.

CHAPTER ELEVEN

Anything the Shadows Can Conjure

I've only been inside the closet space with Victoria for a few seconds, and already I can feel the walls closing in on me.

In the quiet, I can hear every breath – both mine and hers – accentuated in the cramped closet. I'm reluctant to shut the door behind us because I don't want to cut myself off from the sliver of air that I can feel breezing through the gap in the door. But Victoria still looks like she expects to be found out any moment, and she reaches past me to shut the door. The click of the door mechanism sounds final in the silence. Victoria seems to get her shit together now that we're shut in. She exhales a slow and steady breath, and glances up and around the tight space.

"Up there," she says.

Looking up at the tall bookshelves, I can see the corners of bulk-buy cigarette cartons poking out over the edge of the top shelf. Quick must get them duty free from some supplier, I guess. Reaching up with my fingers outstretched as far as they'll go, I can almost touch the nearest carton – but not quite.

"We need a boost again." I cup my hands together, thinking she wants a leg up, but Victoria shakes her head.

"Too crowded in here," she says. "We'll try something else."

I watch as she pulls a few weighty hardcover tomes from the shelves and begins piling them up on the floor. Victoria is so intent on her labors that she fails to see something that was hidden away behind the stacks she has just removed. It seems cigarettes aren't the only thing that Principal Quick must be getting duty free. Victoria sees me looking and stands up from her book pile to peer at the shelf.

"Score. Principal Quick, you dirty old bird!" Victoria picks up the bottle of vodka and turns it over in her hand.

I take a look, too. The text on the label is indecipherable. I think it's all written in Russian.

Victoria grins at me before placing the bottle back on the shelf. She crouches and piles up the last couple of books. Stepping away from the pile, she gestures for me to climb up. The book pile wobbles slightly as I do so, and I hold on to the nearest shelf to steady myself. Standing on the makeshift step, I can just reach the corner of the carton with my fingertips. Teetering on the unstable stack of books, I brush my fingers against the carton to dislodge it, moving it closer to the edge of the shelf. With one last effort, I use the force of gravity to rock the carton upward. It tips up and then falls off the shelf. Victoria hisses in victory. But with the carton comes something heavier – a metallic Zippo lighter, which hits Victoria on the forehead with a loud crack.

Victoria cries out in pain and admonishment, then clamps her hand over her mouth to stop the sound of her own voice. As she does so, she knocks against me, and that's it. The stack of books gives way and topples, and I come down with it, hard. I tumble into Victoria, knocking her over.

Cursing as she hits the deck, Victoria rubs her sore head where the lighter hit her. "I'm okay, don't worry yourself." She sighs, glancing around the closet floor. "We have to find that lighter, or Quick will know we've been in here. You can, like, actually help me this time."

"She'll *know* we've been in here anyway," I remind Victoria, "when she finds her cigarettes have been stolen."

"We won't take all of them," Victoria says. "Just a couple of packs. She'll never even notice. Especially if she's knocking back that vodka as often as I suspect she does, the old lush."

Together, we move the fallen books but there's no sign of the lighter. Victoria peers underneath the bookcase and I see her hair flutter like a flag in a breeze.

"There's an opening," she says, "and it's just big enough for a person to crawl through. I can see a stone floor on the other side. There! I can see Quick's lighter."

I hunker down next to Victoria and peer into the space beneath the stacks. Cool air washes over me and it feels like a memory of being outside. But it smells of dust and age. Kind of musty. I don't like it, so I'm relieved when Victoria announces, "Keep watch. I'll have to go. I'm thinner than you."

Victoria searches my eyes for a response. What kind of response, I'm not altogether sure. She's right; she is much thinner than me.

"Really nothing bothers you, does it?" she asks. Then she positions herself flat on the floor before wriggling head first through the opening into the crawlspace.

"Can't quite reach it," she says, her voice muffled from within the tight space. "You'll have to push my legs…."

I look down at her legs. They appear disembodied now that her top half has vanished under the bookcase. Such a weird image. I don't really want to touch them.

"Grab my ankles and push my legs!" she insists.

I position myself between her ankles and take hold of them. Victoria wriggles against my grip and I push. It's working. With a bit more wriggling, and some more pushing, the rest of her body disappears into the gap under the book stacks.

"Shit!" Victoria's voice echoes from the space beyond the bookcase. It sounds oddly like she's been trapped between their dusty spines, her muffled tones yelling at me from within their yellowed pages.

"Did you get the lighter?" I ask.

"Well, no, I didn't," comes her muffled reply. "There are

some steps in here, and I knocked it down there when I grabbed for it. Hold on, it can't have gotten far."

I lie flat and peer into the gloomy space. Sure enough, I can make out Victoria's feet descending from view down some steps a little way from the mouth of the opening. I wait, listening to the sound of my breathing. I see a flicker of light against the stairwell wall on the other side of the opening. She must have found the cigarette lighter at last. Maybe it's a trick of the light but I see a dark shape move across the wall. It looks like the shadow of a person, and then it's gone. It must be Victoria's shadow, or at least that's what I tell myself.

But the shadow was moving down the stairs, not up.

I hear a piercing scream. It echoes around the space behind the bookcase. The light flickers and goes out. And then I hear something else. Crazed laughter.

"Victoria?"

I can hear footsteps now, coming back up the stairs. I recognize Victoria's feet as she nears the top. She sounds like she's...chuckling to herself.

"Spooked myself good and proper down there," she says, breathless. "Thought I saw someone looking at me from the shadows, but it was just my reflection in an old glass picture frame." She chuckles again and I don't know why, but the sound unnerves me a little.

"We'd better get out of here," I say through the gap.

"You won't have to tell me twi—" Victoria says, but then doesn't finish her sentence.

I see the shadow move across the wall near the floor again, and it's as though it's followed her up the stairs. A dark band loops around Victoria's ankle and she topples backward before she can place her foot down on the top step. She issues a garbled, panicked shriek as she tumbles back down the steps.

"Victoria?" I call out to her. "You okay?"

I hear a slight and distant groan, and then only stark silence.

Maybe she's broken her leg or something. I don't know what to do. But the onus is on me now to figure something out. This smoke run was a bad idea, I decide, contemplating going to rouse Principal Quick for assistance. But she'll crucify us if she finds out we snuck into her office. Only one thing for it, I guess. I begin to wriggle through the gap.

It's smaller, even, than it looks. Victoria was right, she is slighter than me and was therefore much more suited to getting through unscathed. I grit my teeth and wriggle, feeling my fingernails scraping against the cold, unyielding stone floor on the other side. I'm about a third of the way through when I see Principal Quick's lighter lying on the floor. It is just inches away from my fingers. I squeeze my upper body further through the gap and the painful pressure on my ribs makes me gasp. Contact. I retrieve the lighter and pass it over to my right hand. I strike it, but it doesn't ignite.

"Oh my god." Victoria's voice is shaky, but at least hearing it means she's alive.

"Anything broken?" I call out. Then I try the lighter again. There's a final wisp of smoke, but still no fire.

"Oh my god, oh my god, oh my *god*." Victoria sounds really panicked now, petrified even. I hear a shuffling, and then the sounds of her tripping her way back up the stairs.

I thumb the lighter and it catches alight, the flame illuminating Victoria's terrified face just a breath away from mine as she stumbles up the stairs and hits the floor.

"Let me through! Oh my God! Let me through!" she shouts.

I quickly extinguish the lighter and clutch it tightly in the palm of my left hand. With my right, I take hold of Victoria's hand and begin pulling her back through the gap with me. Her skin is cool and clammy to the touch. Her eyes are wide with fear.

"What happened down there?" I ask between grunts as I help her wriggle through the opening beneath the bookcase.

Victoria ignores me. Or she doesn't want to say. Her eyes are so wide I can't help but wonder what they've just seen. She emerges fully, and now I can see the fear written all over her face. She looks really shaken up, so I decide not to pursue it any further. I guess I'm getting better at reading people the more time I spend with them doing insane activities like, *oh I don't know*, stealing stuff from Principal Quick's office closet. Still, I do wonder what it was exactly that freaked Victoria out while she was in the basement. Freed from the confines of the crawlspace, we both get to our feet and dust ourselves down.

Victoria frantically starts stacking the books into a pile.

"Help me out here! Put it back! Put the lighter back!"

I pick up the carton of cigarettes from the floor and pocket two packs. I climb up onto the wobbly stack of books and place the carton and lighter back where we found them.

"Oh my God, oh my God, hurry...." Victoria begins shelving the books the moment I step down from them. I get to work and help her shove the last of the books back onto the shelves.

"What the hell is wrong?" I ask. "Did you whack your head down there?"

The look on Victoria's face sends a chill right through me. It's as though something has gone from behind her eyes. She backs out through the closet door, terrified. I'm about to follow her when I think of something. I turn back and grab the vodka. I think we're going to need it. After closing the closet door firmly behind us, I turn the key in the lock.

Wasting no time, I cross to Quick's desk and pull the drawer wide open. I lift the picture frame up and replace the key beneath it. Then I slide the drawer closed again.

Mission accomplished. No fatalities. Well, apart from Victoria's mental health and the jury was out on that long before anyhow.

"What's—?" I begin to ask.

But Victoria is already out the window.

I clamber out, then slide the window shut. After crossing the shadowy recreation yard, I catch up to her in the corridor just around the corner from the main door to Principal Quick's office.

There's a loaded silence between us as we begin to retrace our steps back to the dormitory. We pause to catch our breath at the next turning. Victoria sees the vodka bottle and swipes it from my hand. She twists off the cap and takes a massive gulp. Wiping her lips with the back of her hand, she sighs heavily.

"Better?" I ask.

Victoria nods and takes another enormous gulp of vodka from the bottle. Then she offers the bottle to me. I take it from her. I wonder how it tastes. I can't remember if I have drunk it before. I'm just about to find out when we both hear a piercing scream.

"Great, someone's having the night terrors," Victoria whispers. "Whoever it is will wake every damn body, Principal Quick included."

"We'd better get back to bed." I look at Victoria and nod to the bottle cap.

She passes the cap to me and I twist it back onto the top of the bottle, sealing it.

Another loud scream echoes down the corridor, and I realize the sound is coming from the opposite direction from the dormitory. I can see from the puzzled look on her face that Victoria has realized it too. As the screams continue I head off, bottle in hand, in the direction of the sound and hear Victoria's footfalls following mine. A few moments later, we arrive at the door to the swimming pool.

"In here," I say, pushing open the door. Victoria follows close behind.

We rush inside, through the empty changing area, and into the pool room. It's an eerie place in the dead of night. Low-level emergency lighting casts a reddish hue over the water.

The ceiling and walls undulate in a red glow cast by the shifting surface of the water. But why would it be moving? As we get closer to the water's edge, I see for myself.

Principal Quick stands beside the pool, as silent and still as a statue. I didn't notice her at first because the place where the shadows end and the principal begins is kind of difficult to discern. Hearing us approach, she turns and sees us. Her momentary surprise becomes a look of intense distaste when she notices the vodka bottle in my hand.

(*Busted.*)

Victoria comes to a halt right beside me and I hear her gasp. At first I think she's just shocked to see Principal Quick standing there waiting for us. But then she puts her hand over her mouth and makes a horrid gagging sound. I wonder if she's going to throw up. She's looking beyond Quick, her eyes wide with horror.

"What the fuck, what the fuck, what the fuck?" she says, over and over.

Saffy lies facedown in the water, deathly still. *What the fuck*, indeed.

Principal Quick's shadow looms over the water, not quite reaching Saffy's prone body. I watch as the blonde tendrils of Saffy's once lustrous hair spiral to and fro with the lapping of the water. For a few breathless moments, I wait for Saffy to come back to life. To roll over on her back and thrash in the water, gasping for air, just like she did when Principal Quick made us swim lengths – when I see the gray girl walking across the water.

Is she here now, I wonder, watching? I glance at the shadows lining the pool but see nothing. The crimson glow cast by the emergency lights has turned the water blood red. My heart starts to beat erratically and I feel a hum growing in my head. The hum stretches out, a sickly, throbbing yawn between my ears that coils into my ear canals before increasing in pitch and then becoming that old familiar ringing sound. My legs feel weak and I swallow against an acidic taste at the back of my throat. Maybe I'm going to throw up instead of Victoria.

Through my numbness and the nausea, I sense movement at my side and see a dark shape launch itself into the water. It isn't until she resurfaces that I realize Victoria has dived in after Saffy.

She reaches Saffy in moments, but looks reluctant to reach out and touch her. Treading water, she turns herself around in the pool to face me, her arms moving constantly to keep her afloat.

"Don't just stand there," she says. "We have to help her!"

Victoria looks to me for help. And I feel that I want to help. But my legs feel distant from me, separated from me by the dull ache that has taken hold of my body. The loud ringing in my ears is at fever pitch.

"Please!"

Moving her arms against the water's surface, Victoria looks up at Principal Quick for help. A look of confusion passes over the principal's face, and she glances over her shoulder behind her.

I understand now that Victoria is looking past Principal Quick, and into the shadows beyond the tiled edge of the pool.

At the gray girl.

I see her too, a silent observer watching from the shadows, that dead-looking, gray girl.

Victoria recoils in fear, arms and legs flailing in the water. And as she does so, her movement turns Saffy's body over in the water, face up.

Saffy's face is horribly contorted in a rictus of fear. A red gash bleeds at her temple. Her jaw is locked open in a silent scream. Her mouth leaks chlorinated water. She looks like she was scared, and battered, to death.

The ringing in my ears retreats, becoming a shrill, cracked scream. It's Victoria. She screams again and backs away, treading water. Victoria points at the gray girl.

"She d-did it!" she stutters, barely able to speak. "She d-drowned Saffy!"

I look back to where the gray girl was standing just seconds ago. But now there's no one there. Only Principal Quick. And Victoria is pointing right at her.

The principal's expression is inscrutable.

I look back to Victoria and see that she now looks more afraid of Principal Quick than anything the shadows can conjure.

CHAPTER TWELVE

Tragic Accidents

My legs are aching from standing at my desk for so long.

At the head of the class, Principal Quick watches over us with an expression on her face that I can only really describe as regal. It's like she's a queen surveying her subjects, watching for any sign of weakness, or of dissent. Her eyes fixate on each of us in turn. When it gets to be my turn, I dare not look away or even blink. She holds my gaze, her face an expressionless mask. The silence in the classroom is so excruciatingly tense that it's becoming almost tempting to make a noise just to shatter it, no matter the consequences.

I watch Principal Quick as she takes a sharp, quiet breath.

"You may sit," she commands.

(*At last.*)

Our chair legs scrape against the floor noisily and the sound grates against the already unbearable atmosphere. I hear Lena groan as she sits down. Her legs must be aching too. I glance at Jess's desk, then at Saffy's. They are notably unoccupied. I wonder if the others are feeling that too – the absence of those two girls. Our fellow inmates.

Principal Quick catches me looking and the dark glimmer of a frown contorts her face. I remember Saffy's face in the pool, the water lit red, and then Jess's face in the bathroom stall amidst so much blood. I try with all my might to blink the unwelcome images away. But it's hard to, especially when their empty desks accentuate their absence. I stare at the weathered wooden surface of my own desk.

Principal Quick waits for us to settle, and then clears her throat.

"Terrible tragedy has hit this noble institution. We must remember our fallen inmates and promise to do our very best in their honor. Only through self-discipline can we avoid such tragic accidents from happening again."

Victoria is at the desk next to mine and I see her bite her lip. It's as though she's fighting to keep something from escaping her mouth.

"You are here to better yourselves," Principal Quick goes on. "To honor the rules and regulations put in place for you so that you may be rehabilitated."

The principal clasps her hands tightly together, as if praying to some higher source.

"As of tonight, lights out will be an hour earlier."

At that, I hear sounds of protest from Lena and Annie. Principal Quick just watches them, coldly, her icicle-sharp eyes daring them to comment further.

"Understood?"

There's an uneasy silence in the room. I can sense the others holding back, each waiting for another to say something first. Victoria appears to be losing the fight to keep her lips sealed.

"Do I make myself clear?" the principal prompts us.

"Yes, Principal Quick," I reply, in unison with the others.

Victoria leans in closer to me. "Tragic accidents…" she whispers, just loud enough for all of us to hear.

Principal Quick glares at Victoria. "Something to share, Victoria?"

Victoria's cheeks burn beet red.

"If you do indeed have something to say," Quick adds, "then by all means share it with the rest of the group."

I can see tears forming in Victoria's eyes. Her hands are

clasped together on top of the desk and she's trembling.

"Very well," Principal Quick says impatiently, "in future, do not interrupt me, young lady."

Victoria unclasps her hands. Making fists, she slams them down onto her desk.

Annie yelps in surprise at the sudden outburst.

Lena chuckles.

Then, Victoria pushes herself up from her desk with a scrape of her chair against the floor and glares angrily around at each of us, Principal Quick included.

"Jess's throat didn't cut itself, did it? Ask her what she's got hidden in her basement," Victoria announces, pointing her finger at the principal, who looks as though someone just pulled a rug from under her feet.

I glance at the others. Their eyes are wide in disbelief, or confusion, or both. A collective 'WTF' hangs in the room.

"I saw Jess's dead body down there," Victoria says, "behind *her* closet."

Principal Quick looks quite at a loss for words.

So am I, to be honest. After we went on the smoke run, what happened with Saffy put anything else from my mind. I never thought to ask again what spooked Victoria so much in the basement beneath Principal Quick's closet. Never would have had the opportunity anyway. As soon as the principal had confiscated the vodka bottle—

(*Luckily we held on to some cigarettes we'd hidden in our clothing.*)

—it was lights out and lockdown for all of us. Victoria has been keeping this revelation of hers all bottled up, and now it's exploding out of her.

"Take a look if you don't believe me," Victoria says.

Then Victoria does the exact thing I was hoping she wouldn't do. She looks straight at me. Like I know what she's talking about. Like we're co-conspirators. Principal Quick catches the glance, of course. She never misses a trick, that one.

"Emily?"

Great. They are all staring at *me* now, and I wish I could be away from this room.

Pretty soon, I get my wish.

* * *

Principal Quick's office looks bigger in the muted daylight from the exercise yard window than it did during the smoke run. Victoria stands next to me, and directly opposite Principal Quick, who is flanked by Lena and Annie.

"I don't imagine I need to show you where the key to my closet is?" Principal Quick says, her voice dripping sarcasm.

She takes the closet key from her desk drawer and hands it to Victoria.

"Show me, Victoria."

Victoria winces and carries the key over to the closet door.

"We will address the matter of why you girls were here at all, in due course," Principal Quick reminds us.

With a trembling hand, Victoria inserts the key and unlocks the door.

"Be so kind as to open it up for us," Quick says. "Come along, girls, let's take a peek, shall we?"

As Victoria opens the closet door, the principal walks around the desk to join us. Lena and Annie follow. Victoria throws me a meaningful look, then takes a deep breath. Dropping to her knees, she looks under the bookshelves.

"Well?" Quick says. "We are waiting."

Victoria starts pulling the books away, then stops abruptly. She looks up at me, panic in her eyes.

"It's...it's not there anymore...I can't even...."

"What isn't there anymore?" Principal Quick says. "Stop babbling, girl."

"The opening! It's gone...just completely gone!" Victoria sounds tearful.

I enter the closet and kneel down next to Victoria. The opening we discovered last night is no longer there, just a neat row of books and papers. And behind them, a solid bookcase.

"I swear it was here, I crawled through! So did you," she says to me. "Tell them, Emily."

It *is* truly strange. But before I can say anything—

(*And I'm not even sure* what *to say.*)

—Principal Quick cuts in.

"You came here to steal from me," she says, her voice rising in pitch, "to break my trust. And now you concoct a wildly unbelievable story to cover your guilt."

Victoria gets to her feet, and I do the same. It's intimidating, to face the principal's stern expression. I flinch, but Victoria isn't done yet.

"We came here for some cigarettes..."

(*Now Principal Quick is the one who flinches.*)

"...that's true. But I dropped your lighter and, you have to believe me, I crawled through and fell down the steps. That's when I found her lying there...poor Jess...."

Victoria begins to sob.

I remember what her frightened face looked like last night after I helped her wriggle through that dark, cramped crawlspace. She looked too terrified for words. Like someone had turned the lights off behind her eyes.

But the solid wall beneath the bookcase now contradicts all of that. I'm beginning to wonder if we didn't somehow collectively dream the whole escapade. But that doesn't make sense either. Principal Quick confiscated the vodka bottle after all. And we still had the cigarettes on us. Still do. When we returned to the dormitory after...Saffy...we hid them behind our bedside cabinets.

"I'm not quite sure that I follow what you are saying," Principal Quick replies, and the patience in her voice is stretched to its maximum. "You say that there's a basement, and you climbed down there and saw.... Well, what exactly?"

"Jess!" Victoria shrieks, and I don't think I've ever heard anyone sounding so scared.

I look at Principal Quick's reaction and beneath the icy exterior see a momentary flicker of emotion in her sharp eyes.

"She's still rotting down there. All bloody!" Victoria cries.

She's really losing it now.

And she's not the only one. Principal Quick puts herself between Victoria and the closet. She raises her hand and slaps Victoria hard across the face.

(*Whoah.*)

Lena and Annie gasp in shock.

Victoria puts a hand to her stinging face. Fresh tears well up in her eyes.

"How dare you try to scare the others?" Principal Quick stares Victoria down with glassy eyes. "You selfish, attention-seeking girl."

Then she glares at me, as though daring me to contradict her. I swallow dryly and lower my head as Principal Quick speaks on, the control in her voice making her even more frightening.

"Upsetting the others with these fantasies. It is heartless, thoughtless, and cruel. Always blaming others for your weakness. For your failings."

Principal Quick turns to Lena and Annie. "You may go. You are all confined to your dormitory."

That's done it. Lena and Annie both file out of the room quickly, but not before looking absolute daggers at Victoria. And Victoria just looks destroyed, really. I guess I should be feeling sorry for her. But I don't know what to say or do to make it any better for her. Either our imaginations got the better of us, or Principal Quick managed to board up the crawlspace in her closet overnight to make fools out of the both of us. Trying to figure out the solution is sending my poor, sleep-deprived brain into a downward spiral.

"Victoria, Emily, you will both accompany me," the principal says.

CHAPTER THIRTEEN

I Must Not Tell Lies

I hear Victoria sobbing in frustration as I follow Principal Quick out of her office.

"Stop sniveling, girl," the principal says as Victoria ducks past her.

Quick locks her office door, using the key from her belt, and then leads us down the corridor. We walk in silence until we reach the classroom door. The principal opens the door and beckons us inside.

"Sit at your desks," she says.

We do as she says, Victoria still fighting back her sobs. I glance at her but she won't make eye contact. She just wipes her nose on the cuff of her sleeve.

Principal Quick takes something from her desk, which she carries over to us. She drops a notepad and a pen onto Victoria's desk, and then the same items on mine.

"If you are going to behave like unruly schoolchildren, you will be punished accordingly," Principal Quick says.

I try not to look, but I can see a vein throbbing wildly at her temple. It looks like it might pop, there's so much blood and anger coursing through it. I catch the same aspects in her eyes and look away quickly.

"You will write lines," she says, "until your notepads are filled. Then, and only then, will you be allowed to go to bed."

I look down at the notepad. There must be at least a hundred sheets of paper in it, maybe more. We'll be here all night long if the principal wants the notepads to be filled.

She leans over my desk and turns the notepad around until it's facing her. She picks up the pen and writes something in the same elegantly spidery handwriting I saw on the manuscript in her office.

I MUST NOT TELL LIES.

"There," she says, before walking back to Victoria's desk and doing the same on her notepad. Victoria sniffs wretchedly, and Principal Quick shoves the pen into Victoria's hand.

I am just about to remind Principal Quick that I didn't actually tell her any lies when I see that vein in her head again, throbbing, and I decide that maybe the best course of action is to remain quiet.

"I shall leave you both to it," the principal says.

We sit in silence as Principal Quick leaves the room and shuts us in. The wall clock marks each passing second as I write line after line. By the time I'm done with a few pages my wrist is aching, and the ticking of the clock seems to have gotten louder.

I risk a glance across at Victoria, who seems to be getting more and more agitated. She's writing her lines, but so frantically that I can hear the paper tearing beneath her pen. I try to catch her attention, hoping I can help her to calm down before Principal Quick returns, but it's no use – Victoria doesn't even seem to see me. She starts stabbing into her notepad with the pen, tearing up the paper. Then she hurls the pen across the room in the direction of the ticking clock.

I see a shadow on the wall beneath the clock. Victoria's pen meets the shadow and then, impossibly, just hovers there – as though the shadow has caught hold of it. I can't quite believe my eyes, but that is exactly what the shadow has done.

Victoria screams as the shadow reveals itself. The gray girl peels herself away from the wall as though she is somehow *made* of the shadows. She holds out her dead, gray hand, showing us the pen. Then she turns her hand over and drops the pen to the floor.

With one swift, dark movement, the gray girl is at Victoria's desk. But, because she is holding her head in her hands and freaking out uncontrollably, Victoria fails to see the gray girl looming over her.

I look, and see, and feel a cold stab of fear as the spectral girl glares at me from behind her matted hair. I hear a ghastly sobbing sound and for a moment I think it's Victoria. But then I realize it is coming from behind that dark, straggly hair. I hear another sound – one that gives me the creeps. A sharp, scratching noise, like fingernails on a coffin lid.

Looking down at my desk, I see letters being carved into the desk as if by an invisible knife point. I look to Victoria, eager to know if she can see it too. Because if she can then it will mean that I'm not stark-staring mad. But Victoria still has her face buried in her hands. I'm on my own here.

The letters form in my desk. 'G...I'.

I stand up, recoiling from the desk and from the horrible scraping noise, which continues as more letters form.

'R...L'. I knock my chair backward and it topples over with a crash.

'A...'.

Feeling terror clawing at my heart, I look at the carved words: 'GIRL A'.

I back away, still hearing that ghastly sobbing sound from the gray specter looming over Victoria. Without realizing it, I've backed up all the way to the classroom door. The door opens and I feel a hand on my shoulder. I turn to face Principal Quick. She does not look pleased.

I turn back to survey the room. No one there except Victoria. The gray girl has vanished – as though she's been carried away by a cold draft that blows through the room.

Principal Quick frog marches me back to my desk, keeping my shoulder in her grip. Once there, she shoves me down into my seat. I see that she holds Victoria's discarded pen in her other hand.

"Careless, Victoria. You seem to have dropped your pen," Principal Quick says.

Then she crosses to Victoria's desk. I see her frown at the unruly state of Victoria's torn pad.

"Back to work, girls," the principal says before dropping the pen on top of Victoria's notepad. She strolls over to her desk at the front of the class and picks up a textbook. She sits down and begins to read in silence.

I watch as Victoria picks up her pen and starts writing her lines again.

I do the same. No point arguing with Principal Quick keeping us company. I take one more look at the shadows, to make sure the gray girl really has left us. When I look down at my desk, the letters that were scratched there have also disappeared.

* * *

It's the early hours of the morning by the time we're done. As we march along the corridors in pronounced silence, following Principal Quick back to our dormitory, I see dark clouds parting outside the windows. A chill wind lifts leaves from the trees, sending them swirling across the sky in an ever-shifting question mark.

Dawn is breaking over the reformatory.

* * *

We sit on our beds and no one is speaking much, except for Victoria, who won't let go of what she says she saw in the basement.

"So neither of you has seen her?"

Lena and Annie shake their heads. Annie looks thoughtful for a moment. I see her hesitate before speaking up.

"I did have a dream. Our first night in here. I think there was a girl like the one you described in my dream, but...."

"A gray girl?" I ask.

"I don't remember. Maybe," Annie says, unhelpfully.

"You?" Victoria asks Lena.

"I don't have dreams," Lena says in a low voice. "Not the kind you'd want to remember, anyway. Gave up on those years ago."

Victoria nods in solidarity. "I know how that feels." She glances at the locked door. "Hey, how long do you think she's going to keep us locked in here?"

"We stole from her," I say, "and you accused her of stashing Jess's dead body away. I think she'll take her time."

"You could have backed me up," Victoria counters.

"I didn't see anything," I remind her. "I was on the other side of the bookcase, until I helped pull you back through, remember?"

I think back to earlier, when the gray girl emerged from the shadows. How she loomed over Victoria's desk. The letters carved in my desk, letters that disappeared when the principal returned. If only Victoria had looked up to see what I saw. Then we would be able to agree on something. But we can't. It is as though the phantom – or whatever the hell she is – has us divided. We're weaker that way, I realize.

"Well, at least you acknowledge there *was* an opening," Victoria says, "but I know what I saw down there, however weird it sounds."

Annie gets up off her bed and starts pacing the room, between Saffy's and Jess's empty beds. It's almost as though by acknowledging their absence she can somehow pluck answers out of thin air.

I'm skeptical.

"There's a lot the principal isn't telling us," Victoria says. "About why she's running this place on her own. She said it's experimental. But what does that mean, exactly?"

Annie looks at me, and I know what's coming. "You were here once before, Emily," she says. "What happened? And why did you get sent back here?"

"I don't remember," I say.

"You must remember something." Annie sounds exasperated. "Anything?"

I don't. And just trying to remember is making my head throb real bad. I can almost hear Quick's metronome, ticking away like some screwed up clock inside my head.

"Jesus Christ, Emily," Annie says, her frustration igniting into anger.

"Fighting each other won't help," Victoria says, diffusing the tension. "I want to know what Quick is up to. Like, why didn't she call the cops about Jess? Or an ambulance? I mean, what kind of fucked up experiment is she running here? And what about the strange girl we keep seeing?"

"*Some* of you keep seeing," Lena says.

"Hey, I'll make it easy for you guys," Victoria says, "the elephant in the room."

Annie smirks. "That's...*you*, isn't it?" A cruel smile curls her lips.

"Oh, fuck you," Victoria retorts, making Annie snort with laughter. "No, I mean...the gray girl's a ghost, isn't she?"

Annie scowls. "Jesus. Don't start that fucked-up shit."

But Victoria is in full swing now. "Emily saw her – I *know* you did, Emily, so don't try to deny it. I think Jess saw her, and Saffy too – and now they're dead."

I have to state the obvious. "And yet we're alive and well."

"Right now we are, yeah. But...." Victoria's eyes darken. "Once you see her, you're dead soon after."

Annie rolls her eyes – and lets rip with the sarcasm. "And you say that like it's a bad thing? Okay. So we're locked in here, at the mercy of a homicidal ghost. Now what?"

"I say screw being cooped up in here," Lena answers.

Lena rises from her bed and crosses to the door. She crouches down and starts examining the lock. After a few moments, she returns to her bed, and then grabs her mattress with both hands and tosses it to the floor.

"What the hell are you doing?" Victoria asks.

"She's going completely freaking nuts, that's what she's doing," Annie says.

Lena drops to her knees and starts twisting one of the bedsprings.

"I might join her," Annie jokes.

It takes some effort, but Lena is determined and strong. She manages to twist the spring out of its hole, then removes it from the bed frame. Next, she lifts the bed, traps one end of the spring underneath. She looks at each of us, breathing heavily from her exertions.

"You. Come sit on my bed. All of you," she says.

She says it with such authority that we each do as she says without any further questions. With the spring trapped under our combined weight, Lena pulls on it with all her might, straightening it out. I watch as she twists the spring between her strong fingers, and snaps it into two pieces.

"Now I have something I can work with," Lena says. She crosses to the door and crouches next to the lock. She starts picking the lock with the wire from the spring.

"Can you really get that open?" I ask.

Lena just grunts, too intent on her lock-picking work to reply properly.

"So we bust out of here," Victoria asks. "Then what?"

"Worry about that later," Lena says through gritted teeth.

Seconds later, I hear a loud click. Lena's done it. She's cracked the lock. With a flourish, she opens the door.

"Okay...worry about it *now*, bitches," she says.

We each exchange glances before joining Lena by the open door. I look through the gap and see the corridor stretching out beyond, and all of a sudden it comes to me.

"I may have a plan," I say.

The open-mouthed looks on their faces should offend me, I suppose. To be honest, though, I'm as surprised as the next girl.

* * *

Weird, isn't it, how you seem to find fault in good ideas the more you dwell on them? That's why I ask Lena to run through our plan one more time as we walk the corridor.

"Seriously?" she says. "It's like the third damn time we've been through this."

"Yeah," I say, "but we only have one shot at it."

Lena shrugs.

"Okay. You losers give me a head start. I bust into the med cabinet, grab some sedatives. Meantime you find Quick, tell her that I went on a one-way ticket to Crazy Town and that I'm headed for the clock tower. You lead her up there and – boom! We whack her, drug the bitch. Then we get the fuck out of here. That it?"

"Sounds about right to me."

We approach a turn in the corridor. Lena brandishes her lock-picking wire.

"Right, this is me, I guess," she says. "Give me a few minutes at least."

"Okay." I nod.

"Later, ladies," Lena says, before she heads off into the other corridor.

We wait there in silence, and already I begin to question the plan. What if Principal Quick isn't even in her office? What if Lena bumps into her on the way to the med store? My head begins to throb with each possible outcome. I shake my head, willing away the onset of that ringing in my ears.

"Do you think we gave her long enough?" Victoria whispers, breaking the silence, and thankfully the maelstrom in my head.

"Give her too much time and she'll be high as a kite," Annie says.

"Shit, I hadn't even thought of that," I say.

We each exchange concerned glances.

"Let's move," I say.

Maybe things will seem better if we start walking to Principal Quick's office. At least we'll have a sense of purpose, and then my plan might not seem so lame after all.

CHAPTER FOURTEEN

Lena

Lena turned the light on inside the med store and pulled the door shut behind her.

She passed the shelves lined with boxes of bandages, packets of gauze, and other medical consumables and walked up to the drug locker. Eyes on the prize. She reached out and grasped the padlock. It was heavy and had one of those sliding metal covers over the aperture. Lena thumbed the cover open and bent over to take a closer look. The barrel looked too small for the wire she was carrying, but she tried it anyway.

Damn. Her lock pick had made light work of the main door, but this baby was going to take something else if she wanted it sprung anytime soon.

Lena surveyed each of the shelves that were in reach for anything useful. She had to use a plastic chair in the corner to check the upper shelves and found them devoid of anything except dust. Then, inspiration struck.

She hopped down from the chair and upended it. The legs were fashioned from black, enameled metal. She slid one of the chair legs inside the padlock. Using it as a lever, she pulled down on the chair, twisting it sharply.

With a satisfying snap, the padlock broke open and fell to the floor. Putting the chair to one side, Lena flung open the cabinet.

Whoah.

Inside was a prescription drug mother lode. Lena began rifling through the shelves of vials and blister packs of needles.

She absentmindedly licked her lips like a kid at a candy store window. In the back of her mind, a vaguely fuzzy warmth. A memory of more carefree times. Of oblivion.

The warmth was snuffed out by a chill at the nape of her neck. She saw a shadow-shape flicker, reflected in the drug bottles. Holy crap, maybe Principal Quick had found her out already.

Lena turned.

There was no one there. But the feeling that someone *was* there lingered.

Lena swallowed, and said shakily, "Hello?"

She felt on edge. But there really was nobody there, and the door to the med store was still closed, as she'd left it.

Lena returned her attention to the contents of the med cabinet. It didn't take her long to find exactly what she needed to make Principal Quick go bye-bye for a little while. Lena knew all of the names on the bottles and cartons. Knew exactly what they did, and how much to use. The printed characters on the labels were as familiar to her as the lyrics to old nursery rhymes. Fair-weather friends, and bad-time buddies each of them.

Lena felt her lips curl into a smile as she released a hypodermic from its packaging. She broke the seal on a vial and plunged the needle in. She loaded up the syringe, ready to use on Principal Quick when the time came. Lena held the syringe up to the light and gave it a couple of flicks with her forefinger. Her slight smile became a wider grin at the tactile memory of performing that ritual so many times before.

A dark shape filled the glass tube of the syringe. A shadow, of someone standing right behind her. Lena glimpsed a darkly glinting eye. She saw a pale hand reach for her shoulder.

Lena dropped the syringe.

"Shit." She stooped to pick it up.

Lena grabbed the hypodermic. Thankfully, she hadn't

broken it. She rose back to her full height again. And as she did, she came face to face with a hideous, gray girl. Or rather, face to hair, because the girl's face was obscured by dark, tangled strands of it. The girl's black eyes blazed into her, through her hair, filling Lena with their darkness.

Lena felt a well of despair bubbling uncontrollably inside of her. Her cry of alarm was cut short when the girl clamped her cold, dead hand over Lena's mouth. The chilly touch penetrated Lena's body and mind with the sharp intensity of an electric shock. Lena fell forward, and she couldn't stop herself. The cold hand pulled her down until she hit the ground, on her hands and knees.

Somewhere...*else*.

The smell from the garbage bags was overpowering. They lay all around her, a nest of filth and decay. Several of them had burst open in the hot sun that Lena could feel beating down on her back. Rotten food baked and basted in the foul juices of human waste. Soiled diapers twitched as engorged rats devoured their contents. The stench made Lena gag. But she knew how to dull her senses to make it go away. She could make all of it go away.

Urgent grunting from over her shoulder told her he was almost finished. His halitosis mingled with the stink of the alleyway and she felt a spike of acid in her throat. He'd better cum soon or she might throw up before he got there. Maybe he'd enjoy it. Maybe not. Lena didn't care. She only cared about the reward. Eyes on the prize. He grunted some more and spurted his slime into her, before coughing and cackling. She pulled away from him but he ran his trembling fingers through her greasy hair and dangled a plastic baggy of junk in front of her.

She reached for it but his fingers snapped it away.

"Ah, ah...."

He laughed like a drain into her ear and she grimaced at the sluice of his breath.

"I'll pay you double for your sister," he grunted.

Lena wriggled free and pulled up her panties. "Leave my kid sister out of this, asshole."

"Aww," he crooned, "you're jealous?"

He dangled the baggie again. A carrot that was just out of reach. Lena hated his games. Hated him, and the things she knew she'd do for that little portion of powder held between his fat, nicotine-stained fingertips.

"Never. I'm number one and you know it," she taunted.

He hit her. That was how it always ended. A bit of pillow talk and then some violence. She'd kill the fucker someday. But first, she just needed a hit. Her lip began to bleed. She sucked at it, tasting the salt tang of her blood. It would taste sweeter with a hit coursing through her veins.

"You're all used up. Bring your sister to me, tomorrow. Or no more candy for you. Just stone-cold turkey." He teased her with the wrap of drugs.

Lena's face burned with tears. She couldn't do what he asked of her. Couldn't drag her sister into this walking death. But she had to make him think she would. So she nodded. His triumphant laugh made her feel worst of all. He dropped the baggie in her lap and then, zipping up his pants, ambled away down the alleyway. She heard him hawking and spitting into the garbage and then he was gone.

The sun ducked behind a cloud. The shade felt good as it cooled her tears. She wiped them from her face, along with the snot from her nose and the blood from her mouth. Then she set about prepping her fix. The track marks on her arm seemed almost to pucker as she held the needle close. Each puncture wound was a little mouth, hungry for succor. She felt it enter her, the opposite of sex, as it spiked into her senses and carried her over the edge and into the sun-kissed never-lands, far, far beyond the corrupt physical world of the stinking alley in which her frail body lay.

But something was wrong.

The horizon tilted and tipped over. She had nothing to cling to, and was sent tumbling in a spiral, down into a black void.

Lena heard a distant scream, quickly subsumed by animalistic grunts.

The scream became cries of anguish. And those only seemed to make the grunting all more aggressive, and urgent. Lena felt sick. She was hearing the sounds of innocence being torn away. The track marks on her arm began to throb painfully. She saw them pulsing in the bruised flesh of her arms, and watched as black tendrils snaked up her arms, filling her veins with poisonous bile. Lena looked away and only then saw a pale shape next to her. Her kid sister lay dead by her side. Her fragile form discarded with all the other garbage. Overdosed eyes fixed wide open. Young eyes that had seen too much to bear.

Lena tried to scream, but could only gasp. She had done this. She had.

She felt freezing cold gripping the sides of her head. Then the cold was gone and Lena felt her body lurch, head over heels through space until—

She slammed back against a hard metal surface.

Lena breathed in stale, dusty air. She was in the med store again, with the cold metal frame of the shelving at her back and the hard floor beneath her.

Glancing around in terror, Lena found that she was alone in there. The gray girl had gone. But the throbbing in her veins still lingered. It intensified as her senses came back to her. She looked down at her arms, turning them over to reveal the source of the pain. Both arms were red raw with jagged needle marks. Lena realized why the throbbing pain was so intense. Her veins had been torn wide open. She was bleeding out all over the floor.

Lena kicked out her legs in a spasm and heard the scraping of glass against concrete. Dozens upon dozens of syringes lay at her feet. Tears welled up in her eyes, clouding her view. Desperate to stand, to get up and out of there, to live and not die – *not like this* – Lena clutched at the shelf behind her and tried to push her body up from the floor.

She slipped in her own blood. The contents of the shelf came crashing down. Lena fell with them. She had lost too much. Too much innocence. Too much blood. The red sleeves of her arms dropped to her sides. As Lena's eyes rolled back into their sockets, she saw a gray shape watching her from the shadows.

She's been with me all along, thought Lena before the dark took her down.

CHAPTER FIFTEEN

Girl A

It doesn't take us long to reach Quick's office. The corridors are deserted, and we move quickly and quietly. We pause for breath when we reach Quick's door. I'm nearest to it. I look at Victoria, and then at Annie.

"Okay, here goes..." I say. I knock. No answer. I knock again.

"Crap," Annie says, "she's not even home!"

I twist the door handle and push. The door is unlocked. It swings open and I step inside. Victoria and Annie join me in the office. I hear a disembodied gasp and realize that the sound is mine.

Principal Quick lays slumped across her desk.

A bottle of vodka stands next to her, half-empty and missing its cap.

"Principal Quick?"

She's not moving. No sign of her breathing, either. We approach her desk together, cautiously. Tension hangs in the musty air of the office. It feels as though the principal may startle into life again any moment. Then I see an empty prescription pill bottle next to the vodka. There's no label on the bottle, just the powdery residue of whatever tablets it contained.

I don't want to touch her, but I have no choice.

I reach out and brush Quick's hair away from her eyes. They're glassy, and wide open. Her face is locked in a silent scream of pure terror. Her hair feels weird against my skin. I wonder if it's still growing, even though she's—

"She's stone-cold fucking dead," Annie says.

"Oh my God. Oh my God," Victoria pants.

"Try the phone," Annie says. "Call for help."

I reach out and pluck the receiver from its cradle. I put it to my ear and can hear no dial tone, nothing.

"It's dead," I say, and wonder if that's an inappropriate thing to say, given the macabre circumstances.

Annie marches over and takes the receiver from me. She puts it to her ear and listens intently. I guess she needs to try it for herself before she'll believe me. She looks crestfallen and then drops the receiver onto the desk.

I see the clipboard on the desk next to Quick's stiff, bony hand. She must have been looking at it before she died. I pick it up and start leafing through the pages.

"Emily?" Victoria asks. "What are you...?"

Each page has one of our psych profiles on it, and I start reading the notes written in Quick's spidery hand.

"This can't be right."

"What is that?" Annie asks, sounding agitated.

"Profiles. Psych evaluations, the whole lot. Look, here's Lena...."

Annie takes the clipboard from me. She reads in silence. I glance at Victoria, who bites down on her lower lip.

"It says she died of an overdose," Annie says, sounding mystified. "Institutionalized since the rape and murder of her kid sister. Jesus, it says here Lena was pimping her own sister out to pay for her habit...."

At that, Victoria reaches across me and grabs the clipboard. "Let me see that," she says.

Annie looks kind of relieved to let it go, and Victoria turns the page.

"This one's *you*, Annie. Oh, fuck."

Annie looks alarmed. "What?"

"Someone's sick idea of a joke," Victoria says, handing the clipboard back to Annie.

Annie examines the page through ever widening eyes. Then she looks up, and appears to be completely aghast at what she just read. "Enough," she says. "Enough of this fucked-up place. I am out of here."

"No," Victoria protests, "we have to stick together, we—"

Victoria tries to stop Annie from walking away from the desk. Annie seizes her shoulders and pushes her away.

"Do *not* touch me! I am out of here! Fuck!" Annie turns tail and bolts out the door.

Victoria looks down at Principal Quick's corpse in disbelief. "She was insane. That's the only explanation. Quick brought us here to fuck with our heads until we were all dead."

"Then.... Why kill herself before she finished the job?" I ask, and even as I do ask it I'm pretty sure I don't even want to know the answer.

Victoria flips through the pages on the clipboard. Something in her body language changes. She stiffens. Then she looks at me, her eyes almost as stone cold as Principal Quick's are.

"You tell me," she says.

"You think.... Whoever this gray girl is?"

"You would know, wouldn't you, Emily? What is it you're not telling me?" Victoria brandishes the clipboard like a weapon. "This 'on the fucking spectrum' act of yours, it doesn't wash any more. You know something and yet you're still not telling."

My head begins to spin. "I don't know what you mean."

"It's all a big act." Victoria holds up the clipboard. "You're the only one without a file, Emily!"

I look at the files she's holding. Victoria has folded back all the pages, to reveal the blank clipboard beneath.

"I did time here before," I say. "Maybe there wasn't any need for a new file."

"Sure you did. And why exactly was that again?"

"I don't.... I don't remember."

(*And really, I don't. I told you, I'm unreliable, I....*)

"You know, that I *do* believe. Principal Quick's little pet fuck up, aren't you?"

Victoria tosses the clipboard onto the desk, careless of Principal Quick's head lying there with her eyes fixed open in death's stare. I turn the clipboard the right way around so I can read it. Then I quickly leaf through each page in turn, to check if what Victoria has been saying is true.

"Okay. There's no file on me, but that doesn't mean one doesn't exist at all."

Victoria's expression is blank.

"It could be filed away somewhere else," I say, and begin to look through the papers on Quick's desk. Still no sign of my mugshot anywhere.

Then the cover sheet of Quick's manuscript catches my eye. *'Girl A' by Mina Quick*. I discard the clipboard, and flick through the first few pages of the manuscript.

"Quick was running some kind of experiment," I say. "Look. 'Girl A'. I think *she* might be the one who's been stalking us, picking us off one by one."

"You think? Let me see that." I've piqued Victoria's interest. She brushes me aside and begins to leaf through the manuscript herself.

"I think I saw her watching us from the clock tower. And she was at the pool too, I'm sure of it. She knows routes through the building that we don't. What if she was in the basement when you fell down there? Maybe Principal Quick lets...or rather, let her roam free, after lights out. That's why she said the clock tower is off limits. She stays up there during daylight hours. I'm sure of it. And maybe Quick thought this girl wouldn't harm her, but...." I glance down at the principal's dead body. And I feel cold.

"Emily." Victoria's jaw drops.

"What is it?" I move back to her side, so I can see the pages she has been reading.

Victoria scoops up the book and holds it to her chest. She backs away and I feel so confused at just how angry she looks right now. Angry, and terrified. "Keep the hell away from me," she says.

But I *am* away from her, so I don't understand what she means. The desk separates us, with Principal Quick's dead body resting head down on it. This whole situation is so fucked up already and the last thing we need right now is more division. I pinch my forearm to make sure I'm not dreaming. My skin feels numb, and cold to the touch.

"No, we have to solve this together. You said so to Annie. We have to catch up to her. And Lena, right? We have to get together and figure out what to do next."

And yet, even as I say the words, I can see Victoria withdrawing further into herself. Away from me.

"No, no, no," Victoria says, and her voice is getting all high pitched and starting to freak me out. "It's *you,* Emily. I don't know how you've been doing it, I'm not sure I want to know, but...."

My ears start ringing, very faintly. Another out-of-body experience? Bring it on. My already pretty limited understanding of other human beings is being stretched to its absolute limit.

"What on earth are you talking about?" I ask her.

"It's *your* name in Quick's research, Emily. You're 'Girl A'."

Victoria throws the manuscript at me. I have to dodge out of the way to avoid it hitting me square in the face. The sheaf of paper hits the wall behind me and drops to the floor.

"Victoria?"

But she's already gone, leaving me alone in the office. Alone except for Principal Quick's dead body. And the manuscript. I crouch down and gather up the sheets of paper from the floor. I carry the manuscript around to the other side of the desk so I can be as far away from Quick's blankly staring eyes as possible.

I leaf through the pages until I see it. My name is there, just as Victoria said it was:

Case study introduction. Emily Drake—

(There's some writing scrawled over this bit, in Principal Quick's hand.)

(NOTE: TO BE REFERRED TO THROUGHOUT M/S AS 'GIRL A'!)

—exhibits symptoms of acute dissociative disorder. Under hypnosis, she refers to a half-glimpsed fellow inmate — a 'gray girl' who lives in seclusion away from the rest of the girls. This 'gray girl' could be a manifestation of an alternate identity and further interviews under hypnosis will explore whether this persona is actually part of a dissociative identity disorder (see footnote 1 about EXTERNALIZED multiple personalities) or merely a projection resulting from what this study will refer to as 'dissociation derealization disorder' or DDD for short. Girl A's case is difficult to pin down within the confines of established prognoses based on prior case studies in this field. Girl A is presenting something new and exciting to the field and treatment must be exploratory and experimental....

Is that who I am? Some new kind of medical definition? My mind feels fuzzy at the concept of having been hypnotized by batshit old Principal Quick. I wonder when exactly that happened. Of course, I wouldn't know if she put me under, wouldn't have any recollection. Would I? My mind flashes with a half-remembered memory of a pulsing light, accompanied by the ticking of a metronome. And then it's gone, leaving yet more questions.

Was the principal writing all of this about me when I was last incarcerated at Greyfriars? She must have been. And, judging from the thickness of the manuscript, this was something she was working on for months. I can't shake the feeling that whatever 'exploratory and experimental' treatment she gave me might have made me even worse. My behavior and my condition. Nor can I ignore the possibility that my out-of-body episodes could be a symptom of Principal Quick's dubious brand of reformatory care. Is that why Jess and Saffy are dead, I wonder? Did they kill themselves because of some wacko treatment that Quick was subjecting them to? But my thoughts circle back to the 'gray girl'. Where does she fit into all this? I'm wondering now if she really could just be the product of my disorder.

If that's true, though, how did the other girls see her?

A sound pulls me out of my spiraling thoughts. A scratching, coming from behind the closet door. I listen intently, hoping against hope that I imagined it. That it is—

(*What did Quick's manuscript call it?*)

—a projection, that's it.

But the scratch-scratching continues and, even worse, it is accompanied by a sobbing, wailing sound. The voice is female, and anguished. My mind conjures images of Jess, all bloody, her fingernails ravaged from her climb up the hard, stone steps of the basement. The shrill wailing gives way to the eerie sound of a musical box's chimes. I swallow hard. Can't just stand here, doing nothing. What if it really is Jess trapped in there? But I saw her throat gashed open, all her life's blood spilled over the tiled floor in the bathroom. It can't be her—

(*So, who* is *it then?*)

—I think, as my hand falls to my side and brushes against the handle of the desk drawer. The key is still in there, I know it is. And I know I'll have to take it from the drawer and unlock the closet door. Then I will have to face whatever is in there, sobbing and wailing and scratching, because I also know that if I don't, the sounds are going to drive me insane. Far crazier than even Principal Quick could have bargained for.

I slide open Quick's desk drawer and root around inside. But, before I can locate the key, I discover something else. I pull out a small, crumpled metal box. It has a metal handle poking out through a tiny aperture in one side. I hold up the box and turn the handle. It chimes discordantly. And all of a sudden, the wailing stops. The music chime echoes out into silence. The scratching on the door has thankfully stopped, too.

I place the music box onto Quick's desk and find the key at the back of the drawer. Clutching the key in my right hand, I steel myself and then walk over to the closet door.

I knock gingerly.

"Hello?" I ask the silence, and of course no reply comes.

I insert the key into the lock and wonder why my hand is shaking so much. I turn the key in the lock barrel and I hear it click against the tumblers. Willing my hand to stop shaking, I clutch the door handle and twist it open. I push against the door and see into the closet.

There's no one inside. Embarrassed relief quickly becomes concern that I'm imagining things again. The extract that I read in Principal Quick's manuscript plays over and over in my mind. I'm about to shut the closet door when the music box chimes again. My mind conjures an image of the principal, dead as a doornail and sitting up in her desk chair. Turning the little music box handle, her staring eyes glistening with madness.

The music box chimes again and I try not to scream in terror.

I turn sharply around to see that Principal Quick is still slumped over her desk, exactly as she was before. A shadow momentarily moves across the wall behind her. I blink and it's gone.

I rush over to the desk and pick up the music box. I turn the little handle. No sound this time. I shake it and still it doesn't chime. I thrust it into my pocket and run to the office door, eager to be away from Principal Quick and the confusing mysteries she's left in her wake.

CHAPTER SIXTEEN

Annie

Annie ran on until she reached the main doors. She reached up and pushed the door release button. Hearing an electronic buzz, she stepped back from the door, expecting it to open.

But nothing happened.

Annie tried the door and slammed the palms of her hands against it in frustration. How could she have been so stupid? Running away from Principal Quick's office without first taking her keys? Now she was stuck inside this stupid goddamned building with no means of escape.

Well, she would just have to find another route out of there. Only thing for it. There must be an emergency exit or something. She would find it. Anything to get away from creepy Emily and insipid Victoria. They were no use to her at all. Whatever sick game old Principal Quick had been playing was not going to be the end of her, no fucking way. Annie grimaced at the memory of what she had seen written about her in the psych evaluation profile on the principal's clipboard.

Annie turned on her heels and began to retrace her steps. Maybe the refectory would be her best bet. Where there were kitchens, there were fire risks. And where there were fire risks, there were also building regulations. There would be a fire escape somewhere out back of the canteen. She was willing to bet her life on it.

Or maybe not my life, she thought, still disturbed by what she'd seen in the profile.

"*Aaannniieeee....*"

The voice was a cold whisper and it stopped her dead in her tracks.

"Emily? Victoria? That you?" Annie asked, even though she knew in her rapidly beating heart that it wasn't them at all.

She heard a laugh. It was an entirely mirthless sound, cold and mocking. And that sound made all the hairs on the back of her neck stand on end.

Annie's eyes discerned a dark shape, moving across the corridor wall ahead of her. It was the distorted shadow of a girl, and it snaked across the wall as though she had been borne out of the fabric of the building itself. Annie tried not to scream in fear, and failed because the shadow stretched out like it was reaching out to find her and entrap her in its darkness. She backed up and, with no choice but to double back on herself, she took another corridor. It was the route to the swimming pool.

No way out through there, Annie thought, her mind racing. *Just keep going.*

"*An-nie!*" The sharp whisper nearly shocked her into losing her footing as she rounded a corner into a wider corridor.

She risked a look back over her shoulder and saw that same dark shadow, moving at speed along the corridor. It wasn't natural, the way the shadow spread out like that. A dark tendril blossoming across the wall, it seemed to suck all the ambient light from the corridor as it grew.

Annie was at the door to the recreation yard. Without a second thought, she gripped the handle and opened it. Closing the door quietly behind her, she hoped that whoever was following her hadn't seen her duck outside.

Keeping to the shadows, which were thankfully still, Annie made for Principal Quick's office window. When she reached the window, she saw the principal's body through the glass, lying slumped across her desk. Emily and Victoria had left. Maybe it was them who were chasing her. Maybe it was their plan to kill her too, like they had killed Principal Quick. Annie took a moment to try and catch her breath, intent on not allowing her fears to get the better of her, and then she tried to open the window. It was unlocked, but it wouldn't budge.

"*Aaannniiieeee....*" The sharp whisper made her cry out in surprise. She couldn't help it because now her fears really were besting her.

Annie spun around.

The courtyard was empty. She looked up at the perimeter wall, then at the branches of the dying tree. Her eyes sought out an escape plan. But there was too much of a gap between the tips of the branches and the wall for her to climb up and leap over. That would have been perfect – an escape route that didn't require her to go back inside the building. Her only option was the window now. She turned her attention back to trying to open it. She bent her knees and used the leverage this posture gave her to force the window up, but only by an inch. It was as though an invisible hand was pushing down on it, preventing it from opening.

Just then, she saw someone move inside the office.

It was too dark in there to make out, but maybe Emily and Victoria hadn't gone after all. Or perhaps they had returned when they couldn't find her in the corridor. She might have been too hasty in her judgment of them. It was, after all, one of her worst traits. One that had gotten her into terrible trouble in the past.

"Emily? Victoria? Help me open the damn window, will you? It's stuck...."

If the window wouldn't move, they could grab Principal Quick's keys and she could meet them at the front door. Then they could get the heck out of there, together. If they kept to the road, they might get lucky and hitch a ride.

Then Annie saw another movement. She was expecting either Emily or Victoria to come to the window when she realized her dreadful mistake.

Principal Quick lifted her head from the desk.

Jesus Christ, thought Annie, *she's not dead. Not dead and she was faking it and*....

Quick's head turned sharply to face her. Annie screamed. The principal's eyes showed no sign of life.

Then, with abject horror, Annie saw a dark shape emerge from next to Principal Quick.

It was a girl, dressed in a gray uniform like Annie's, her facial features concealed behind her tangled dark hair. She was holding Principal Quick's lifeless head aloft, her fingers gripping on to the dead woman's hair.

Annie put her knuckles into her mouth to stop herself from screaming her lungs out. The gray girl held Quick's head as if it were a prop dangling in a sick puppet show. And then she slammed the principal's head back down onto the desk with a horrible crunch.

Annie blinked. And the strange girl was at the window.

Annie staggered back, terror making every step an ordeal, as the girl's dirty fingernails skittered across and down the glass. She was reaching for the bottom of the window. Her bony fingers appeared through the one-inch gap like worms through soil and Annie saw her begin to lift the window upward.

That was enough for Annie to find her footing again.

She turned and bolted across the recreation yard for the door that led back into the corridor. But as she reached to open it, a freezing-cold hand grasped hold of her wrist, stopping her. At the icy touch of that almost skeletal hand, Annie heard a scream inside of her that was horribly familiar and yet not her own.

Impossibly, the gray girl was standing right in front of her.

Annie tried to wrench her wrist free, but that cold grip was all too strong. She tried again, shrieking with the effort as she used all her body weight to escape it. Annie heard a ripping sound and for a horrible moment thought it might be the tendons in her arm. She wriggled free, crying out in terror and clutching on to her frozen wrist in pain. Annie's uniform sleeve dangled loose from her arm – the source of the ripping sound. As she broke contact, the scream from within her echoed and diminished, leaving only the wind whistling through the dead branches of the tree.

Annie recoiled from the grim visage of the gray girl. Her eyes sought out the window in the moonlight. It was still almost shut. Then, she felt those bony fingers clutching at her exposed shoulder and knew she had to find a way to rid herself of this spiteful apparition.

The tree. It was the only option left. She brushed away the unwanted touch of those cold fingers and ran to the center of the recreation yard. Annie reached for the lowest of the branches and leaped for it. Contact. She swung her legs up until the soles of her shoes found the tree trunk. Then she pushed herself up higher until she was on the branch.

Without looking down, Annie shimmied along the length of the branch until she could reach the next highest. It was just out of reach. Her terror was all the inspiration she needed, and she set about tearing the rest of her sleeve away from the shoulder of her uniform. She was in such a panic that she managed to wrench a length of the underarm away with the sleeve too. No matter. That only made it easier to twist the fabric into a makeshift rope. Annie swung the frayed fabric over the tree branch and grabbed hold of the loose end, making a loop. She tried to use it to pull herself up and onto the next branch.

But the fabric of her sleeve was not strong enough. With a stomach-churning tearing sound, it gave way until it was rent in two and Annie fell sprawling back from the tree. She hit the ground hard, with such force that it knocked the wind from her.

Annie rolled over, groaning and tried to get her shit together. She saw the dark glint of the gray girl's eyes and realized that the hideous creature was crawling toward her across the yard. Annie grunted with the effort that it took her to get back onto her feet. She had to scale the tree to escape her pursuer, but how?

Annie's eyes found a coiled shape that lay against the roots of the tree. A jump rope. Annie reached down and grabbed it. She slung it over the branch nearest her and pulled herself back up. Without daring to look below her to see how close the gray girl was, Annie let loose one end of the rope and swung it higher, over the branch she couldn't quite reach before. It worked this time. Unlike her torn sleeve, the rope was strong enough to hold her weight.

Once she'd used it to pull herself up and onto the high branch, she risked a glance below.

The mysterious gray girl had disappeared.

Annie clung on to the branch and waited until her heavy breathing subsided.

She peered over to where the branch ended. Quite a distance to the wall, but it didn't look so insurmountable now. Not from up here, anyway. Annie decided to stand up, to get a better perspective. Looping the skipping rope around it, Annie held on to the trunk as though she were some kind of crazy tree-hugging activist. From there, she worked her way up until she could stand on the branch, with the topmost length of the tree at her back.

She closed her eyes for a moment and caught her breath.

When she opened them, the gray girl was standing in front of her. Annie gazed in disbelief at the girl's bare feet, corpse-pale and balancing on the narrow branch as though she were a prize gymnast.

"Please..." Annie began to plead.

But it was no use.

The gray girl was upon her before the word had fully formed from her lips. Those icy hands clamped on to the sides of her head and Annie's strangled cry became caught on a gust of freezing air that wafted over the wall. For a moment, Annie saw the trees and fields beyond the wall. She saw the road like a ribbon of black through the wilderness. And then she realized she could only see those things because the gray girl had lifted her from her feet and high into the air.

Annie felt the rough fibers of the skipping rope wrap around her throat.

For a moment, there was silence. Even the night wind had stopped blowing.

Then there was a rushing sound as Annie felt her body drop.

She waited for the makeshift rope to pull tight around her neck. A death-noose of her own making. Annie shut her eyes again, expecting it to be for the last time.

But the noose did not tighten. On and on she fell, and that was somehow worse. The pit of her stomach protested queasily at the sensation. It was as if the world had opened up to swallow her whole.

Then there came a sharp bang.

It sounded – crazily – like a hammer.

Annie opened her eyes.

She recognized the space she was in, though her reeling senses could hardly comprehend what she saw.

It was the courtroom.

She was in the courtroom, but how? And the hammering sound she had heard was exactly that.

The judge slammed the hammer down again on the wooden block before him and called for order. A reluctant hush settled in the courtroom. Disoriented, Annie felt as though she might topple over. Her hands gripped on to something to break her fall. At first, she thought it was the branch of the dead tree. She looked down and saw that it was, in fact, the wooden rail of the witness dock.

Annie swallowed, wishing her dizzy spell would end.

"The jury's verdict is unanimous," the judge was saying, "and it is the opinion of this court that the accused did knowingly commit the crime of which she stands accused before us…"

Annie was being sentenced.

All over again.

The judge's voice sounded weirdly distant and muffled.

Her vision blurred and she blinked in an attempt to focus on what was going on around her. She had a horrible feeling that she had been drugged. Was that even legal, considering she was on the stand?

"…therefore it is my solemn duty to give sentence. Taking into consideration the testimony of mental health experts during this trial, the accused should serve a minimum of two years detention in a youth correctional facility for her crime – a crime that left an innocent young woman, with a promising life and career ahead of her, permanently disfigured…."

There were gasps and murmurs from the gallery. The judge again called for order.

A woman screamed obscenities at her. *Bitch, murderer, perverted psychopath.*

The crowd roared its disapproval. She deserved to die in jail for what she had done.

For what I did.

Annie blinked.

She saw a memory of liquid. Saw its arc describing a shining, wet hook in the air. The opposite of a rainbow. Annie heard the splash and then the sizzle of acid eating into flesh as it hit her victim in the face. Saw the victim's hand clutching at her cheek, too late. Watched as the woman's skin came away with her hand. It was as though she was peeling away a beautician's face mask, Annie remembered. She'd never be beautiful again. Not for him. Not for anyone. If she could bear to look in a mirror ever again, it would be to despair at her hideous reflection.

"…a crime committed to seduce a young man whose bravery to attend court today is a testament not only to his decency, but also to the failed plan of the desperate wretch you see before you in the dock," the judge concluded.

Annie looked through her tears at the young man on the witness stand. His eyes burned with hatred and betrayal. She knew – all over again – that he didn't love her. The fact looped around in her skull until she was sick to the core from its persistence. He could not, and would never, love her. She felt as though the life was leaving her body with each breath she exhaled. Her legs buckled and she clung on to the railing, but fell anyway, down from the dock.

As she dropped, she became aware of the skipping rope, still coiled around her throat.

She clawed at it with frantic fingers, but it was too late.

Her neck snapped as the noose held her in death's embrace.

CHAPTER SEVENTEEN

A More Permanent Form of Oblivion

I'm running in the direction of the medical storeroom when I realize I've been along this corridor before.

It's as though the reformatory is playing tricks on me, folding in upon itself like some kind of puzzle to prevent me from getting to where I need to be. And where I need to be right now is with Lena. Unless Annie or Victoria got to her first, she doesn't know that Principal Quick is dead. She'll be waiting for us to bring the principal along to be syringed into oblivion. Lena has no idea that Principal Quick has found another, more permanent, form of oblivion all by her sweet self.

I stop running, and try to get my bearings as I catch my breath.

My heart is thundering in my chest, and my head is near exploding from the pressure of the blood in my veins. I try to slow my breathing, but can't. I wonder if this is what a panic attack feels like. I read about those in Principal Quick's spidery handwritten notes. I read about a lot while I was in her office that I'd rather forget.

My skin, already coated in a film of clammy sweat from running, turns cold. What if there really is no actual way out of here? What if the building really does, somehow, have me trapped inside of it? That makes me nothing more than a rat in a maze.

I lean against the wall for support, and that's when I feel it beneath the palm of my hand. It's just a vague sort of *thrumming* at first, but as I focus my mind on it I begin to feel its rhythm.

Thrum, thrum, thrum.

The wall – yes, and I'm aware how crazy that sounds – has a heartbeat. It really does feel as though the reformatory is alive. A living, breathing creature. I almost laugh at the idea. This crummy old shell is alive, somehow? But there it still is.

Thrum, thrum, thrum.

The rhythm pulsing in my palm is now so defined that I feel compelled to put my ear to the wall in order to hear it, too. I lean in and press my ear against the wall. The surface feels pleasantly cool against my cheek, which is still warm from running.

The throbbing beat seems to come from deep inside the building. I'm amazed the walls don't crack and crumble under its repetitive force. But as I listen intently to this strange heartbeat, I begin to wonder if it's maybe what's holding the building together.

Thrum, thrum, thrum.

I feel my heartbeat begin to slow, in time with the reformatory's. My breathing becomes relaxed and less labored.

Thrum, thrum, thrum.

I'm in sync with it now, my ear canal becoming a conduit for the beat at the heart of this dark old place. Something tightens – inside of me, or the building itself, I can't be sure – and I feel a little lightheaded. My heart skips a beat and falls out of time with the rhythm of the reformatory. One heartbeat becomes a slight echo of the other.

Thrum-thrum, thrum-thrum, thrum-thrum.

The staccato sound is now less like a heartbeat and more like the immense ticking of some vast, subterranean clock marking time that's running out.

How odd, I think.

I really want to pull my ear away.

And yet I can't.

The sound becomes deafening, and I clamp my eyes shut against it. My vision flashes red behind my eyelids, and I feel my blood again, coursing hot through my veins, making my head throb from the pressure of it all.

Tick-tock, tick-tock, tick-tock.

The cacophony rages in my skull and I begin to lose feeling in my nerve endings as they become numb. My legs grow weak, forcing me to push harder against the wall for support, but that's where the noise is coming from. A vicious cycle.

I feel a spike of darkness enter my head, carried by the ticking beat of the wall. My ears begin to ring. For a moment, I feel as though I am floating, borne on the soundwaves that are holding me fast. I open my eyes and try to focus on another sound, any other sound. One that might bring me back to the here and now and place solid ground under my feet.

The wall seems to shiver as I look at it. The drab, gray paintwork flakes outward, as if something is pushing through the layers of masonry beneath, eager to free itself from its hiding place. I gasp as the gray girl's head appears from the wall, followed by her shoulders, and then her upper body. She is birthed by the pulsing rhythm of the reformatory's ominous heartbeat. Where she ends and the wall begins is hard to make out. It's as though the building has made her from bricks and mortar, before coating her in the paint-gray pallor of its own skin. One hand emerges from the wall and I hear her fingers snap into existence. She uses them for leverage, in the same way that a moth might flutter its wings to spring from its cocoon. When the vertebrae in her neck begin to click too, I know that she's turning her head slowly, but ever so surely, in my direction.

That clicking sound is my terror, and my salvation.

I scream.

I push with all my might against the wall. It holds me to its dead, cold bosom and I'm terrified that even as it gives birth to her, it might swallow me up. Life from death, and vice versa. I decide against going down without a fight. Balling my hands into fists, I beat against the wall and feel that *tick-tick-thrum* just stop for a second.

And a second may be all that I need.

I snap my head away from the wall. The rest of me follows its momentum. The ringing in my ears stops. I see her, spreading across and out of the wall like an obscene stain. Her fingers claw the air. I can't see her eyes beneath her dusty mane of hair, but I can feel their malevolent gaze on me. She's almost free of the wall now.

I run.

Crashing around the corner, I slip and lose my footing.

I twist my ankle badly and bang my knee against the floor. Every instinct is telling me to crawl to the wall, and to lean against it for support. But I'm too scared. Remembering the hideous heartbeat, and the gray girl who must have freed herself from the wall by now, I cry out, the sound giving new names to my agonies. Avoiding the wall, I push myself up from the floor. My ankle hurts like fuck but hey, that's good. It's something tangible, something real that I can focus on. And while I have my focus maybe I can find my way out of this hellish place. I start limping along the corridor. When I blink, it's like a whiteout. But I can concentrate on the pain.

I don't get very far before I hear it.

A distant shriek from around the corner.

I follow the sound as quickly as my ankle will allow me to.

Wincing at the pain with each step, I glance behind me to see if the gray girl is catching up to me.

I can see only shadows.

I grit my teeth and push on, then turn the corner into another corridor. A shaft of silver moonlight creates a sharp rectangle on the floor. The light is coming through the window to the recreation yard. I hear another shriek, and I know now that someone is out there. I continue limping toward the door that leads to the yard. Then the shrieking stops and I hear another sound. This one even more chilling than the last.

Thunk.

There's a finality to the sound that freezes the blood in my veins. I know it sounds weird, but it's like it's the last sound in the world. I wrap my arms around my body and hug myself tight, searching for warmth that isn't there. I keep moving and, as I reach the door, I see a long, dark shadow swaying across the rectangle of moonlight on the corridor floor.

I open the door and limp into the exercise yard. The moon hangs brilliantly white in the night sky, illuminating the façade of the clock tower. I hear a creak and turn to see the dead tree at the center of the yard, its branches shaped like gnarled fingers clawing at the sky. Another creak and I see the source of the long, swaying shadow cast by the moonlight into the corridor.

Annie.

It comes back to me, clear as day, what I saw written in Principal Quick's psych evaluation of Annie. On the clipboard. 'Suicide by hanging'. That's what it said. This is so fucked up. Did Quick know how this would happen, or did that…*thing* in the wall have something to do with it?

"Annie," I say, because I really don't know how else to articulate what I'm seeing.

Annie's body hangs limp from a high branch. Her head lolls at an odd angle and looks as though it could topple from her neck at any moment. The branch creaks under her weight as the rise and fall of the wind causes her body to sway from side to side.

I notice that one of her arms is bare and then see why. The sleeve of her uniform has been torn away. I take a couple of nervous steps closer and, as her body rotates slowly in the wind, I can see that the recreation yard jump rope has been fashioned into a noose around her livid neck. Her tongue protrudes from between her teeth. But her eyes are the worst of all. They're wide open and the moonlight catches them, making them gleam with an iridescent white. Then, as the wind rises again, her body turns and that light goes out from her eyes.

I turn away, still not quite able to process the abjection of all that I've seen, and all that I've endured. I can't quite believe that Annie managed to climb all the way up into that tree in order to hang herself. I tell myself that maybe I don't have to. I know that somehow, the hideous gray girl I saw emerging from the wall is to blame for this.

For all of this.

I look at the door that leads back to the corridor, willing the gray girl to be standing there. But I'm alone. I glance up at the clock tower and its empty windows. I look to Principal Quick's office window and see someone there. A cloud obscures the moon, and she's gone. I realize that what I saw in the window was my own moonlit reflection.

Recalling that deathly glow in Annie's fixed, open eyes, I limp a retreat to the door. Then I head back inside, in search of Lena.

CHAPTER EIGHTEEN

The Specter Took Its Time

Victoria ran, each breath snagging in her throat because of her panic. Her heart pounding because of her fear. Fear of Emily, and of Principal Quick's dead body. Rising panic at the prospect that she had been in such close proximity to Emily when it could have been her all along, killing the girls, and now Principal Quick. Emily had been found in the bathroom, which was awash with Jess's blood. Sure, Quick had said that Jess had committed suicide, but what if she was merely covering for her star pupil? The thought almost made Victoria gag.

Emily's name in the principal's manuscript could only mean one thing. Victoria unpacked the evidence as her mind raced.

Item one: Emily had been valuable to Principal Quick, for whatever whacked-out research number she was doing on her.

Item two: Emily had been an inmate at Greyfriars Reformatory before. Maybe the principal had to hit the pause button on her research when Emily had been released from her care. No way Quick was going to lose out on a chance to make her name with Emily around once again. Hell, she had been nothing short of eager to welcome her back into the fold, from what Victoria recalled of the first couple of days. So what if it meant losing a few no-hoper inmates along the way? Emily was back under Principal Quick's loony microscope.

Well, Victoria mused, it had backfired on Quick, and spectacularly. Emily had sure made it look like suicide. The bottle. The pills. The only thing that had been missing was a 'goodbye cruel world' suicide note. Victoria's skin crawled at how Emily had feigned her ignorance, and how she had even looked surprised, when they found the principal facedown on her desk like that. But not *too* surprised. Oh, no. There was something very wrong with Emily, and it began to dawn on Victoria that she was lucky to be alive. How easy would it have been for Emily to kill her while they had been on the smoke run? Maybe Emily was as smart as she was crazy, after all. By having Victoria go with her, and then to discover Jess's body—

She's still down there! All bloody.

—down in the basement, it would make her look the total innocent. Then, when Victoria had spoken up about it, she had thought it extremely odd that the principal was so keen to have her show them the closet. The old bitch had been so eager to prove her wrong in front of everyone. The principal had no doubt done it to show Emily that her secret was safe; Victoria was convinced of that now. It was supremely messed up to think that Emily was being allowed to toy with them like that, and to pick them off one by one, while Principal Quick covered up for her each time.

Well, Principal Quick was dead now, too. And good goddamned riddance. Victoria intended to go on living. And she was out of there, just as soon as she—

Victoria stopped and slapped her hand onto her forehead in frustration at her sudden realization.

No keys.

How in the living name of heck was she going to escape without Principal Quick's keys? She glanced up at the barred window nearest to her in the corridor and, for just a moment, considered doubling back and retracing her steps to Emily. But if she was being brutally honest with herself, she was too scared. Afraid of what Emily might do to her if she showed up at Quick's office looking for the keys. And that was if Emily hadn't taken them already. She was too sly not to have done so. Add to that the fact that Victoria didn't want to be in the principal's office with the corpse of its owner ever again. She felt a shiver pass over her skin at the memory of that room and its sickly sweet, charnel smell. Victoria gazed at the shadow of the window bars, which stretched across the floor in the moonlight. She refocused on her next best option. There was only one person in the building who could get them out of there. Lena had made light work of lock picking, and hopefully she could do so again. Setting off at a running pace, Victoria headed for the medicine store.

* * *

Breathlessly, she opened the door. It was dark inside. Too dark to see properly.

"Lena?"

Victoria took a couple of tentative steps into the storeroom and heard glass crunch beneath the sole of her shoe.

Not good.

Turning around, Victoria felt along the wall beside the doorframe in search of the light switch. She found it and clicked the light on. Turning back to the room, Victoria let out a strangled cry at what she saw illuminated there.

The floor was awash with dark blood. The storeroom looked more like some nightmarish abattoir. Victoria's eyes followed the pool of blood to where Lena sat, slumped at the foot of the open med cabinet. She was bleeding out. Jesus, she must have lost liters of the stuff. Syringes littered the floor around Lena's still body. One still dangled from Lena's forearm, and Victoria gagged as she took in the carnage that had been visited upon poor Lena's body. Her arms, her wrists, had been torn to ribbons. It was as though someone—

Lena? No it couldn't be Lena, no one would do that to herself. Least of all her. She's tougher than that. Was tougher....

—had been trying to dig something out of Lena's flesh. Victoria threw up, and she had to grab on to a nearby shelf to stop herself from collapsing in sickness and fear.

She backed, trembling and sobbing, out of the room.

Then, Victoria felt a cool breeze on the back of her neck. She put her hand there. Her hand turned cold, too. Victoria looked down and saw a dark shadow looming all around her. She turned on her heels and saw the girl—

The gray girl!

—standing just a breath away. Her features were indistinct, but Victoria knew it wasn't Emily. This was something else. Something inhuman. As though hearing her thoughts, the girl reached for her and Victoria saw how emaciated the girl's fingers looked. Her fingernails were lined with dirt. Like she had crawled out from the grave. As that bony hand reached for her, Victoria screamed. She swatted in terror at the hand and ran away, in fear for her life.

Victoria didn't stop running until she reached another door, and only then slowed her pace to pass through. It was the sliding door of the refectory. As Victoria slid it shut behind her, she glimpsed the darkly distant figure of the gray girl in the corridor. She was following her.

Victoria hit the light switches and then looked for a latch on the door—

If only I'd grabbed those goddamn keys!

—but there wasn't one. She glanced frantically around the refectory, her heart beating in time with the flickering of one of the strip lights. All the furniture was bolted to the floor; no way that she could barricade the door. Feeling queasy from fear, Victoria pushed on between the dining tables, and to the back of the room. There was the door to the kitchen. Victoria prayed to gods she didn't really believe in that the fucker wasn't locked.

Hallelujah, Amen.

It was unlocked, and she didn't waste any time ducking

inside. The only light in the kitchen came from an emergency exit lamp above a door, its eerie green glow doing nothing to calm Victoria's frayed nerves.

She dashed to the emergency exit door and slammed both her hands against the metal door release. Then she realized her mistake. The door was chained and padlocked shut from the inside. She would have to confront the girl in the refectory, or find somewhere to hide. But Victoria couldn't face going back out there. She was too afraid that those claw-like hands might latch on to her.

Mind made up, she skirted around the kitchen's work surfaces. There were some larger storage bins and cupboards closer to the ovens. Victoria dropped to her haunches and opened one of the cupboards. She might be able to fit inside. Anything other than facing the apparition that had been following her since she'd found Lena's bleeding body. Anything to avoid a similar fate at those cold, dead hands.

There was a flicker, followed by a flash. Victoria thought it might be a lightning storm – and then she remembered that the kitchen was windowless. The flickering continued, along with the *tink-tink* sound of the fluorescent lighting tubes overhead, and she realized that someone had turned the light on in the kitchen. She listened intently and heard the faint creak of the door as it closed. She was still facing the kitchen cupboard.

Tink-tink.

Her heart had almost stopped beating in her chest, she was so terrified. Too frightened now even to look, Victoria clamped her eyes shut. She felt warm tears spill down her cheeks. Heard a distant whimper, and then realized it was her own voice. She could feel that chill in the air again, could feel it penetrating her skin. She knew what was coming, and every second was loaded with dread as it passed.

Tink-tink. Buzz.

The specter took its time.

Cold fingers brushed Victoria's cheek and she screamed. She felt those fingers wrap around her face, on either side. Her scream sputtered and died in her throat as she felt her head being twisted around.

And Victoria opened her eyes.

★ ★ ★

She sat up in bed, all pink pastel and plush throw cushions.

She looked around at all her gender-stereotyped belongings, neatly laid out on cerise shelves. The little alarm clock, also pink, told her it was still nighttime. Just before one a.m.

A pervasive, unpleasant smell made her nose wrinkle.

Confused by the strange odor, and feeling half-asleep, she walked over to where her robe was hanging. Her toes thudded against something heavy and soft on the carpeted floor. Strange. Why was her dad sleeping facedown on her floor like that? Weirdly, her gymnastics trophy lay on the floor too, by his side. She course-corrected and walked around his ever-so-still body, so as not to wake him.

Victoria took her robe down from the little plastic hook on the back of the door. She clambered into her robe. Following the hissing sound, she drifted out of the room.

Holding on to the handrail because she was feeling so woozy, Victoria yawned her way downstairs and headed for the kitchen. She passed the line of framed photo portraits on the wall. A half-dozen versions of herself, pictured through the years from chubby-cheeked kid to young adult. Smiling. But not *really* smiling.

Victoria's throat was dry and she needed a glass of cool water. She entered the kitchen. The lights had been left on, their reflections gleaming off the polished tile floor. Squeaky clean, just how Mom liked it. But instead of the quiet of the hour, Victoria could hear an intense hissing sound. As she moved into the domestic space, she saw her mother sitting on a breakfast stool. Her upper body lay slumped across the kitchen island, with a near-empty liquor bottle next to her. She appeared to be unconscious.

Victoria yawned, and a bad taste clung to the back of her throat. She really did need that glass of water. Strange, she thought she had walked to the kitchen sink, and yet here she was, over by the cooking range. Her limbs were so very heavy, and she felt so tired all of a sudden. Victoria felt something cold and hard in her hand and looked down to see she had turned one of the gas dials. Matter of fact, they were all open. The hissing sound intensified, along with the toxic levels of dryness clutching at her throat.

She approached the kitchen island and reached out a leaden hand in the direction of her mother. All the while the hissing grew louder and louder. She was standing right next to her mom now. Feeling lightheaded, Victoria sat down beside her. She touched her mom's shoulder. But her mom did not react. Victoria pulled her mother's shoulder back, gently but firmly. Her mom's head lolled over to one side. Yellow streaks of vomit glistened on her exposed cheek. Her eyes were fixed open in a sightless gaze.

All that Victoria could hear was the hissing.

Victoria stood up, walked from the kitchen to the back door, and out onto the rear porch. She heard the wooden gate bang shut behind her, though she didn't remember even passing through it. She was halfway across the front lawn when the blast knocked her from her feet and onto her face. She tasted dirt and her nose felt numb from the impact. A sharper taste than that of the soil invaded her senses. Her nose was bleeding into her mouth. She liked the taste. Savored it.

Victoria rolled over onto her back, which felt oddly numb. She wondered if the skin had been burned away from her back. It certainly smelled as though it had. Meat residue blackening on a summer barbeque. She lay there, propped up on her elbows like a sunbather, and watched the house go up in a massively glorious ball of flame. The gas explosion rocked the earth beneath her and she laughed. She thought of the line of photographs at the foot of the stairs. Pictured them peeling and disintegrating in the heat and the flames. All those past versions of her, gone forever.

She watched the house burn until her eyes stung. And then she watched it some more. When the smoke finally made her blink, she felt tears at the corners of her eyes. She wondered if her father was still conscious even as his body burned, facedown on the floor of the bedroom in which he had hurt her, so many times. She hoped so. Her mom was already dead before the gas ignited, which seemed apt somehow. Mom had lived her life in ignorance, always looking the other way. Never listening to what Victoria had so desperately tried to tell her. Not a care to notice the warning signs. Her last voyage to the bottom of a liquor bottle had taken her down, long before her cremation.

As the heat from the fire began to dry the tears on Victoria's face, she realized without doubt that they were tears of joy.

She blinked, and then opened her eyes.

The house had gone, the blaze replaced by a halo of light from the reformatory kitchen overheads. Cold breath cooled her face and her eyes filled with abject terror at the sight of the gray girl's fathomless, empty eyes staring into her own.

CHAPTER NINETEEN

Is This Hell?

I keep on moving so that the shadows can't gain on me.

At every turn, I hear an echo of that awful sound, repeatedly in my head.

Thunk, thunk, thunk.

I try to put Annie's dead face from my mind. Try not to linger on the way her lips had already turned pale blue by the time I'd found her, hanging from the dead tree in the recreation yard. I try to ignore the gray phantom that must have tormented her in her last moments.

But I can't.

Why aren't my ears ringing? I wonder if they ever will again, after all that I've witnessed during this night. I wish I could retreat, instead of running. I crave the numbness, now, in a way that I never have before. Floating out of body and out of time would be just the thing, please and thank you. But in truth, my senses feel sharper than ever. I'm aware of every breath I take, and each footfall I make as I rush down the corridor.

I find the door to the medical store wide open. Blood covers the floor. Lena's body is slicked red with blood. Jesus, there are so many needles everywhere. What the hell happened in here?

She *happened*.

The thought arrives with such stark clarity that I whirl around to see if someone has whispered it into my ear. But I'm alone on the threshold to poor, dead Lena and so much blood. I don't want to go inside. Don't want to tread in all that blood.

I feel as though it would be the wrong thing to do. The blood still belongs to Lena, and to Lena alone.

I back away from all of the broken glass, all of the horror and death inside that depressing little storeroom, thinking what a waste of a young life, and how Lena was the last of us I'd have expected to die here at Greyfriars Reformatory. The clever way she got us all out of the locked dormitory – that was neat. We'd still be locked inside and arguing about how we were going to escape if not for her. The way she kept watch each night, by the dormitory door, makes me think she wasn't looking out for Saffy, or for herself. Rather, I think she was looking out for all of us. For whatever reason, I believe she saw herself as a protector. Sure, she was happy to have Saffy be the alpha, probably because Lena wouldn't be interested in that self-aggrandizing nonsense. Lena was always there, only speaking when she needed to. She was tough as nails, she was resilient, she kicked ass.

And now she's dead.

I'm nowhere near as resourceful as Lena was. Her survival skills would have made her a useful ally. My best shot at surviving the wilderness outside the reformatory. But she's gone, and I'm on my own now.

Then I notice the bloody footsteps leading away from the medical storeroom, and begin to figure that Victoria must have come here first. She must have been looking for Lena's help too. I'm already walking, and following the blood trail before I even realize it.

The bloody footprints become an expressionistic flourish as I follow them around the corner into another corridor. Victoria must have slipped as she navigated the corner. Must have been going at quite a pace, and I bet I know who, or what, she was running from.

The corridor darkens as I walk further. There are no lights on in this part of the building. Not sure exactly where I am now because I'm feeling a little light-headed all of a sudden. Not in my usual way. This is something else. There's a sick feeling in the depths of my stomach that makes me swallow. I keep walking and become aware of a noxious smell in the air. Is that what's making me feel unwell, I wonder?

I see the familiar door to the refectory and get my bearings. The door is halfway open. From inside, a light flickers. The smell is strong now, and unmistakably gas. I take what breath I can before I reach the door and go inside. The light flickers madly overhead – a malfunctioning starter lamp in one of the overhead lights – and the potentially deadly combination of toxic gas and erratic electricity sets my teeth on edge. I find my way between the refectory tables and a memory of my fight with Victoria comes back to me. It strikes me that we were both focused on the wrong fight. Instead of battling each other, we should have been finding ways to team up. Stronger together, not apart.

I push on toward the kitchen door and I know I'm going to have to breathe soon. But not yet. I clamp my arm over my mouth and nose and kick the swinging door into the kitchen open. A loud hissing alerts me to the fact that the stove gas switches are all open.

Victoria is on the floor, a crumpled mess at the foot of a stainless-steel storage unit.

I move in her direction as fast as I can. A shadow spreads and sweeps across the wall to the left of me. I don't stop to look. I hear a metallic clang as a pan or some other utensil falls to the floor somewhere behind me. Again, I don't hesitate. Eyes on the prize. Stronger together. Not apart. Holding my breath, which wants to burst free from my agonized lungs, I quickly close each of the gas switches.

I stoop and curl my free arm under Victoria's upper body. I try to lift her and have to remove my other arm from in front of my face because she's a deadweight. Clutching her tightly with both arms, I pull her up from the floor. Her head lolls forward, chin balancing on her chest, and I wonder if she's dead already.

I can't hold my breath any longer. I have to breathe. I open my mouth and gasp.

The putrid stench of the gas is overpowering.

I hold on to Victoria and drag her limp body backward through the kitchen. Her heels drag across the hard floor surface, making it harder for me to move her. My head is swimming now from the effort of dragging her, and from breathing in so much gas. I have to take another breath and this one nearly finishes me. I tumble back through the swinging door and into the refectory. I lose my footing and slam down hard on my ass. Victoria's dead weight topples on top of me. I cry out at the pain and feel Victoria moving on top of my legs.

She's alive.

"Victoria?" I rasp, my throat burning as I speak her name.

She replies with a groan. It's not much, but it's the most human sound I've heard for what feels like a long while. It urges me on somehow, encourages me to double my efforts.

"Can you walk?" I ask.

She grunts, and then nods, as I get to my feet and help her to stand. We lean on each other for support and stagger across the refectory toward the still-open sliding door. It might just be the effect of the gas playing tricks on my powers of perception, but the room looks much bigger than it did before, and the door much farther away. The strip light flickers overhead and I wonder if it's all been in vain after all. Surely the place will go up any second with so much gas in the air, and no windows.

"Come on! A spark from the light might be enough to make the gas explode," I say.

Victoria increases her pace along with mine.

We struggle on together and reach the door. Maybe I really did turn off the gas just in time.

After tumbling through the door, we fall to our knees together in the corridor. Even the musty odor of the reformatory smells blissfully sweet after the tainted air of the kitchen and refectory. I breathe in and out a few times to clear the nasty taste from my airways. Then I turn and slide the refectory door closed. Victoria has taken on much more of the gas than me. She crawls to the corner of the corridor and throws up. The vomit keeps coming. Her upper body convulses as she dry heaves. Her throat is making sounds more likely to come out of a blocked drain, and I'm feeling pretty queasy myself now.

"All done?" I ask.

She dry heaves again.

There's clearly nothing left for her to puke up, but her body needs to be rid of the poison in her system. She groans and sits back against the wall before wiping the perspiration from her forehead. She looks pale and drained. Victoria looks at me groggily, eyes streaming with tears.

"What *is* this place, Emily? Is this Hell?"

I don't know the answer. So I just shrug.

"Lena's dead," she says.

"I know," I reply.

"Where's Annie?"

"Annie's dead," I say.

"Oh no." Victoria looks like she is struggling to take it all in. "How?"

"I found her hanging from the tree in the recreation yard."

"Jesus Christ," Victoria says. "That's how her file said she died." Then she coughs to clear her throat. "Except it said she hanged herself in detention. Why would it say that?"

"I didn't—"

"I know, okay. It's her. That...gray girl. It's like she knows every bad thing you ever did in your life." Victoria coughs again, then struggles to her feet. "Lena's case file said massive blood loss from torn veins. Said it was intentional self-mutilation – in case the drug overdose didn't do the trick. That's how she died, for sure. But Principal Quick entered it in her case file like a premonition or something. At first I thought you and she were in cahoots somehow..." She catches my look. "...and I'm sorry about that, but you can understand why I thought that, right?"

I can't. But I nod anyway because it seems the right thing to do at this particular time. Maybe I'm getting better at navigating this kind of human interaction after all, because Victoria seems to accept my nod.

"I just don't understand it, Emily. How could Principal Quick know? And why did she choose to top herself like that? She was studying you, right? For her book?"

I nod again. I'm getting good at this.

"Well," Victoria goes on, "she had you back, right where she wanted you. And then Jess died, and Saffy. Followed by Principal Quick herself. Then Lena and Annie – not sure who went first...." Victoria winces, as though she's said, or thought, something truly terrible. She takes a deep breath before continuing.

"So the only thing left to puzzle out is the gray girl. Do you think she's real, Emily?" Victoria asks. "Do you think she really can be killing us off, one by one?"

"There was something in Principal Quick's manuscript about her," I reply. I try to remember the exact words, but can't summon them. "That she was...a projection or something."

Victoria's eyes widen. She starts pacing the corridor, thinking aloud. "That manuscript of Principal Quick's. That's your case file, Emily. I think it must be the key to all of this." She stops pacing and looks right at me with excited zeal in her eyes. "We have to go back and take a proper look at it. You game?"

Again, I nod.

"And *your* file?" I ask. "Is it true, Victoria?"

"I fucking hope not," Victoria says before marching off along the corridor.

* * *

"Emily..." Victoria says, and I've seen it too.

Principal Quick's body has gone. Her desk is unoccupied. The empty pill and liquor bottles are still where they were before. The phone receiver lies, silent and useless, on the desk where Annie put it down. The manuscript is still there, too. I rush over to grab it.

"Do you think she faked it?" Victoria asks. "Her death, I mean?"

"She could have, I guess," I reply. "If anyone would know how, it would be Principal Quick. She seemed to know a thing or two about meds, after all. Maybe there was something she knew she could use to look stone-cold dead. But why would she want to fool us like that?"

Victoria shakes her head. "I think she's insane, Emily. I mean was...or is.... Jesus, you know what I'm saying – completely off the scale batshit mental. I think she's been playing a game with us since we arrived here. And I'm not sure it's a game we can win, unless we can stick together, okay?"

"Okay."

But there's always the chance that someone just moved the body, I want to add, but I can't bring myself to say it. And I wonder why – before I realize that it's because if the body was moved then it means whoever moved it was very probably the gray girl who's been haunting us every step of the way. My skin turns cold at the thought, and I shiver.

Then the phone starts ringing.

Off the hook.

I look to Victoria and she looks back at me as if to say *no way, I'm not answering it*. But it rings on, and one of us has to do something. So I reach over the desk and pick it up.

"Emily...?" Victoria says feebly.

At first, I can't hear anything except a weird kind of whispering sound, like the breeze through some trees. But then, down the line I hear a faint musical chime and remember the small music box in my pocket. Then comes a burst of shrill laughter.

"*She's coming for you, Emily,*" a voice rasps, after the laughter has died out.

The voice sounds weirdly familiar, and utterly alien all at the same time. It chills me to my core, and I slam the receiver back down on its cradle. But the voice is inside my head now, laughing and taunting, and I clamp my hands over my ears in the vain hope that this will block it out.

"*Coming for you, coming for you, coming for youuuuuuu....*"

All that my hands over my ears are doing is to keep the voice inside my head, looping and echoing, growing in intensity until—

Victoria screams.

—and the horrible voice stops.

But then I look at Victoria and see the fear etched into her features and I'm almost too scared to look at the corner of the room. To see what she sees. But Victoria is gasping and pointing now, and I have to see what's gotten her so terrified.

There, in the shadows next to the filing cabinet, stands Principal Quick. And she still looks dead. Worse still, her face is still locked in that look of horror, her glassy eyes betraying no emotion. She's just standing there and watching us, and I wonder if she's been there this whole time. There's a jangle of keys and I realize with dread that she has taken a step toward us both.

Victoria screams and moves beside me.

Principal Quick's body moves stiffly, like a mannequin's, as she takes another step, and then another. Each time she moves, there's another jangling sound, and as she emerges into the light from the desk lamp, I can see the bunch of keys in her hand.

"*Looking for these, girls?*" Her voice has the sound of something that's been buried deep in the earth and then dragged to the surface again, bringing some aspect of that grave along with it. When she giggles, a foul, yellow fluid spills from the corners of her mouth and Victoria and I both turn and run to the door.

We clatter out of the office and into the corridor.

But the jangling continues, and I know we are being followed.

"Oh my God, oh my God, oh my God," Victoria says breathlessly, her terrified eyes fixed on the office doorway.

Mirthless laughter echoes down the corridor as Principal Quick follows us out of her office. She lifts her dead hand and jangles the keys in the air, taunting us with them.

"*God can't help you now, foolish girl,*" she says in that charnel voice, her face still locked in that look of life-extinguishing horror.

Then Principal Quick's entire body twitches like a mad puppet's before dropping to the floor in a crumpled heap.

The keys are buried beneath her.

Victoria screams again. And I try to, but I can't. The sight of Principal Quick, back from the grave, was harrowing enough. Now I just clamp my hand over my mouth because there she actually is, as plain as day, standing behind Principal Quick's fallen body. The gray girl, her dark eyes blazing through her mane of tangled hair. She shoves Principal Quick's dead body aside with one foot and it's as though she's discarding an unwanted Halloween costume.

Then she creeps toward us as lithe, and as quiet, as a spider.

I feel Victoria clutch at my hand. Her hand trembles against mine, and I hold on to it tightly.

We run.

CHAPTER TWENTY

Those Dead Eyes Seem to Find Us

We turn a corner at breakneck speed and Victoria loses her footing.

I skid to a stop and help her to her feet, glancing over her shoulder to make sure the gray girl hasn't caught up to us.

"Emily," Victoria says.

But there's no time to talk. I see a muddy shadow stretching across the wall at the corner we just turned.

She's gaining on us.

"She's coming," I say, and see panic in Victoria's eyes.

I let go of her hand and we run on.

"We've been down this corridor before, haven't we?" Victoria asks breathlessly. "It's like we're running in circles."

I stop worrying about the shadow that's pursuing us for a moment and look. Really look. Damn it all to hell. Victoria's right. We definitely passed by this spot before.

"How is that even possible?" Victoria asks, seeing the look on my face, and the fear in her voice provokes my own.

I recall how the gray girl was at one with the reformatory, not just part of its fabric, but woven into it somehow. That immense heartbeat—

thrum, thrum, thrum

—comes back to haunt my memories, and I remember how the gray girl emerged from the masonry, and was knitted together as if from the dust of time. I wonder if she's as trapped in this building as I feel. Perhaps she knows she can't get out, and so puts all of her dark energies into keeping people in. Her playthings. Her pets. The mazelike corridors caught me up inside of them once before, and now I'm beginning to wonder if she can manipulate the physical layout of the building. To keep us trapped inside and chasing our tails until we weaken. In this game of cat and mouse, or rather – *mice*, it's clear which roles Victoria and I are playing. We're already both out of breath.

How long can we keep up the pace on her mad treadmill until she catches up to us?

Victoria has slowed to a jog.

"I have a stitch," she says, and grimaces.

She stops still and clutches her side with one hand. With the other, she reaches toward the wall for support and I swear I actually see its drearily painted surface shiver.

"Don't," I warn her. "Don't touch the walls."

She withdraws her hand and looks at me, puzzled.

"You wouldn't believe me if I told you why," I say.

"I don't know *what* to believe anymore," she replies.

Then I hear a sharp, rasping breath and can see from the panic-stricken look on Victoria's face that she hears it too.

"I believe you though, Emily," she says. "If you say we're in danger, then we're in danger."

"We're in danger," I reply.

And I'm not kidding.

We take off again at speed. Victoria clutches at her side. Her trust in me seems to give me renewed energy. And I focus on that energy until I feel sharper, and more alert than ever.

We run on until we reach a T-junction at the end of the corridor. Victoria veers to the right, but I reach out with my hand and grab hold of her sleeve. She looks at me, eyes wide from our flight.

"This way," I say, feeling sure that this is the correct thing for us both to do. "We should go this way."

She nods, and we take a left down the corridor, picking up our pace as much as we can. The green glow of an emergency exit sign reveals a door beneath it. We slow to a stop and then check out the door. It's chained and padlocked shut.

"No health and safety restrictions at Greyfriars Reformatory," Victoria sighs.

"Come on," I say and we push on along the corridor.

Another left turn is the only way we can go except back on ourselves, so we follow it around into another corridor.

The dormitory door is up ahead, to the right.

It's still open from when Lena sprung the lock.

We run to the door and steal inside. I give the corridor a quick, nervous scan before I shut the door. Impossible to say for sure, but I think I saw a shadow flicker at the corner of the corridor. I decide to keep that to myself. Victoria already looks petrified.

Closing the door, I catch my breath. Victoria doubles over in pain, complaining about her stitch. But I know we have a bigger problem.

"Can't lock the door without any keys," I mutter.

The high windows are no use as an escape route, either. They're out of reach and, even if we could climb up to somehow reach them, they're all barred. Keeping the door shut has to be our priority, so I start looking for a solution.

The beds all stand in rows, empty and white, except for the bed that Lena cannibalized for the lock-pick spring. That one stands, skeletal looking, at the center of the room. It's all we have, so I march over to it and grab one end of the metal frame.

"Help me barricade the door," I say.

"What use will that be? Against a phantom?" Victoria protests.

"We have to try," I say.

Victoria groans, and trudges over to the other end of the bedframe. At least she appears to be over her stitch. Just in time for me to give her a new one.

"On three," I tell her. "One, two, three."

We lift the heavy bedframe and carry it over to the door. I take the lead, and maneuver the bed around until we can stand it on its side. Shuffling it into place, I manage to trap the door handle with the bedsprings beneath it.

Having a physical boundary feels good. But only for a moment, because then I hear a faint scratching sound. And another.

Scritch-scratch.

I look to Victoria, whose eyes fill with fear. The scratching intensifies, then there's a loud knock and we both jump back from the door.

"We need more weight," I say, looking around the room frantically. "The mattresses."

We rush over to one of the unoccupied beds and grab a mattress. It's bulky, but far lighter than the bedframe. We carry it to the door and place it over the bedframe, adding more bulk to our barricade.

Scritch-scratch.

"Another," I say, wiping sweat from my eyes.

Scratch.

"Another," Victoria agrees.

Knock.

We both rush over to another unoccupied bed. I grab hold of one end of the mattress, and Victoria the other. We lift the mattress up and away from the bed.

Victoria screams – and I see the pure terror etched into her eyes.

There, curled up on the floor under the bed, is a girl, dressed in the same gray uniform that we wear – but hers is spattered in dark blood.

"Oh my..." Victoria begins to say.

But before she can find religion once more, her words become another scream of fear as the bloodstained girl we've inadvertently revealed twitches and jolts over onto her back. Her face is a tortured mask of perversity, her contorted expression locked between pain and delight. Her eyes pop open, hideously white, and glare up at us from the floor. She opens her mouth and, with a sick gurgle, thick blood spills from the corner of her vomit-smeared mouth.

And she laughs. Jesus H. Christ, she actually *laughs*. And I swear it's the most harrowing, and soul-destroying, sound I have ever heard.

Victoria is yammering away now, her mind apparently unhinged by what's she's seeing. She screams in fear again as Jess – or what used to be Jess – claws at the air suddenly, her fingers all bloody. Jess's body twists with the momentum and her pelvis thrusts upward. Her head dangles, upside down, and she licks those vile lips of hers as she looks hungrily at both of us. Then, crablike, she starts to scuttle from under the bed and toward Victoria. Her laughter dies away, only to be replaced by the hideous snapping of her teeth.

"Jess, oh my God, Jess, no!" Victoria says, and gasps as the Jess-thing clutches at her ankle with its bloody fingers.

Victoria hops up onto the bed behind her and the crablike cadaver circles around the bed, its teeth snapping.

I take my chance and run for the door.

The scratching and knocking continues and I feel trapped between the threat of what's outside the door, and what we've inadvertently barricaded ourselves in with.

"Emily!" Victoria's warning cry echoes around the room.

I turn sharply to see Jess scurrying over toward me, her twisted body making horrible snapping sounds with each tortured movement. I can't help but notice with disgust how her hands and feet leave bloody prints on the dormitory floor behind her. The awful chattering of her teeth grows louder and more intense as she nears me, and I have only seconds to act.

I hop to the side of our makeshift barricade and grip the bed frame with both hands. When those chattering teeth are inches from my feet, I pull with all my might, and bring our barricade – mattress and all – down on Jess's head. Her body crumples and her legs twitch violently. Her arms flail by her sides madly, as though they're attempting to free themselves from the rest of her body. There's blood everywhere now and, even worse, the clatter of teeth on the hard floor surface as Jess spits them from her mouth.

"Victoria! Now!" I shout, and she jumps down from the bed, giving Jess's madly flailing body a wide berth.

Joining me at the door, Victoria grips the handle. I do too, my hands over hers, and we open the door, ready to face whatever nightmare is out there.

We stumble into the corridor and look frantically around.

"There!" Victoria says, her voice almost crushed by terror.

I see it too.

A dark figure watching from the shadows. We both run the other way. I can almost feel the darkness snapping at my heels, like Jess's blood-smeared teeth did. We turn a corner, and then another, and I see the familiar entrance to the recreation area up ahead of us. We increase our speed and slam into someone coming the other way.

One moment the corridor was empty, and then....

The *someone* is sent sprawling from the impact onto her back in the corridor. She groans, and chuckles dryly. I see with horror that her body is unnaturally bent and distorted. She sits up, with a horrid cracking of bones, and I see why her body looks that way. It's Annie, her neck still broken from her fall in the noose. But her eyes are wide open and looking straight at us. They are the same lifeless, milky white as Jess's were.

"*She's coming for you,*" she drawls, her voice as broken as her neck.

Victoria wails, and I grab hold of her hand, willing her to keep her shit together even as I'm wondering if I'm about to lose my own.

Annie shuffles in a twisted and broken gait along the corridor, something slippery trailing along behind her. I realize with fright that it's the skipping rope. The one she was hanging from the tree by. It slithers along, limp and gray, like a decaying umbilical cord.

"*She's coming for you, and you can't stop her,*" Annie intones.

I blink away the tears that, strangely, have formed at the corners of my eyes and look at Victoria. She looks like she might pass out at any moment, so I squeeze her hand. Realization dawns on her face as I make my move.

She follows me, more as a result of my still holding on to her hand than any other reason.

If we knocked Annie down once, together, then we can do it again, together.

I hear Victoria roar as we rush Annie. Victoria sounds like a berserker going into battle. And that is exactly what she has become. Annie's hideous cackle is cut short as we slam into her upper body. Our hands are still locked together, our arms becoming a limbo pole. Annie is lifted from the floor on impact and actually tumbles, head over heels, before landing with a crack of her head on the corridor floor, the rope coiling beside her.

Neither one of us looks back.

We reach the door to the swimming pool and pause to catch our breaths. Victoria pulls at my hand and I realize I'm still holding on to hers. Her mouth curves into an awkward smile as she retrieves her hand. The fear is gone from her eyes now and she almost looks amused.

"That felt good," she says.

I'm glad for her that it did, but I'm not sure if I'm feeling anything in particular about it. The act of rushing Annie and knocking her over seems to have been some kind of rite of passage to Victoria. To me, though, it was just an act of survival.

"Does anything faze you at all? Ever?" Victoria asks.

I don't really know how to respond. I don't think she noticed my tears back there. She was probably too preoccupied to notice. You know, what with the running and the screaming, and all of that.

Her smile becomes a bemused look. "You're a strange girl," she says, "really very strange."

I don't have time to reply – can't reply – because behind Victoria, I see a pale, gray hand slither from the doorway. It slides across the surface of the wall, dripping wet.

I try to speak but can't.

(*I guess some things* do *faze me a little bit, after all.*)

Victoria sees something is wrong and turns to look in the direction of my gaze.

She gasps as Saffy emerges from behind the swimming pool door, her clothes plastered wetly to her skin. Saffy's eyes are dead to the world, almost completely white but with sickly traces of yellow where her pupils used to be. And those dead eyes seem to find us, out here in the corridor, and she smiles.

"Oh, no," Victoria says.

As Saffy smiles, water spills from her mouth and trickles onto the floor. She lurches toward Victoria, who screams and backs away before holding on to my shoulder for support.

More water spills from Saffy's mouth as she speaks, along with a foul, sewer-like smell. Her speech is guttural and half-drowned. And there is a disturbing, childlike glee in her voice.

"*She won't stop now. She's coming for* you, *Emily.*"

Saffy lurches toward me now. Each footfall makes a wet, slapping sound.

I look down at the floor and see her feet leaving wet footprints on the floor as she walks. I look to Victoria and see the rising terror in her eyes. A feeling begins to grow inside of me, a coldness that starts in the pit of my stomach and then quickly spreads out into my arms and legs. My veins turn to ice, and I feel my skin growing cold. My heart beats faster.

I'm not fazed. This is something else. This must be what it's like to be truly afraid. To be stripped down to what's at the base of being human. And it's a useful feeling, because it gives my mind new focus. It feels like energy, similar to what I experienced with Victoria a short while ago, but even more powerful and focusing.

I look at Saffy and her mouth is leaking so much water it is as though she has an entire swimming pool of the stuff inside of her body. I decide that I don't want to feel her touching me with those dead, moist fingers. I decide that I don't want to hear another word from that drowned throat of hers.

"Fuck you, Saffron," I say.

And then I turn and run.

Victoria isn't far behind. And neither is Saffy, her wet footsteps increasing in speed as she pursues us both.

We turn a corner into another part of the building. The corridor splits. I hang a right, purely on instinct. Then I curse my shitty instincts and skid to a halt, seeing another lurching figure up ahead.

It is Jess, all covered in blood.

"*She's coming for you, Emily,*" she says, her lips flecked with vomit.

Seems like everyone just wants to join the party.

Jess grins, and it makes me feel sick to see all but a couple of her teeth are gone from her mouth, exposing bare and bleeding gums. The whites of her eyes glint in the darkness. Her bony fingers claw at the air, searching us out. Where Saffy left a watery trail behind her as she walked, Jess leaves bloody footprints on the floor with each step.

It's a gruesome sight.

Victoria catches up to me and stops dead in her tracks, seeing Jess's cadaverous body lurching toward us. We retreat, but our backward trajectory means that Saffy will be upon us any moment. No choice now but to head the other way along the corridor, to the left.

"This way," I say and – even as the words escape my lips – I know they're useless.

With a sickening series of bone-sharp cracks, Annie rounds the other corner, skipping rope dragging behind her. Annie's head dangles so limply from her broken neck that it's upside-down. Her white eyes gleam blank from their shadowy sockets.

"*She's coming for you,*" Annie says, her voice a hideously drawn-out whisper.

She drags her twisted limbs down the corridor toward us and each movement sounds as though it is unlocking some deeply broken part of her body.

"*Won't stop until she gets you,*" Saffy cackles wetly.

We're trapped between three phantoms, and they're each closing in on us.

I feel Victoria clutch on to my arm in fear. Together, we back away from the unholy trio of dead inmates. Then I realize where we're standing.

Right beside us, the entrance to the clock tower staircase looms.

CHAPTER TWENTY-ONE

To Haunt Us Again and Again

"We can't go up there," Victoria says.

There's no real panic in her voice; she's just stating a fact. And I know she's speaking the truth. If we climb the stairs to the clock tower, there will be no other way down. But with a glance in each direction from the stairwell alcove, all I can see are the dead, white eyes of Saffy and the others closing in. All I can hear are the horrible clicking sounds of Annie's bones, the dragging rope, and the wetness of Jess and Saffy's footfalls on the hard floor as they creep ever closer to us.

"We could try to rush them," I suggest.

"We managed against Annie," Victoria says, the panic entering into her voice now, "but against three of those bitches? I'm not so sure."

The shadows of our pursuers fall dark across the wall opposite the alcove.

We have to act now or they'll be on us.

"I'm not so sure, either," I admit.

Victoria bites her bottom lip. I can see from her expression that she knows we have no choice about where to run to next. We turn together and face the steps. They're shrouded in gloom, with just a tiny sliver of light coming from the opening at the top of the stairs.

Scritch-scratch.

The sound comes from within the walls, and makes the hairs at the nape of my neck stand on end.

"Did you hear that?" Victoria asks.

"Yeah," I reply.

"What the hell is that now?" she says, sounding as creeped out as I feel.

"It's *her*," I say, and Victoria's sudden silence tells me that she knows who I'm talking about. "We have to move. *Now*, Victoria."

We begin climbing, our footfalls echoing loudly in the confined space of the stairwell.

Scritch-scratch.

The stone steps beneath our feet are damp and slick. As we reach the halfway mark, I feel the next step crumble beneath my right foot and lose my balance. I stumble into Victoria and almost knock her over. She cries out, and we cleave to each other in the gloom for support.

"Sorry," I say, "the damn step just crumbled away."

Victoria takes a sharp intake of breath. "I don't think it crumbled," she says in a tense whisper. "It *moved*."

"Moved?" I can't quite get a handle on what she means, but then I look down and see it.

Scritch-scratch.

The bricks that form the steps are moving. Undulating, in the same way that soil moves when something is burrowing to the surface. And I know now that something is moving to the surface of the clock tower steps. Something cold. Something gray, and relentlessly malignant.

"Let's go back?" Victoria says, panicking.

I glance back the way we came. I can see them, their white eyes in the darkness as they stumble and crawl up the steps after us.

"We can't," I say, hoping that Victoria won't look back, but she does.

She screams, and the sharp sound in the claustrophobic confines of the stairwell is like a starter pistol that wills me to act against this new nightmare.

I grab her wrist and pull her with me as I push on up the stairs. Each one moves beneath my feet, willing me to fall and break my neck – and Victoria's too.

Only three more steps to go now. I can see the light from the night sky bleeding out across the stone landing at the summit of the stairs.

Two more steps and I've broken into a run now. The less time my feet are on the steps, the better. I actually manage to use the insane movement of the bricks to my advantage. As I feel them move upward beneath my foot, I use that movement as a springboard to the next, and final, step.

"Last one!" I shout.

Victoria stumbles, but I dig in and just about manage to hold her upright, dragging her across the threshold and into the clock tower.

We fall, sprawling onto the cold stone floor. I unclasp my hand from Victoria's wrist so that I can break my fall. She twists her body sideways to land beside me, the impact against the hard floor knocking the breath from her body in a last gasp. I feel a sharp stab of pain at my hip and I wonder why. I roll over onto my back and move my hand down to my pocket. The little music box is still there where I tucked it away earlier. No wonder it hurt when I fell; the thing is made of metal.

For a few moments there's silence, save for our labored breathing. As we both catch our breath, I become aware of the wind that buffets the interior of the clock tower room as it blows through the open arched windows.

I clamber to my feet and help Victoria to hers. We both dust ourselves down, and Victoria inspects a raw-looking scrape on her knee. It looks sore. She must have caught it against the top step as she lost her footing. She spits on the fingertips of her right hand and rubs the spittle into the wound.

"Best antiseptic known to humankind," she says after she realizes I'm watching her.

"Really?" I ask.

Victoria nods.

I have never heard this wisdom before. With all the bacteria swimming around in the human body, I find it difficult to believe that saliva isn't going to achieve much else other than making her wound ten times worse. I'm about to say as much when I see a look of fresh terror on Victoria's face.

The gray girl is with us in the clock tower.

She stands in one of the windowless alcoves, her tangled hair blowing forward over her face, teetering on the precipice. It's just how I saw her in my dream, and I feel ever colder at the memory of it. Then I see the gray girl quiver slightly, and I realize that she's sobbing.

I move through the wind, which whips at the ends of my hair, and Victoria reaches out to grab hold of my sleeve, intent on stopping me from taking another step.

"Emily! Don't go near her! She'll—"

Victoria's voice falters. I look her in the eye and see pure fear embedded there.

"It's okay," I venture, wondering if I even sound convincing.

"Don't—"

I pull away from Victoria and approach the gray girl.

As I walk slowly toward her, I retrieve the music box from my pocket and place it in the center of my palm. I hold it aloft so the girl can see it. It's like a totem. An offering. I turn the handle slightly and the music box chimes. The gray girl's entire body snaps to attention at the sound. She stops quivering, poised in the archway and as still as a statue.

"You don't have to do it," I tell her. "You don't have to be angry anymore."

I turn the handle slightly again, and the damaged little music box emits more chimes. The girl cocks her head to one side with all the animalistic curiosity of a bird of prey circling a scurrying morsel far below.

I clear my throat to speak again. And I try to focus on an image. The gray girl and the wall of the reformatory as one. The way she emerged from concrete and dust as a living, yet not living, thing. Her doomed birth's only purpose to haunt us again and again.

"I think you're trapped here," I say, "for whatever reason, but you don't have to be. We can all leave here together."

I see a flash of something from behind her dark curtain of hair. Her eyes, twinkling in an echo of the exposed metal casing of the music box.

I keep moving toward her, peering at her and trying to discern any human expression in those eyes. The wind blows and parts her hair for just a second, and I see her eyes flash with a look of malevolence. And something else—

Recognition?

—and then she bares her stained teeth as her mouth forms a hateful snarl.

She leaps from the archway, right at me.

Victoria shrieks.

Still holding the music box out in front of me, I shield my eyes with my other hand. I hear her feet hit the stone floor. Hear her run the short distance it will take to attack me. The wind gusts around and into me, impossibly cold, and I wonder if it is the wind after all or her spectral force that chills me to my core. I feel her freezing hand swipe the music box from my hand. Hear it clatter to the floor. My face is blasted by a freezing tumult of wind that seems to pass right through me. I force my hand away from eyes, expecting to see her standing a hair's breadth from my face—

But she's gone.

Victoria stops shrieking.

I turn and see her crouching in unutterable horror on the floor. The gray girl stands over her, indomitable. The discarded music box rings out in one last discordant chime before falling silent. Pale hands emerge from the darkness and I see Saffy, Annie and Jess close in around Victoria. They latch on to her, their bony fingers digging deep. Annie laughs, a horrid guttural sound made all the more hideous by her twisted neck. Saffy drips fetid swimming pool water over Victoria as she entwines her fingers around her wrist. Jess grips the other in her blood-encrusted hands. Victoria screams, struggles and yells at them to let her go, to please stop, but they're deaf to her pleas.

The gray girl nods at her undead foot soldiers and Saffy clamps a wet hand over Victoria's mouth, turning her protests into a single, muffled cry for help. Victoria claws at the air, desperate, and I realize that Saffy is suffocating her.

But it's their ringleader who poses the worst threat.

Victoria's eyes open wider as the gray girl looms over her and then swoops down. She clamps her hands on either side of Victoria's head, an eerie hissing sound emanating from between her foul teeth.

Victoria's legs kick out on the stone floor spasmodically.

Saffy's face contorts into a hideous grin of cruel pleasure. Her hand drips wet over Victoria's mouth. I hear a disgusting gurgle come from Victoria's throat and I wonder if Saffy is somehow drowning her where she is being held, pinioned by four spiteful phantoms.

I have to help her.

"No," I say. "Leave her alone."

But I don't think they can even hear me through the intensity of their single-minded hate. And even if they could, they would pay no heed to me.

But maybe Victoria can.

If she can hear me through her fear, she might fight back. I know I did when we fought side by side in the corridor.

"No!" I shout.

And I see Victoria writhing against them. She manages to move her head, first to one side, then the other. She wriggles some more and breaks free of Saffy's grasp for just a second. Then Victoria bites down, hard, on Saffy's hand—

(*Atta girl!*)

—and, even in that limbo state between life and death, Saffy can apparently feel pain because she howls and withdraws her hand. The gray girl snaps her head around, looking over her shoulder at me, that sharp twinkle in her eyes describing pure hatred. But Victoria's brave fight is all for nothing. The gray girl's hands are still clamped firmly on either side of Victoria's head.

"Leave me, Emily. Run!" Victoria says.

And then, with a muffled splash of liquid, Saffy clamps her other hand over Victoria's mouth.

But somehow, despite this assault, Victoria keeps speaking.

"I'm dead already," she says, her voice decisive and clear, "just like my case file says. I died in the gas explosion."

I feel sick to my stomach when I realize that I'm hearing Victoria's voice, but that it's coming from the gray girl's lips. It's as though the mere contact of her hands is allowing her to be inside of Victoria's head.

"I said you don't have to do this anymore," I say. "Stop now. Let her go and we can all go."

The gray girl grins through dark strands of hair and then speaks again, in Victoria's voice. "I killed my family, Emily. I'm...dead...already...."

I can see now that Victoria's losing the fight. She can't breathe. All the color drains from her face. Her legs flail beneath her, and then stop moving. I look at the quartet of phantoms holding her down. They're abusing her with their spite, and draining her of life.

And I know what I must do.

CHAPTER TWENTY-TWO

Nature Versus Nurture

The gray girl looks almost as surprised as I feel when I reach her.

I don't have a plan as such, nothing as noble, nor as fancy as that. I just have a – well, I guess you might call it an instinct. I've been watching her, you see, the way the gray girl's hands clamped around Victoria's head seemed to be the tipping point for her victim to begin losing the fight. And I wonder if I can turn a negative into a positive, somehow.

It's worth a shot.

We're trapped up here in the clock tower after all. Nowhere else to go. The only survivable exit is blocked by the four hideous un-dead things that are attacking Victoria. And I know that when they're done tormenting her to death, I'll be next in line.

She's coming for you, they kept saying as they pursued us to this dreadful, lonely tower. And you know what? I'm not even sure if they meant it collectively. I suspect that I'm the main course in their murderous feast, and Victoria is just the appetizer. So I have to intervene to stop them from killing Victoria. Together, we might have a chance.

Like I said, it's worth a shot.

I have the element of surprise. Dead girls don't expect you to rush them, I guess. Annie didn't, in the corridor earlier, and she was thrown down on her face. I'm hoping what I'm about to do next will have a similar effect, but on their ringleader, and she seems infinitely more powerful. Victoria was at my side to help overthrow Annie. I'm on my own facing the gray girl. But now is not the time for self-doubt.

Now is the time for decisive action.

I slam the palms of my hands on either side of the gray girl's head. Her hair feels as slick and cold as pondweed beneath my skin. She's real to my touch, and reality can hurt. She twists around against my grip until she's facing me, her dark eyes registering surprise—

(Yeah! Surprise, bitch!)

—through the dank strands of her cemetery hair. She bares her disgusting, yellow teeth and I can smell her. She stinks to high heaven of the grave, of rot, and of ruin. I dig my fingernails into her head, just behind her ears. She jolts, and snarls in pain. What a sound she makes – a dying animal. And she loses her grip on Victoria, just as I hoped she would. Without a second thought, I lash out with my left foot. I feel Saffy's face, soft beneath the sole of my shoe. She emits a strangled cry as I knock her sprawling wetly back toward the staircase. I feel a surge of elation as Victoria stirs and then elbows Annie away. With only Jess to contend with now, Victoria manages to get to her feet. Jess still has hold of Victoria, but Victoria is fighting back. If my hands weren't otherwise occupied, I'd punch the air in triumph.

But my elation quickly turns to fear as the gray girl starts fighting back, too.

She clamps her rotten teeth together and begins twisting and writhing within the confines of my grip. Her hair is so slimy that I can feel her almost breaking free. If she gets loose, I know that she'll gain the upper hand, and too quickly for me to be able to do anything about it. I can't lose the advantage, not now that Victoria has managed to throw off a couple of the other girls.

I have to go on the offensive.

I grit my teeth and pull the gray girl's head toward mine. The struggle makes my arms burn from the effort of just keeping hold of her. The act of pulling her toward me is excruciatingly counterintuitive. Every fiber of my being is telling me to push her away, not to pull her closer. But I focus all my efforts to get on with the horrible task that is – quite literally – in hand. It's working. And, even though it's an almighty, almost superhuman struggle, I manage to pull her closer to me.

All the blood rushes to my head, and I feel my temples almost bursting from the effort. I wonder if that's what she feels, too, as I grip her head ever tighter and pull it toward mine. I wonder if she can feel anything at all. She growls, and the sound makes me think that the only thing she must feel is hatred. I smell the ripe decay escape from between her dead lips and almost gag at the stench. I have to fight against hate, whatever the cost. And what's the opposite of hate? I redouble my efforts and lean my body closer to hers.

Until our foreheads touch.

There's a sonic boom inside my head.

A psychic blast.

So much pain, and so much fury that it shatters the fragile mirror of my mind.

No, of *our* minds.

It's insane.

I can see myself through her eyes, and I can see her through mine, all at the same time, overlapping and separating, and overlapping again, until…we are one, but not the same. The intensity of it rocks me from my physical reality, shocking every nerve ending in my body into submission. And I feel like I've been ripped from my body. I'm cut adrift in the cloying air of the clock tower, my sense of being divided into a mad sprawl of untethered atoms. I wonder if the wind that still blows steadily through the open arches will blow me away.

Then I hear a ringing sound and it's so distinct, and so musical, that I wonder if the clock tower has a bell that I simply haven't noticed before.

It takes me a few moments to focus on the sound. And when I do, I realize that it's coming from the discarded music box. The discordant chimes seem to grow louder as I concentrate on their source. I've heard this tune before, but there's a different quality to it now. As it plays on, I realize that the chimes are playing backward. And with that realization comes another sound.

Tock-tick.

The clock tower clock starts ticking in time with the music box chimes, also in reverse. The effect is such that the sounds seem to draw the air from around me with each shuddering, backward, *tock* and *tick*.

God, the chiming in my head is so loud now, it's deafening.

And my feet start moving in time with each *tock-tick*. I look down and see that I'm walking backward, but I can't feel my feet or my legs. It's as though I'm floating above the floor as I move. It's a horrible sensation, because all the while I am reminded of the drop from the open archways.

Then I come to a halt.

I'm standing in the open archway looking out over the wilderness at night. I can see my breath in front of my face, only it *isn't* my breath – and it's moving in reverse. The whole world seems to change, subtly. The black night sky beyond the clock tower arches becomes dark blue. I realize that I'm watching sunset – in reverse. The deep blue sky turns magenta around me, and then brightens to a pale gray. Clouds drift by, unnaturally fast, as impossible afternoon light creeps in around me.

Or rather, around *us*.

I can feel her shadow.

It envelops me like a cloak. The gray girl is standing here with me. And not just that, but she's *inside* of me – and all *around* me. I can feel her. And the feeling is soul-shocking despair. A melancholy so deep that it's unfathomable. My vision swims and even though I can't feel their cold, bitter kisses against my cheeks, I know that tears are there. We're seeing through each other's eyes and as I – as *we* – glance down at the ground far below, I know what's coming and I'm powerless to stop it.

And we fall.

Into the rush of air that leads to the impermeable finality of hard earth.

We fall.

And keep falling.

That discordant ringing in my ears subsides as we plummet from the tower until there's only a sharp intake of breath. Mine, or hers, I'm not sure.

And then—

I'm sitting—

We're sitting—

In Principal Quick's office.

Her manuscript lays open on the desk. 'Girl A'. She made us her case study. But she's barely started writing it. There are only a few pages. This must be a long time ago. We're not sure because we don't know how the past feels. We've been living the next day for so long now.

Sunlight streams in through the window. She's smiling at us. Holding something up to the light. The light catches her eyes and they sparkle. She's saying something to us and we do try to focus but we're drifting again. We're neither out nor in of this little room and its private meeting. We gaze at how the sunlight makes dust motes look so very pretty as they float across its beam, like fireflies. The window is open, just a crack, and the breeze that blows in from outside smells like Pease Blossom. Principal Quick places the something on the desk in front of us. We recognize the shape and the logo emblazoned on it. It's a carton of cigarettes.

We hear her voice, then. It is soft and melodic. A voice describing a dream state.

(Are we hypnotized? It feels like we're hypnotized.)

"Take them. Use them. They are currency in this place, and the dividend is friendship. Buy their confidence with them, one cigarette at a time. Tell me what they tell you. In strictest confidence, of course. Run along now."

We run along, though we can't remember leaving Principal

Quick's office. We run along to the recreation yard. We pretend that we managed to steal the cigarettes. Aren't we clever? The others are highly amused by us. Especially Saffy. She smokes two back-to-back. Even puts her arm around us at one point. It seems to be working. We listen hard to everything she says so that we can remember it and then tell it all to Principal Quick. In strictest confidence, of course.

Yes, she made us her case study all right. 'Nature versus nurture'. It says so in her book. We have a sneak peek when she's pretending not to look the next time we're in her office. And she gives us more cigarettes, more instructions. We follow. And they give us what we think Principal Quick wants. Only they don't tell us the truth, they tell us lies. We don't know that yet. They pretend to be our friends, but they're not. We don't know that yet, either. We won't notice their conspiratorial smiles until it's too late.

"Happy Birthday," Principal Quick tells us, so it must be.

We don't recall having had birthdays before, so we remain quiet. We watch as Quick opens her desk drawer and reaches into it.

"I got you a gift," she says. "I hope you like it." And her eyes twinkle, even though the sun isn't shining today.

We wonder if the gift will be more cigarettes. We hope so, because we like it when the others are our friends. It's a good feeling when they confide in us like they do. Spill their secrets beneath a cloud of tobacco smoke. Allow us to join in when they torment one of the others. It feels kind of grown up, you know, fitting in like this? It feels like friendship. And that friendship feels more real than anything else.

"Happy birthday," the principal repeats. "You're doing so very well. And I'm so very proud of you."

She reaches over the desk and ruffles our hair. We laugh along because we feel how a pet dog might feel, only not as unconditionally grateful. Principal Quick misinterprets our laughter, of course, perhaps because this is the only tenderness she's ever shown. She reaches out again. There's a good little doggy. But this time, we recoil from her touch.

"You can't make me snitch on my friends anymore," we say.

We still have our bite as well as our bark, you see.

Principal Quick almost looks hurt for a moment, and then looks indignant. The sparkle in her eyes solidifies into ice.

"They're not your friends. You don't *have* any friends. You only have me. Your mother." She withdraws from us and paces the small expanse of floor behind her desk.

We tell ourselves it's not true. We spend more time with them than we ever do with her. They know us, the *real* us. She doesn't. Whatever she's writing in her book barely even scratches the surface of who we really are. Which is weird in a way, because by forcing us to play inmate with them, she has made us into what we are now. One of the sisterhood. A girl amongst girls-behind-bars.

She sighs, then speaks again. "I remind you that your father didn't want to know. He walked out on me – walked out on the both of us – just as soon as he found out I was carrying you." She pauses at the framed picture on the wall. Her graduation day. Her professor, and her former lover. "You want me to look after you, don't you? Studying your disorder will make us both rich. We'll show your neglectful bastard of a father what we can achieve. A new life, far from here. And you can have more new friends to play with than a thousand cigarettes can buy. You'd like that, wouldn't you?"

Oh yes, my disorder. Or is it *our* disorder? No, mine. All mine. I've been thinking about that. What if I didn't have a disorder until she decided to imprison me here with them? I never committed any crime. Never did anything wrong. Recently, in our office sessions, she's told me that I did. That I just can't remember. But I don't believe her. I think every time she hypnotizes me, she makes me more forgetful, more befuddled. I'm not one hundred percent about it, but I think the ringing in my ears began soon after she started putting me under. I look at the smirk on her tight lips and I think—

(You *did this to me.* You *made me like this.*)

—I would have been fine if she had just let me go. And it's such a clarifying thought. Just let me be a normal girl, on the outside of this forgotten place with all its fragile and forgotten fuck-ups. Well, now I'm one of them. And for what?

I see her absentmindedly run her fingertips across the surface of her book. The manuscript looks fuller now. The pages have multiplied as Principal Quick has unpacked each day we've spent behind bars. Incarcerated even though I…even though *we* have done nothing wrong. Nothing except the accident that was our birth. We wonder if we ever really were 'Emily'. Maybe for a little while? Until the rot set in. Until Quick's anger and resentment took hold and she saw fit to weaponize us against our father. Against the world. 'Girl A'. That's us. She doesn't love us. Not really. We are just her ticket out of here. Each day of our lives more empty words for her best seller. She wanted to see how we'd react to being institutionalized with a criminal element. Well, the damage is already done. She gave us our disorder. And our disorder made us begin to shut down just as soon as we became aware of the betrayal.

Be careful what you wish for, I guess.

We leave her smirking face in her office and go back to the dormitory. The little music box is hidden in our pocket. A birthday present we can never use, because if we do, they'll know what we are, and what we've been doing, and who we've been doing it for.

They're waiting for us when we return. Saffy and the others. She sits cross-legged on her bed, flanked by Victoria, Lena, and Annie.

"How was your little one-to-one session with teacher?" Saffy says, and there's something crueler than ever in her voice, so I don't answer. I just swallow and wonder why my throat is so dry.

I'm on my own here. Vulnerable.

"Did she give you any cigarettes this time?" Saffy asks. She chuckles mirthlessly, and the others join in.

"I don't..." I begin.

But I can see it on their faces. They know I've been snitching on them the whole time, telling Principal Quick everything they have confided to me in the dark. And it's then that I realize my throat is dry because I'm shit-scared.

"Grab her, girls," Saffy says.

Their hands are on me in a flash. Their fingernails dig into my flesh. I know that bruises will form where they twist my wrists painfully as they drag me over to where Saffy still sits, patiently waiting. She looks at me pityingly, then slaps me hard across the face. I taste blood on my lip and know that she's split it with her first blow. Then the others rain down hard on me with fists, nails, and – as I curl up to protect myself on the floor – feet. My whole body becomes numb as they punch, and kick, and scratch. Their laughter rings in my ears. I try to call out for help, but I know she won't come. This is just another part of the narrative in her book. Part of my life story as an inmate of her fucked-up reformatory. And the ringing laughter becomes a series of musical chimes. They've found the music box. Saffy holds it up close to my face so I can see it, even though my vision is blurred by my tears.

"Give you this, did she? For being a good little snitch-bitch?"

Saffy turns the handle, faster and faster, until the music chimes become a parody of music, notes flying off the handle. Then she stands over me. She drops the music box to the floor and stamps on it. The others laugh. Somebody spits and I feel it warm on my face.

Then they drag me into the bathroom. Saffy goads them on, telling them to take me to the mirror. They hold my head up by my hair and I can feel it being torn from my scalp. They make me look at myself.

"Take a long, hard look, bitch." Saffy grips my chin and holds it up.

I can see myself in the mirror, but I don't recognize my face through the blood.

"You're not 'one of us'," she says, her hateful mouth intimately close to my ear. "You're nothing. You're pathetic. And mark my words. Each and every day you spend with us in this shithole will be – from now on – a living hell." She unclamps her hand from my jaw, letting my head drop. "Flush her, girls."

They drag me into the nearest bathroom stall and force me to my knees. I try to breathe before they push my face into the toilet bowl, but the wind is knocked from out of me. My gasp is cut off as a torrent of cold water drowns my face. When it's over, they drag me to the next stall and flush my head under the water again. And again, and again, until I'm in the last stall. Then they leave me, broken, drenched, and spluttering water. All except Saffy, who pauses for a moment before throwing the crumpled music box at me. I'm too numb to feel its impact. It clatters to the tiled floor beside me and Saffy saunters out. I hear the door shut behind her and I try to scream. But no sound will come. So I scream in silence. Over and over, until I can't any more. I remain where I am, curled up on the floor, unable and unwilling to move.

And then I see her.

One of the girls is still in the bathroom. I can see her feet under the gap in the stall. She's just standing there, in the bathroom. I wonder if one of the girls is going to give me another kicking. They certainly aren't here to help. No one helps. I lie there for what feels like an age. Then, as the feeling begins to return to my body, I feel pinpricks of pain where they've injured me. I struggle to my feet. The room tilts because my head is swimming from their blows, and from the water. I stumble out of the stall toward the motionless girl. Her hair hides her face. I reach for her, hoping she'll help me to walk out of here. But as I do so she moves – almost drifts – to the door. I follow, my feet slipping and sliding on the tiles.

I emerge into the dormitory.

They're all asleep in their beds. A shaft of brilliant moonlight illuminates my empty bed and for a moment I consider climbing in and curling up to sleep there. But the strange girl, her pallid skin a deathly gray in the moonlight, stands over by the door. I feel a strong sensation as I look at her, one that I can only describe as a kind of bond between us. It's as though there's an invisible rope connecting us and whenever she moves, I have to follow. Like schoolchildren roped together in the snow so they won't get lost. She moves again, and I follow, leaving the softly snoring girls behind.

I'm in the corridor, and the pain from my injuries really takes hold. My right leg falters where it's been kicked and I support myself against the wall. I can hear my heartbeat in my head. I take deep breaths, the strange girl waiting for me up ahead, and when I take my hands away from the wall I see that I've left bloody handprints there. I didn't know I had so much blood in me.

It's okay, she seems to say, and it's totally weird because she does it without actually speaking. *We can go somewhere they'll never find you. Somewhere they can't hurt you again.*

Oh, but I'd like that. That would be a *real* birthday present. One to treasure forever. So I follow blindly on and feel my mouth curl into a smile. My split lip spills more blood down my chin, but I don't care. If anything, it just means that I'm still alive.

We turn a corner into the next corridor and I see the recreation yard through the windows. As I limp past it, I admire the twisted shape of the dead tree beneath which I'd sat so many times with Saffy and the others, smoking and feeling like I was part of something. One of the girls. A fellow inmate. But I know that was all a lie, so I move on. I feel the tug of that invisible rope guiding me. After a while, I follow the gray girl to an opening in the wall of the next corridor and realize where she has brought me.

The clock tower stairs.

Of course. We can be alone up there. No one goes – not even Saffy. It's out of bounds. My silent guide goes first and it strikes me how strange it is that she seems to walk without really moving.

We reach the top, and the pain racking my broken and bruised body is excruciating. I hear a horribly distorted chime. Strange, I wasn't even aware that I had picked up the music box, let alone carried it with me all this way. And yet, here it is. A broken birthday present for a broken life. I hurl it to the floor and stamp on it, just as they did. With each stomp, the box lets out an agonized little chime. I want to put it out of its misery. When I'm done, I see her standing in one of the open archways. The wind ruffles her hair and I see a flash of intent in her dark eyes. The invisible rope pulls me toward her, and I go willingly because right now she's all I have.

I climb up next to her.

She wraps herself around me, a cold cloak made of night.

And together we fall.

As we tumble together into space, I see the rage in her eyes. And the despair. And I know that she's my dark mirror. Too late, I understand that she's made a victim of me. And that I've made a victim of myself. And, even as we plummet toward the hard ground below, I begin to fight back. But she grips me tightly in her melancholic tourniquet. I rail against her, pummeling her frozen, un-dead body with my bloody fists. But she won't let me go. And the wind whistles ever louder in my ears until it howls at fever pitch. We fall faster and harder, conjoined twins dragged down by the sheer weight of despair.

And we're going to hit the ground.

I scream.

CHAPTER TWENTY-THREE

A Shadow Self Revealed

I slam down onto solid ground.

But not *the* ground. I'm standing once again in the clock tower room, its aged stone floor beneath me.

And she's right in front of me. The gray girl.

Our foreheads are pressed together so firmly that it feels as though our flesh is fusing. I rock on my feet, and she moves against me, a perfect mirror of my actions. I circle around, walking on the balls of my feet, and she follows my trajectory. We're like two rutting stags with our horns locked. And then she's pushing against me, and she's stronger, so much stronger. I try to push back, but my feet slide across the stone floor and I'm forced to take rapid steps backward. I cry out at the force.

"Emily!"

Victoria is near, I can tell from the sound of her voice. I can't see her, because the gray girl is blocking my line of sight. But then I see Victoria's hand at the gray girl's shoulder. She's trying desperately to separate us. But it's no use. The gray girl is just too strong. She hisses between her stinking teeth and swipes at Victoria with her left hand. Victoria is swatted away like a fly. I manage to pivot around so that I can see Victoria. She's on the floor, her hand pressed to her forehead where the gray girl struck her.

And then something moves behind her.

A sickly, crawling form lunges from over the lip of the staircase. It scuttles across the floor in horrid, jerking movements.

As it reaches Victoria and clutches at her hair and clothing, I see it for what it is and realize with terror that this is – or was – Lena. The pockmarked skin on her arms oozes black filth from each of a hundred or more needle punctures. She opens her mouth in a gleeful snarl, and more fetid black ooze trickles out. Victoria screams in horror as Lena's vile cadaver envelops her in its corrupt limbs.

But there's nothing I can do to help her.

Seeing my fear, the gray girl propels her body forward like a battering ram. I skid and slide backward, all too aware of the open archway – and the deadly drop – behind me. I'm losing ground, but I can't lose the struggle. Not now. Not now that I've remembered some of what happened to us – to me.

I redouble my efforts.

"I'm not afraid of you," I say, and I really do mean it.

I slam my hands down on her shoulders, clutching them tight.

The gray girl seems to lose some energy from this. *Good.* I push back and feel her give a little. She is rage, and despair, for certain. But she is also fear. And the thing about fear is that if you deny it, it has nowhere else to go. It has to fold back in on itself. Devour itself. Fear, I think, lives in fear of being rumbled. Of being found out. So long as we're in its grip, well that's fine, isn't it? Fear has taken hold of you. But when you rise above it – what then? You have the opposite of fear, that's what? And as I formulate these thoughts I push back harder still – until I have the upper hand.

"I'm not afraid of you," I go on, "because you're me. And I'm you. If I can love myself for what I truly am, then you don't have any purpose anymore. And *that* is the opposite of fear. And in the spirit of all that, dear sister, I release you."

I headbutt her away from me.

The impact knocks her back. Her hair moves from her face. And for a moment – just a split second, really – I'm looking at a dark reflection of my own face. A deathly gray, mirror image. A shadow self, revealed.

She looks shocked, then appalled. Lost, even.

Then her gray face mutates into a hideous, twisted mask of hatred and anguish. Her mouth contorts, issuing forth a hiss of pure rage. She charges at me.

"No!" I hear raw terror in Victoria's cry and I don't know if she's crying out for her life, or mine, or both. But I swallow that terror. I make it a mere discordant musical note in my mind. The death knell of fear itself. I don't feel anything except serenity. I close my eyes and hold my arms out wide, ready to embrace my dark sister.

And a cold wind blows right through me.

Because that is *all* she is, after all.

I open my eyes and turn to see her. She's frozen in time, framed in the moonlit archway. There's a mere second of realization in her angry, blazing eyes.

And then she plummets from the tower.

Everything stops dead. Victoria's cries of terror, Lena's feral snarls, and all of the sound and all of the fury, gone.

I falter. It's like something has been ripped from inside of me – all the adrenaline and urgency. My legs give way, but then someone is at my side, supporting me, and I don't fall. Not this time.

"Thank you," Victoria says.

I glance around the tower and see that we're alone. Lena and the other hideous, groping phantoms have gone. Bad memories, scattered to the wind.

I nod. "I guess," I say.

"Really. Thank you, Emily. Without you, I think I would have been swallowed whole by what she made me feel. What she forced me to re-live. When you got between us like that.... Well, you inspired me not to give up. To fight back."

I don't know what to say. So – *you guessed it* – I say nothing.

"I thought you were going to fall," Victoria continues.

"So did I," I say, and that is the stone-cold, honest truth.

"I'm glad you didn't."

Now I *really don't* know what to say.

"Principal Quick was right about one thing," Victoria says.

"What's that?" I ask.

She rubs her sore head. "You learned something. By coming here. I think we both did."

I wonder what I learned. I think of Principal Quick's classroom, and of her words so elegantly inscribed on the blackboard there. The seven virtues. "My first step toward rehabilitation? My mother always said I still had a lot to learn."

Victoria looks puzzled by this, and then amused. "Well, I'm no expert," she says, "but I do think you're doing just fine." Then she adds, "I think you're the kindest person I've ever known."

We each put an arm around each other, and it feels like friendship. And it feels true. And it does feel good.

Together we stagger to the archway and peer over the edge.

The gray girl is nowhere to be seen.

I sense shadows gathering behind me and wonder if she's still lurking there. Ready to spring out from the shadows and push me over the edge again, just as she did in my nightmares. I turn to look, and find the tower really is empty and still.

The shadows really are only shadows.

CHAPTER TWENTY-FOUR

The Reformatory's Dark Heart

Together we descend the stone staircase from the clock tower. It's a struggle because we're both feeling battered and bruised after the events of the night. But dawn light glimmers through the high windows at the far end of the corridor and with it, the atmosphere in the reformatory feels changed. I wouldn't say that it's actually warm in here, but it's not as cold, either – if that makes sense?

I know that Victoria feels it too. She looks up and down the corridor with a serene expression on her face. She breathes in and out slowly and steadily, as if savoring the air. I try it too, and feel calmer already. It's hard to believe that just a short while ago we were being pursued in this very same corridor by visitors from beyond the grave, hell-bent on harming us.

Victoria must have caught the look on my face because she appears thoughtful and says, "Did it really happen?"

"Did what happen?"

"Saffy, Lena, and the others. Coming after us. That horrible gray girl. Attacking me like that." Victoria puts her hand to her head again, as if in a daydream. "It seemed so frightening and real back there, in the dark. But in the warm light of day I'm not so sure.... You know?"

"I know."

It is indeed the weirdest feeling in the world, but I also feel that our mutual understanding requires no further comment from either of us. Enjoying the silence, I watch the dawn light as it begins to creep slowly across the corridor floor, and then up the wall opposite us. The light sun-kisses the gray paintwork, giving it a peach-colored glow. A warm section of a rainbow. I walk toward the light, following its progress as it spreads.

"What's up?" Victoria asks.

"I just…I can't really explain, but I need to check something."

"Okay," Victoria says quietly and reassuringly. "Whatever you got to do, just do it."

I reach out and hesitate before my fingertips touch the wall.

The gray girl was as much a part of Greyfriars Reformatory as she was part of me. She was definitely gone from the clock tower, and we couldn't see her on the ground below it, but now I need to know if she's still part of this building. I take a breath and steel myself.

I place my fingers on the spot where the sunlight meets the gray of the wall, at the intersection between the light and the darkness. The wall feels cool and indifferent to my touch. And then, as the sunlight spreads across the rough surface, a warmth grows beneath my fingertips. There's no thrumming of energy anymore, only the settled molecules of bricks and mortar. The gray girl is no longer here, and it's as though some aspect of the building, the part that was alive, has died with her. The reformatory's dark heart has stopped beating.

I let my fingers fall from the wall and I turn to watch sunbeams dance further along the corridor. Eager to be amidst their warmth, I follow them.

"Where are you going now?" Victoria asks.

"To see," I reply.

"To see what?"

"To see what we can see," I say.

Victoria chuckles at that and begins following after me.

The reformatory is so quiet and still as we move through it that I almost feel the need to chat with Victoria to break the silence. But I do like the silence too. There's a clarity to it that I've

never noticed before. As we walk, I replay Principal Quick's—
 (*I still can't bring myself to think of her as 'Mother'.*)
—tour of the building in my mind. I remember how adrift I felt, and how the ringing in my ears was a bell calling me home, to my safe place in my psyche. I don't need it anymore. The silence is no longer threatening to me. If anything, it now feels calming. Ordinary. I begin to bask in that normality, and to focus on the sounds of our breathing, as I lead Victoria in the direction of the main entrance.

Our path takes us to the door of the med store. The door hangs open and I pause for a moment, and then look at Victoria. She nods, and that silent gesture gives me all the courage I need to step inside and check it out.

I find that it's empty. Lena is nowhere to be seen.

And not only that – someone has done one heck of a clean-up job in here. There are no hypodermic needles on the floor at all. I glance around at the shelves, with their boxes of bandages and other medical supplies. Everything is neatly packed away and organized. The place looks, and smells, dusty and unused.

"Weird," I say.

"Totally," Victoria replies.

She looks disturbed, and I'm not surprised by that. I feel it too, seeing the empty space where Lena had lain bleeding.

"Let's get out of here?" she asks, with a slight tremor in her voice.

"Yes. But I just want to check around the building first."

"Do we *have* to?"

"If Lena's not here then...."

It's difficult to articulate my feeling that the other girls might still be alive in the building and hiding somewhere. Luckily, I don't have to, because Victoria takes my hand and leads me out of the storeroom.

"We're near the recreation yard. We'll check it out, together. Agreed?"

"Agreed."

We begin walking in that direction.

"Emily, if we don't find Annie there – do you think that means – well, I don't know exactly, but do you think we might have completely lost our minds?"

"I'd be inclined to think so," I say.

"That is the most *Emily* answer I could ever have hoped for," she replies.

And I see that she has tears in her eyes but quickly brushes them away and attempts a laugh. It doesn't sound all that convincing, I have to admit.

We near the door to the recreation yard in what feels like no time at all. That lovely, peachy, orange light streams in through the windows. I pause as soon as I step into the light, and Victoria waits with me. We both look to each other for moral support before walking on through the door to the yard.

The tree is bare. No Annie, no jump rope, nothing. The way the bare branches of the tree describe twisted shapes against the dawn sky is something approaching beautiful. I've never seen it look that way before. As the clouds roll by, the sky becomes brighter with each second that passes. The small patch of soil beneath the tree glistens with morning dew, tiny beads of water, air, and twinkling light.

We move on and check the refectory, and then the kitchen. Both look completely untouched, just the same as the med store. Then we go to the dormitory and find the beds neatly made and lined up in rows. No sign of Jess, nor anyone else for that matter. Not one of the beds looks like it's been slept in, let alone used as a barricade against the forces of darkness trying to penetrate the door. The place really is empty, deserted. We're the only living souls here. And now there's only one place left on our itinerary.

Principal Quick's office.

I can tell from Victoria's body language as we approach

Principal Quick's office door that this is the room that scares her the most. And she has every right to be scared. I experience a vivid memory of Quick's dead body, puppet-walking down the length of corridor we're now standing in. I wince, remembering the terrifying way that her body dropped to the floor to reveal the insane puppet master that was the gray girl standing behind her. But I refuse to be rattled, so I don't dwell on such things. Instead, I choose to focus on the here and now. On the facts in the warm light of day:

The corridor is clear. Fact.

The bunch of keys that were dropped on the floor are nowhere to be seen. Fact.

Principal Quick's lifeless body is gone. Fact.

And the gray girl, too. All facts.

But if we want to get out of here, we do have to check the office first.

We both pause for breath at the door.

"Listen," I say, "we didn't find hide nor hair of the others. So we *know* Principal Quick isn't going to be in there, don't we?"

"Yes," Victoria says.

I wonder if she really believes it.

"But if she is," I say, "then we just get the hell out of there, together, okay?"

"Okay," she says, and I can see beads of sweat have formed on her brow.

We have to do this, and now, before either of us loses our nerve. So I grip the office door handle. I twist it and open the door.

We step into an unoccupied room.

The musty smell is gone. Principal Quick's manuscript lies open on her desk. Atop that, I see her bunch of keys. I walk over to the desk and retrieve them. As I grasp the keys, a passage from the exposed pages of the manuscript catches my attention—

Girl A is presenting something new and exciting to the field and treatment must be exploratory and experimental. It is my intention to expose the subject to an extensive program of hypnosis, alongside social experimentation built around my formative thesis on nurture/nature and the role that peer groups inform the retreating (and projected) self....

Words. They're just words. They're not me. I'm me. My thoughts and actions make me who I am. I'm no more a series of tests and measures than I am my own mother. And yet, I still can't shake the feeling that her thoughts and her actions still have some kind of a hold on me.

"Let's get out of here," I say, before closing the manuscript.

"One second," Victoria says, and then takes the phone from its cradle. She holds it to her ear and listens. "Line's still dead."

We're halfway to the door, when I see the closet door. It's closed. I stand still.

"Should we check in there, do you think?" I ask.

Victoria looks at the door for a moment, then at me. "Oh *fuck* no," she says.

I grip the keys tighter and we leave the office.

★ ★ ★

A couple of minutes later and we reach the front door. No phantoms on our tail, no ominous gray shapes moving from the shadows. The building's foyer feels bright and airy for the first time since I've been in the reformatory – starkly different to the rainy day when I made my bid for freedom and gave Principal Quick a well-deserved bloodied nose in the process. I picture her look of surprise as I outwitted her before sprinting off into the wilderness. Of course, her smug superiority had returned just as soon as I had, mud-bedraggled and soaked through from the rain. But that was then, and this is now. I rifle through the keys on the ring and try a few until I find the right one to unlock the door.

"Hit it," I say to Victoria, before nodding at the gate release button mounted on the wall.

Victoria reaches up and slams the flat of her hand against the button.

With a click of the final bolt I push the main door open and a shaft of daylight greets us.

"Shall we?" I ask.

"We shall," Victoria answers.

We link arms and step into the light.

CHAPTER TWENTY-FIVE

A Gap in the Clouds

It's been so long since I've exposed my eyes to raw, natural daylight that I have to blink tears away. I glance at Victoria and see that she's doing the same. Or maybe she's crying? Maybe both.

Whatever, it does feel truly wonderful to be outside and breathing the cool, fresh air of morning.

The main gates are wide open to the sweep of wilderness beyond, which looks verdant beneath a gap in the clouds. I take another restoring breath and prepare myself for a long walk ahead. With our arms still linked, we walk down the front steps.

It's only then that I notice them. Five ambulances are parked at the side of the building. They look pretty old, automotive relics from a forgotten decade. Each one has its rear doors wide open.

I stop with a crunch of gravel beneath my foot as I see two black-clad paramedics emerge from the side of the reformatory. They carry a stretcher between them. The unmistakable shape of a body lies beneath a white sheet. It has a cloud-like quality in the way it appears to float a few feet above the ground as they carry it over to one of the waiting ambulances.

Then another pair of paramedics, carrying another stretcher, emerges. This is followed by another, and another, until there are five stretchers in total. One for each waiting ambulance.

"Five of them," Victoria mutters.

I watch as each pair of medics loads the stretchers onto the ambulances.

"Jess, Saffy, Annie, Lena – and Principal Quick," I say, seeing the shapes of their bodies under the sheet-covered stretchers.

Their grim cargo stowed safely and silently away, the paramedics shut the rear doors and walk to the sides of the vehicles. They climb inside, almost in a synchronized dance of sorts, one in each passenger's seat, and one in each driver's seat.

It's a weird, and more than a little macabre, spectacle.

I unlink my arm from Victoria's and wander across the gravel toward the ambulances. As I do so, a hand grips my arm and pulls me back, almost toppling me. With a burst of engine noise, I see why. A large vehicle skids to a halt just inches from where we stand, kicking up dust and gravel. It's the prisoner transport bus – the same one that delivered us here. With a loud hiss, the door of the bus opens. The driver – also the same one that drove us here – sits at the wheel, staring straight ahead through the windscreen.

I look back through the dust at the ambulances. They're already moving off, each one peeling away as the other passes by until the convoy exits through the main gates. The cloud of dust has already made them indistinct, a fading memory.

I feel Victoria's hand in mine, and she's leading me onto the footplate of the bus.

"Who sent you for us?" I ask, as I climb aboard.

But the driver remains silent behind a pair of impenetrable aviator shades.

I follow Victoria toward the back of the bus and take a seat beside her.

The door hisses shut, and the entire vehicle rumbles so hard with the revving of the engine that it feels like we're in the belly of a mechanical whale. The driver circles around, past the still-open front doors of the reformatory, and we both take a look at the building for one last time. The dark doorway into the foyer reminds me of an open mouth, screaming.

* * *

Greyfriars Reformatory looks much smaller by the time the bus reaches the gates.

I turn my attention to the view out of the window. A drab, gray sky hangs heavy with rain clouds that look too miserable to burst. Inhospitable wilderness unfolds as far as my eyes can see. Still, I'd much rather be on this road than within the labyrinthine walls of the reformatory. I begin to relax a little and lean back in my seat.

Just then, I feel something at my breast. A little scrape. I tuck my fingers beneath my uniform and find the chrysalis there. I had forgotten all about it. I retrieve it from my clothing and cup it in my hand. It feels so warm and dry. It twitches slightly against my skin and I wonder if it's because of the movement of the bus.

Then, with amazement, I watch as it cracks, then splits open. The chrysalis becomes dust in my hand as a butterfly emerges from it. It flaps its new wings tentatively, testing them. They're golden like the sunrise. I laugh and turn to look at Victoria. She smiles, seeing it too. The brilliant creature flaps its wings fully, and darts up and away from my hand. I watch it flutter above the aisle to the very back of the bus. The butterfly escapes through an air vent.

Free.

I turn in my seat and catch a glimpse of the butterfly through the window opposite as the wind carries it away. Just then, there's a crack in the clouds. Brilliant sunlight washes over me, blinding me for a moment. I hold my hand over my eyes and see the countryside transformed by the sudden sunlight. It really is beautiful. So beautiful.

I turn back to Victoria to share the moment.

But she has vanished.

I look around the bus, but I'm alone. I stand up and walk toward the front of the bus, gripping the backs of the seats as I go.

"Did you see where she went? My friend?" I ask.

I know how completely ridiculous, and pathetic, my question must sound. The driver neglects to answer me anyway. The bus jolts to one side as the driver navigates a sharp bend in the road and I'm thrown sideways. I manage to grab a hold of a handrail to prevent myself from falling. As the driver course-corrects, I decide to return to my seat.

I hunker down in the seat where Victoria was sitting. It feels cold, now that I'm alone.

I stare out at the wilderness.

Dark clouds gather again.

Dusk begins to fall.

CHAPTER TWENTY-SIX

Principal Quick

Principal Quick stared at the blank sheet of paper, but still the words would not come. After a heavy sigh, she dropped the pen onto her desk, casting it aside like some damaged and useless limb. She put her hands to her temples and rubbed them with her fingertips in a vain attempt to subdue the tension headache that was brewing there.

She glanced at the closet. Visualized the vodka bottle hidden on the bookshelf. Imagined how easily it would slide down, each swallow numbing the pain inside of her head. But if she started, she wouldn't be able to stop, and she couldn't risk that right now. It would only be another long night of self-recrimination and self-loathing. Yet another night when her word count drifted into the negative.

Christ, why wouldn't this headache go away?

All the old worries started coming back. Someone else would beat her to it, pull the research rug from beneath her feet and publish their findings first. It had happened so many times before, to academics she once knew, before she had exiled herself at Greyfriars. They had tended to give up afterward. They never seemed to have the same bright spark anymore. After being usurped – by a man, it was always a man – they had settled into teaching positions that were beneath them, and took out their bitterness on the doctoral researchers under their care. Perhaps they were right to do so, let the poor saps know disappointment and critical rejection before the real world sank its teeth into them. Grooming them to fail.

Was that what she was doing? Quick wondered if it was.

William Drake had been a wonderful supervisor at first. They had laughed a lot during their progress meetings. He had never let her dupe herself by submitting substandard research, and always picked her up on her referencing – a weak point if ever she had one. And that hadn't been the only one. He had acted with professional decorum throughout her research period. She had fought her feelings for him at first, too, unwilling to become the clichéd starstruck student. And she was never starstruck. If anything, she felt sorry for him. He seemed only to have his work and nothing else. But he did have a dazzling mind, and that was irresistible to her magpie mentality. She had identified that as a trait during her undergrad years, when she collected a series of partners and then discarded them just as soon as she had identified what made them tick. Convincing herself that it was going to be different with William had been all too easy. The age difference framed things differently for a start. She knew this was not a partnership based on physicality. Difficult to feel aroused when he made that 'old man' sound whenever he sat down, the symptom of a botched disc operation when he was younger and from which he had never recovered – and never would recover. Easy to feel differently when they chatted until the wee hours of the morning, initially online in the guise of an extended tutorial, and eventually – after she had graduated – in bed. Another damn cliché, but William really had been a warm blanket.

And then he had torn it away from her, and left her cold and alone.

How she hadn't seen it coming was perhaps the source of all the bile she now felt in later life. She had been so sure of him, and of her skills in reading him, that she had missed the signs. The way he often looked to the window while he was 'listening' to her. She had convinced herself that he hung on her every word – the curse of the researcher who is too close to her material to see anything else – when really he had just been biding his time. His endgame, of course, was to steal her research. To repurpose it and dress it up as his own. He had been so careful, and she had only made it easier for him. When they had attended a drinks reception together after a research seminar, he had introduced her to other seasoned academics as his 'assistant'. Jesus Christ! And she stood there and smiled politely along with them. What a fucking sap love had made of her. Only now, in stark retrospect, could she see behind their sardonic smiles. They all must have been thinking she was sleeping with him for grade inflation. And she wasn't,

she wasn't,

she wasn't.

Was she?

Quick stood before the closet door and realized she hadn't been aware that she had strolled over to it. Disturbing. It was almost as though she was disassociating from the present the more she dwelled upon the past. Which was pretty laughable when she thought about it, given her methodologies toward her daughter's treatment. Maybe she should hypnotize herself and ask herself probing questions about her motivations. She laughed, and then felt the tears forming in her eyes. She sobbed at the void in her heart and slammed the flat of her hand against the closet door, fighting what awaited her on the shelf inside. Quick folded her hurt inside of her. She had learned to do that soon after William's rejection, and now had it down to a fine art. She imagined her tears withdrawing back into her body, an outpouring of grief in reverse. Visualized each tear solidifying and curving into a black thorn. She allowed these dark barbs to hook into her insides, gouging away at her being until she was full of blood and rage again. Like she had been that night after he had referred to her as his assistant, in public, and after all the intimacies they had shared. His introduction had rattled her, it had been so unforgivably fucking patronizing, and it had sparked a blazing row between them later. She respected him the least when he was dishonest in his answers.

Quick had frozen him out for a couple of days after that, until he called her late one night and apologized. He had told her exactly what she had wanted to hear – that he had been floored by the depth of his feelings for her, and that he hadn't wanted anyone to figure them out. Not yet, anyway. He had told everyone she was helping him with research not to belittle her – oh no – but rather so that he could justify being with her so much, and so often. She had melted, and their bond seemed even stronger after that. Because that is how psychological abuse works, by dressing up misdemeanors against you as benefits. Yes, actual benefits. It would have been more honest of him to have said, "You know, dear…"

(*She had liked how he had called her dear – up until that moment.*)

"…it really is in your own best interests to be my subordinate. Everyone will believe that our relationship is purely professional that way."

Well, fuck him. And fuck the patriarchal academy. Fuck them all to fucking hell.

Where was she?

Oh, yes. She was on to something with her research. She'd be an incendiary device going off in his face. He'd see her name everywhere. She'd be at every conference, would deliver every keynote, and he (and his new 'assistant', the latest in a rapid succession of other poor saps) would either have to send their apologies, or suck it the fuck up.

She was feeling better already. The curse words definitely helped. And the closet door was remaining shut.

After wandering back to her desk, she paused and looked at the photograph on the wall. A constant reminder of a different time, and of a different woman. She had left it hanging there for its motivational qualities. To reach. To do better. His smile was nothing more than a dark slit to her now. And she'd wipe away that smile forever when she was done.

She reminded herself how far she had come. From the grief-stricken wreck she had been after that night. She had dressed in his favorite outfit, styled her hair in the way that she had long since outgrown, but which she knew would remind him of the first heat of their relationship. All of this because the news that she had to tell him that night would change their lives. He hadn't seemed to even notice what she was wearing, or what an effort she had made for him. He seemed more distracted than ever, because he had been, of course. Probably lining up his next protégé. But she had been too blind to see it. She had made a show of refusing a drink – completely out of character, that should have been a big-ass clue, but nope, he hadn't even blinked – and had sat down at his behest. He had returned to his laptop then, clearly in the middle of typing something. An email? An instant message to her incoming successor? She had already been on the off-ramp and she hadn't even realized it. If there were doctorates in naiveté she would have defended her viva voce with flying colors.

And he had laughed when she told him. Actually laughed. Even when he did that, she thought for a moment that he might be laughing with joy. Far from it. The unencumbered cruelty in his eyes had pierced her heart. He had looked at her as if to say, 'And what do you want me to do about it?' She had lost it, then. She had hurled every insult in the English language at him, probably in the hope of getting some other reaction from him, some semblance of the man she thought she knew. The man she had fallen in love with. The man with whom she had created a child. And the man who didn't give a damn about either of those things. She had threatened him, then. Had even swung at him. The calm way that he told her – even with a split lip – how everyone knew she'd been sleeping around had shocked her to the core. Oh, he had done a number on her and covered his deceitful ass long ago. If she ruined him, he lectured her, he'd take her down with him. As he mopped his bleeding lip, he reminded her that no right-minded institution would take her on with a reputation such as hers.

Lecture over, he had invited her to show herself out.

And as she'd sobbed all night into glass after glass of liquor – he didn't care about their child, so why should she? – she had realized that her wonderful life had become nothing more than a trashy romance novel with the best pages torn out. She had considered a termination. Had booked an appointment and had met with her doctor, who gave her a fake smile, some leaflets, along with an estimated bill for the procedure.

And then, as the world turned beneath her, aloof from any of her problems, she had decided to keep her child. Crucially, she had also decided to continue her behavioral research after the child was born. The birth was not without its complications. The baby had become entangled in its umbilical cord. Quite the visual metaphor. But it had lived, and it was female. Quick nursed the child with formula, and named her Emily. She had tried one last time, confronting William in the parking lot with Emily crying the whole time in her papoose. He wasn't interested. But by the time he had called security she had made enough of a scene. Enough, it turned out, to secure her position as principal at Greyfriars through one of his contacts at The Consortium Inc., where he was earning a fast and significant buck as a consultant. Career academics were often company men at heart, and William had proven no exception. Greyfriars, he had explained to her, had been shut down some years ago due to newer facilities being built closer to the city. It would provide the perfect laboratory for her to continue her research with a steady income, away from prying eyes, while providing a home for her and Emily. She didn't really have any choice but to accept. William held all the cards. She needed his reference, and he had hand-picked a role for her. Even though they were separated, he still had a hold over her life.

And so, she had started a new life at Greyfriars. She took to her new role with gusto, and began researching the personality types she could harvest from detention centers for her experiments. But it was a lonely existence. And as each day passed, she knew that the isolation of Greyfriars Reformatory wasn't meant to help her at all. William had merely wanted her and their daughter to be far away. Out of sight, and out of mind. So he could focus on his new protégé.

(*Thanks a bunch, baby daddy.*)

The kid had her father's eyes, which helped. Helped Quick to focus on the endgame. To use the gift he had put inside her belly against him.

She had weaponized Emily, over time. And time was something she had in abundance.

It had been a natural progression really, for her to begin to see Emily as one of the inmates, rather than as her own daughter. Every time she looked at her, she saw William Drake in those eyes. She used that to accentuate the distance. Keeping his surname attached to Emily's helped to consolidate it. Emily Drake became as alien to her as any of the girls in her care. And it was all too easy to work a backstory into Emily under conditions of hypnosis. With regular sessions, she had Emily believing that she had done something terrible in order to be locked up in the reformatory. After several treatments, she was someone else entirely.

She was 'Girl A'.

The next stage in Emily's usefulness was for her to develop a bona fide set of symptoms via careful conditioning under hypnosis, and in meticulously orchestrated social situations with other inmates. William Drake's daughter had been reworked from out of Quick's mortar and pestle of rage and revenge, and was reborn as 'Girl A' into the pages of her research.

Principal Quick flicked through the sheaf of pages forming her manuscript.

She was getting close now. So much closer. She was almost certain she had succeeded in demonstrating that it was possible to create a disorder in the raw materials of her subject. Emily had been a healthy and happy youngster. Now she was a fuckup like the rest of the inmates. Like her dear old dad. And she was exhibiting symptoms of an actual disorder, when she had no history of ever having had one before. The imaginary friend, the lapses in concentration, and the disassociation from everyday reality.

It was beginning to feel exciting again.

Quick glanced at the blank page in her manuscript. It no longer looked so insurmountable to her. Now it posed only possibilities. She looked from the page to the slit of William's smile depicted in the photo hanging on her wall. Now, more than ever, she needed to focus, and to get on with her research. All the darkness and doubt had seemed to leave her. A cloud giving way to the clear light of day. She decided to refine her focus the very next day. She would step up Emily's 'treatments', and get her next chapter written up. And that was the endgame. Publish, and someday, after she and 'Girl A' had taken the world by storm, she would reveal who William Drake really was.

A smile curled her lips. She glanced at the closet door. The drink would have to wait until after she had achieved her next milestone. But she had another way to celebrate. She slid open her desk drawer and pulled out a pack of cigarettes, followed by her lighter. The words on the pack caught her eye. 'WARNING. Smoking can cause serious heart complaints.'

That was a good one. Her oh-so-serious heart complaints had started the day she had met William.

She closed the desk drawer and crossed to the window. The moon was high in the night sky, casting a steely glow across the center of the recreation yard. The bare branches of the tree made crazy paving of the ground with their geometrical shadows. Quick placed her cigarettes and the lighter on the windowsill, then unclasped and opened the window to its fullest extent. The cool, crisp night air flooded in, awakening her senses. She put a cigarette to her lips and thumbed the lighter. The flame felt warm on her face as she lit the cigarette. She placed the lighter back on the windowsill. She drew hungrily on the cigarette before exhaling a plume of gray smoke out of the window and into the night.

When the smoke plume cleared, Quick saw the shape.

It stopped her heart for just a second, the sight of the girl's body. Even in the cold silver of the moonlight, the girl's hair was unmistakably auburn.

No, no, no. It couldn't be.

She stubbed the cigarette out on the brickwork surrounding the window, and tossed it out of the window. Pausing only to snatch her keys from atop her desk, Quick dashed to her office door. By the time she was out in the corridor, she had broken into a run. The clatter of her heels echoed off the walls like machine-gun fire as she ran, full pelt now, down the corridor and into the one that led to the recreation yard door. She shoved a key into the lock and turned it. But the door would not open. Wrong key. Careless of her. She tried another. Wrong again. She heard a strange sound, akin to a horse's whinny, and realized that it was coming from her own throat. Her hands began to tremble, and she rifled through the keys over and over, for what seemed like an age, until she found the right one. Her hand was now shaking so badly that she couldn't get the key into the lock. She had to clamp her free hand around her wrist in order to slide the thing home. Still holding on to her wrist to steady her hand, she turned the key – and the lock clicked open.

She flung the door open and felt night's chill wash over her.

So cold that she felt as though she had fallen into an icy lake.

As she stepped into the recreation yard, her eyes found the dark, prone shape on the ground, half-hidden by the shadow of the dead tree. The shadow around the body had the aspect of a dark cloud. Quick glanced up at the sky and saw only the bright moon, the twinkling stars, and the sightless eyes of the clock tower's arches, high above. As she reached the body, she realized with fright that the shadow was blood. It had pooled around the poor girl's broken head. She must have climbed all the way up there, and then she must have—

So much blood.

—fallen from the tower.

Quick took a step back and knocked against something with her foot. She looked down to see the crumpled shape of the music box lying discarded just a few feet away from Emily.

Just a few feet away from her dead daughter.

And there was so much blood.

It had all been for nothing. She'd be ruined. A laughing stock. William and his 'assistants' (she was picturing dozens of them now, a harem of fucking bitches eager for distinction) would see her name in the headlines – but as a murderess, a failure, a fuckup like all the others under her care.

One harem led to another and soon she began to blame the girls. It must have been Emily's fellow inmates who drove Emily – literally and figuratively – over the edge. Emily had said as much, and she hadn't listened.

Her fatal flaw again. She had been so focused on her research that she had failed to see the telltale signs. Why hadn't Emily come to her? She must have been scared, that was why. Scared of what the others would do to her. Quick knew that beatings were all part of the process of desensitizing Emily, but this? This was too much.

They were the fuckups – the lot of them. Concluding thus, she retreated to her office. Began to read through their case files. She had been blind to them, too. Her eyes so fixed upon the prize that she had missed the cracks in the firmament. Each girl would have ended her meaningless life if it hadn't been for her care. If it hadn't been for her carefully constructed reality of punishment and virtue.

She could read between the lines of each and every one of them. Quick took up her pen – no point now in completing her other research – and began adding their epitaphs, concocting fitting ends for each life less lived.

Jessica? A sad, navel-gazing specimen who misspent her every waking moment clutching at an umbilical cord that had long since been cut. A little leech, sucking the life out of anyone who came near. Her only purpose in life was surely to slit her throat and to stop being such a pathetic burden on the world.

Next page. Victoria. The universe was still trying to course-correct itself around Victoria because she really had no place in it. She should have died in the gas explosion that wiped out her family and all its tawdry secrets.

Next page. Annie? By rights, she should have been sent to death row for the despicable things she had done. Any court in the land would agree with her, Quick was sure of that, but instead she was supposed to take her under her wing and look after her. Because of her age. There was no justice in this world.

Oh, but there would be.

Next page. Saffy. Self-styled 'Queen Bitch', inflicting her own crippling insecurities upon others. A perpetual, entitled teen, stuck inside a tawdry love affair with a man old enough to be her father. Drowning in self-delusion.

Next page. Lena. To what depths had she sank to feed her addiction? She would almost certainly have died from a drug overdose if she hadn't been picked up by the authorities.

An overdose.

And that was Quick's eureka moment.

All good doctors have them, after all.

She began the next morning by dismissing the kitchen staff. They hadn't questioned her when she told them that Greyfriars' funding had been pulled. She had thanked them for their service (and she had almost meant it) and packed them off to the minibus that awaited them outside on the gravel forecourt.

Singing a jolly tune to herself as she went, Quick had made her way to the med store. Once inside, it didn't take her long to find what she needed. The correct combination. A corrective cocktail, as she liked to think of it. After taking her dark bounty to the kitchens, she set about grinding the pills into powder in a large pestle and mortar. The crunching, grinding sound as she pummeled the pills using the heavy utensil was not unpleasant to her as she worked. She wondered if Emily's skull and bones had made the same sound when they had hit the concrete.

Quick added the powder to a huge pan of bubbling porridge, which she mixed and stirred at a slow simmer over a low flame.

Once it was a pleasingly slushy consistency, she set it aside to reheat later. Oh, but she could have been quite the domestic goddess, given half a chance. Shame. But now she was more – so much more.

She made the girls line up after their morning shower, beside their beds. Emily's was, of course, notably empty. She informed them that there would be no breakfast ration that morning until they had performed a special task. She added that the task would be physical, and so would help them work up an appetite.

Quick sensed their apprehension as she led them in silence through the corridors until they reached the door to the recreation yard. She led them over to the spot where Emily's body lay, facedown on the concrete. The pool of blood had begun to dry, forming an indelible stain.

Victoria, ever the weakling, was the first to scream. Quick felt like beating the snot from the miserable girl's face, but managed to control herself. Decorum was so important when setting an example for disaffected youth. She had set out an assortment of shovels, trowels, and rakes in a neat line for each of the girls to use – the tools of the groundskeepers' trade. Those workers had been dismissed, too. Good for their gardening implements to be put to use in their absence. She instructed her charges to dig in the small area of bare earth surrounding the dying tree. Small, and yet ample to be dug into a grave for Emily.

One of the girls began to vomit into the soil as she dug alongside her fellow miscreants. Principal Quick ignored it. The girl's bodily fluids, a symbol of her guilt and of her complicity, would be buried in the cold soil along with Emily's remains.

And once the hole was deep enough, Quick allowed the girls a breather before setting their next task.

"Lift her up," she said.

Victoria started sobbing again, and bolted for the door. Quick intercepted her, and this time she slapped her hard across the face, a violent backhander that sent the tears and snot flying.

"Lift her up. Lift her together. Just as you put her there together."

Not one of them dared argue with her. Through their pathetic sniveling and wailing, they each grabbed a wrist or an ankle and heaved Emily's deadweight over to the waiting grave. At Quick's signal, they lowered her in.

"Now replace the soil," Quick commanded.

They each grabbed a digging implement and set to work.

Quick noted how eager they seemed to cover the body over. With each scoop of soil, they were concealing the guilty consequences of their actions. It took them a while, but Quick had all day, and when they had filled the grave with soil Quick instructed them to use the rakes to return the topsoil to some semblance of normality.

When they retreated to the outskirts of the recreation yard, Quick was able to take a step back to look at their handiwork. It was as though nothing had happened. Only the dark red stain remained, and that would fade with time, and rain.

"Good work, girls," Quick said. "Get cleaned up. You have earned yourselves a meal."

After washing, they trudged after her in silence as she led them, single file, to the refectory.

"Line up, and I will dish up," Quick said.

"Where are the kitchen staff?" Lena asked, first in line. Brazen of her, really.

"Union dispute," Quick replied, smiling inwardly at her jibe. She ladled a generous portion of lumpy porridge into Lena's bowl.

A look passed over Lena's face for a moment, and Quick thought she might be planning some act of retaliation.

"Next," Quick said, fixing her gaze upon Jessica, who was sniveling and clutching her bowl to her chest like some ridiculous Dickensian parody.

"Please, Principal Quick," Jessica said, "I don't think I can eat anything, I feel too sick."

Quick looked at the wretched girl. So thin. An extra ladleful of the slop went into Jessica's bowl. Well, why not? Quick ignored her ridiculous sobs as the girl dragged her feet all the way to one of the tables.

She watched them eat, counting each mouthful and wondering if she had seasoned the mixture with enough 'corrective cocktail'.

Only time would tell.

And it did.

Lena began gagging first. She made a sort of grunting sound initially, which grew into a cough and then a series of frightened yelps before she fell, choking, facedown onto the table. Her convulsions set the other girls off, each of them shrieking in terror before the lethal cocktail of drugs took hold. Quick watched as each successive girl clawed at her throat, thinking perhaps even in their last moments that they could save themselves. How stupid of them. They had each signed their own death warrants as soon as they had sat down to partake of their first spoonful.

Except for Jessica.

She didn't seem to be dying, and that troubled Quick. She marched over to the apparently hysterical girl and saw that her porridge was untouched. Her eating disorder – of course. Quick grabbed hold of Jessica's hair and wrapped it around her fist, pulling down hard until the deceitful little bitch opened her useless mouth wide.

She wasted no time, then.

Scooping up porridge in the spoon, Quick rammed it into Jessica's protesting mouth. She tilted the spoon, ensuring the mixture went down. Quick refilled the spoon and this time, Jessica tried to close her mouth. Quick heard the girl's teeth shatter as she rammed the metal spoon between them and right down her throat. Jessica's scream died in her throat and Quick released the girl's hair from her grip.

Quick then took a seat opposite the girl as she continued choking, spittle and porridge slicked around her lips – and watched her die.

She left them all there, slumped over the dining tables. No burial for the likes of them.

Afterward, Quick's closet door had not remained shut.

Violently drunk, Quick set about completing her case notes, adding an imagined cause of death for each girl. The contents of her clipboard had become a ledger of the damned. But when she got to Emily's case file, she faltered. With a sigh, she accepted that it would remain unfinished, just like her manuscript.

Quick rose from her seat, swaying uneasily from so much vodka. She took the framed picture down from the wall, kissed William Drake's slit mouth goodbye, and placed it facedown in the desk drawer. She took the crumpled music box from her pocket and placed it inside the drawer, too. Then she slid the drawer closed before emptying the remaining bottle of pills she had taken from the med store into her hand. She shoveled them into her mouth and drank them down with hit after hit of vodka, straight from the bottle. A fire began to rage in her throat, mirroring the one in her heart. Soon enough, she had run out of pills. Moments before she fell unconscious, she glimpsed something in the shadowy corner of her office.

It looked like a girl.

Her skin was a pallid gray color. Quick could not make out the girl's face because her hair had fallen over it.

"Emily?" she asked, her voice sounding distant through her inebriation.

And then everything went black.

* * *

Principal Quick awoke as if rising to the surface of a fathomless nightmare.

The foul aftertaste of liquor and narcotics coated her throat. She coughed, which only made it taste worse. Daylight flooded the office through the window to the recreation yard. She must have been out for the count all night. Quick almost knocked the vodka bottle over as she staggered to her feet. She had to lean against the desk for support. A surge of bile hit the back of her throat and she had to swallow hard to prevent herself from throwing up all over her manuscript.

The manuscript.

Oh, yes. She would have to finish it someday. But first, she had work to attend to. She straightened herself out as best she could, then picked up the keys from her desk. She left the office and locked the door behind her. Her heels clicked against the hard surface of the reformatory corridor floor as she made her way to the main entrance. She hit the button that would release the main gates and set about unlocking the front door.

Stepping out into the cold daylight, Principal Quick watched the prisoner transport bus drive between the gateposts before it circled around and drew up in front of the steps.

She carried her clipboard over to the bus, ready to greet her inmates.

CHAPTER TWENTY-SEVEN

You Will Learn

I'm on the prisoner transport bus again and the sky outside the window looks as gray as I feel.

I say 'again' because, well, I've been institutionalized a few times. All my adult life actually. I've had a few problems, shall we say. But before you ask, my meds are so strong I can't remember what any of my problems were, or are. I guess that kind of makes me an unreliable narrator? If that bothers you then look away. I know I would. Or at least, I think I would.

The four other girls on the bus have been real quiet since we crossed the county line into Dustbowl, Nowheresville. Not that any of them spoke to me at all in the first place, you understand. I'm not what you'd call the approachable type. A couple of them whispered to each other, some nonsense about 'making a break for it during the pee break'. Yeah, good luck with that in your handcuffs and leg irons, ladies. Probably just trying to style it out before they realized for sure that they were going to be banged up like the rest of us. No special cases here, just a bunch of head cases.

I glance at a couple of the other girls, and find myself wondering what they might be hiding. And then again I don't wonder at all. I mean, what's the point in trying to figure that out anyway? We're all hiding something. That's partly why we're here.

I glance out the window and try to decipher where 'here' is, exactly. The window is almost as grimy as the sky, making me doubly separated from the landscape as it smears across my vision. I can see the skeletal forms of trees, clinging to the wind-battered hillsides. The country road begins to twist and turn, as if coiling in on itself to keep us moving into its spiral.

The driver makes a bad gear change as the road gets rougher. The torturous sound of the grinding gearshift gives way to a burst of static on the bus radio. The signal is weak, probably because of the mountainous terrain on either side of us, but I can hear a few faint bars of a song coming through the tinny speakers. The lyrics say something about ghosts, and regret, and about not saying sorry. Soon enough, the song becomes lost in another crackle of static and I turn my attention back to the window.

"Turn the fucking thing off if it's not working properly." The voice from the back of the bus is petulant, and clipped with indignation. I look around, on instinct, and my eyes meet the baby blues of the tall blonde who decided to take the entire back row for herself. She gives off that vibe, you know, where she's just daring you to sit near her so she can make a scene. Best ignored, those types. Which makes it all the more unfortunate that I made eye contact with her I guess.

"Would you like a fucking selfie with that?" she says.

I break eye contact. Then I go over what I saw, but in my mind's eye. It's a thing I do. A thing I *have* to do, to try and make sense of whether or not what I'm seeing is real. Unreliable, like I said. One thing's for sure, that blonde girl wears her entitlement like a swipe card. She groans theatrically, and I think I'm in for an earful from her. But then I see the apparent source of her disappointment, looming dark beyond the small clear section of driver's window that isn't caked with dirt.

The building is solid looking, hunkered down into the landscape like it knows more bad weather is coming. A clock tower is the only vertical part of the structure, looming darkly at the center of the building. The bus swerves and the road narrows further as we approach the brick perimeter wall and wrought-iron gates. Lichen casts a rusty glow over the weathered bricks, and thick black paint is peeling from the iron railings. There's a sign next to the gate, the painted letters almost destroyed by the elements. It reads 'Greyfriars Reformatory for Girls'. Whoop-de-doo. The way the paint has deteriorated makes the words 'Grey' and 'Girls' stand out. Yup, that's us in our drab uniforms I guess, the gray girls.

The driver slows the bus to a halt and a few seconds later, the gates swing open, activated by an unseen hand. The driver makes another horrendous gear shift and the bus proceeds through the gates and onto a graveled forecourt. The centerpiece of this gloomy space is a dead-looking tree. A few dry leaves flutter in the wake of the prisoner transport bus as we pass by. I glance back through the rear window, careless of the arrogant blonde, and see the gates swing shut behind us. They close with a loud clank, and the driver swings the vehicle around so we are adjacent to the front steps of the building. With a hydraulic hiss of the brakes, we lurch to a halt.

"Finally," the blonde says, with a wisdom beyond her years.

"Right, ladies, disembarkation time. Front rows first. Single file. No talking. Watch your step at the bottom."

The chains we're wearing tinkle like Christmas bells as we file off the bus. I'm ahead of the blonde, so I stand up but she gives me that superior look of hers and pushes past me. As the heat of her body rubs against me I notice that she smells overbearingly sweet, like a bag of boiled candies. I don't like the scent.

"Come on, come on," the driver urges, and I follow as quickly as my leg irons will allow me to.

The sky looks just as grimy as it did from inside the bus, but at least the air is fresher outside. I take a few calming breaths—

(*In, then out, count to three in your head, and breathe in again.*)

—like they taught me to, and then line up with the others

alongside the bus. The reformatory looks huge now, up close, its dark windows giving nothing away. The front steps look cracked and worn. Several hopes and dreams must have been deposited there on the way into that—

(*And I'm just being honest here.*)

—frightening shithole of a building.

But even more terrifying is the woman waiting for us on the steps.

She's in her fifties, and wears a functional black trouser suit. Her auburn hair is bunched and her lips pursed, making her look pretty tightly wound. She carries a clipboard, tucked under her arm. In her free hand I see a bunch of keys on a dull, silver ring. They too make the sound of little silver bells as she walks across the gravel to face us. She doesn't look at us yet, instead giving the driver a sharp nod. The driver clambers back onto the bus and I hear the engine grumble back into life behind me. The air around me fills with exhaust fumes. After a hiss of the brake release, the bus moves off, kicking up dust as it goes.

The woman quickly pockets the keys, pulls out her clipboard and makes a show of leafing through the pages of the document that is clamped to it. She shakes her head, slowly.

"More lost souls," she says. Then, after taking a breath, she begins to walk the line of girls.

"I am Principal Quick. Welcome to Greyfriars Reformatory. Your new home."

I can see the blonde's smug, smirking face poking out from beneath her plumage-like fringe at the head of the line. The principal stops still and stands in front of her. Glancing at her clipboard, she says, "Name?"

The blonde flinches for a second. Blink and you'd miss it. But I didn't.

"Saffy," she says.

"Full name," Quick replies.

Then Saffy speaks her full name, real fast so it almost comes out as a single word.

"Saffron Chassay."

I'm not the only one who sniggers. I mean, who wouldn't? *Saffron Chassay*. What a ridiculous-ass name. It suits her. She rolls her eyes at the barely contained laughter from me and a couple of the other girls. But she does look rattled. Interesting.

Quick takes a pen from the little holder on the clipboard and makes a ticking motion on her document before moving on to the next girl. She's the waif of the group, real skinny and pale. I notice her tousling her hair as Quick approaches, which makes the older woman purse her lips even tighter.

"Hands by your side girl. Name?"

"Jessica Hope."

Another tick, then Quick moves off. Jessica starts fiddling with her hair again as soon as Quick's back is turned.

"Name."

I hear a loud hawking and then spitting sound as the next girl deposits a ball of freshly drawn phlegm onto the gravel. I lean forward a little so I can get a better look and see that the clever girl has spat right in front of Quick's feet. Oh, boy. I remember seeing her on the bus because the dark circles under her eyes stood out. I recall thinking that she looks as though she has grown up way too fast. She has the punk rock look about her, and could pass for thirty thanks to those dark rings.

I see Quick reach out and for a moment I think she's going to whack her. But instead, Quick places a finger under the girl's chin and lifts her face until their eyes meet.

"Nasty habit," she says. "Name?"

The girl jerks away from Quick's touch, then stares at the floor. "I'm...Lena Turner," she says, and I'm surprised at the defeat in her tone.

"Yes, I suppose you are." Quick makes her mark on the clipboard again, before moving on. "Name."

"Annie. Annie Chastain."

Quite perky sounding, this one. And I can see a distinct look of displeasure on Quick's face before she makes another ticking motion with her pen. Then Quick moves to the end of the line. It's my turn.

"Emily Drake. Surprised to see you back here so soon."

I can almost sense Saffy's ears pricking up at this. A couple of the others seem pretty interested too. I can see them out of my peripheral vision, but I try not to look away from Quick in case she interprets it as a sign of weakness. I vaguely remember Principal Quick, and this place. But I'm not sure if I really do remember, or if it's just my meds messing with my head again. I try my breathing exercises again.

"You'll learn," Quick says, her eyes on me, "someday." Then she takes a step back and addresses all of us. "You will *all* learn, as I live and breathe."

Quick tucks the clipboard under her arm with military precision. "Inside. Single file."

One by one, the girls ahead of me file across the gravel forecourt, up the steps and into the main entrance of the reformatory. I am last in line and as I follow the others, a shadow catches me. The sudden chill turns my skin to gooseflesh and I have the compulsion to look upward. The clock tower looms over me, obelisk-like against turbulent skies. The increasing wind is bringing with it dark clouds that look heavy with rain. I notice that the clock's hands are not moving – stuck close to six. Above the clockface is an arched window, open to the elements. For a moment, something gray flutters within the archway. It looks like a girl, standing there in an inmate's uniform and watching me through her long, dark hair. The wind is making my eyes water and I blink to clear my vision.

No one there after all.

I keep walking, eager to be indoors and away from the biting wind.

FLAME TREE PRESS
FICTION WITHOUT FRONTIERS
Award-Winning Authors & Original Voices

Flame Tree Press is the trade fiction imprint of Flame Tree Publishing, focusing on excellent writing in horror and the supernatural, crime and mystery, science fiction and fantasy. Our aim is to explore beyond the boundaries of the everyday, with tales from both award-winning authors and original voices.

•

Other titles available by Frazer Lee:
Hearthstone Cottage

Other horror and suspense titles available include:
Snowball by Gregory Bastianelli
Thirteen Days by Sunset Beach by Ramsey Campbell
Think Yourself Lucky by Ramsey Campbell
The Hungry Moon by Ramsey Campbell
The Haunting of Henderson Close by Catherine Cavendish
The Garden of Bewitchment by Catherine Cavendish
The House by the Cemetery by John Everson
The Devil's Equinox by John Everson
Hellrider by JG Faherty
The Toy Thief by D.W. Gillespie
One By One by D.W. Gillespie
Black Wings by Megan Hart
The Playing Card Killer by Russell James
The Portal by Russell James
The Siren and the Specter by Jonathan Janz
The Sorrows by Jonathan Janz
Castle of Sorrows by Jonathan Janz
The Dark Game by Jonathan Janz
Will Haunt You by Brian Kirk
We Are Monsters by Brian Kirk
Those Who Came Before by J.H. Moncrieff
Stoker's Wilde by Steven Hopstaken & Melissa Prusi
Creature by Hunter Shea
Ghost Mine by Hunter Shea
Slash by Hunter Shea
The Mouth of the Dark by Tim Waggoner
They Kill by Tim Waggoner

•

Join our mailing list for free short stories, new release details, news about our authors and special promotions:

flametreepress.com